DATE DUE	

A Novel of Cannes

THE LUMIÈRE AFFAIR

SARA VOORHEES

SIMON & SCHUSTER
NEW YORK   LONDON   TORONTO   SYDNEY

SIMON & SCHUSTER
Rockefeller Center
1230 Avenue of the Americas
New York, NY 10020

For information about special discounts for bulk purchases,
please contact Simon & Schuster Special Sales at 1-800-456-6798
or business@simonandschuster.com

Book design by Ellen R. Sasahara

Manufactured in the United States of America

1   3   5   7   9   10   8   6   4   2

Library of Congress Cataloging-in-Publication Data

Voorhees, Sara.
The lumière affair / Sara Voorhees.
p.   cm.
PS3622.O696L86 2007
813'.6—dc22   2006052242

ISBN-13: 978-0-7432-9195-8
ISBN-10:   0-7432-9195-6

To my beloved Penguinis:
Dayton, Coert, Emily, Molly, and Dayton.
You are the heart of everything that matters.

There are two cinemas:
the film we actually saw
and the one we remember.

Molly Haskell, *Popcorn in Paradise*

THE LUMIÈRE
AFFAIR

PROLOGUE

FRANCE

The High Alps of High Provence

April

$\mathcal{A}$ ll they could ever tell me was that the lightning came in through the top of my head. Not that I couldn't have figured that out for myself. When the storm was over and we'd all been carried down the mountain, I woke up with a splitting headache and a numb place in the center of my scalp.

The lightning had come and gone in less than three milliseconds, but in my imagination it lasts for minutes, playing like a trailer for an art-house film, the camera panning languidly from clear blue sky to meadow and to picnic: an ant treks along the sticky rim of a spoon, a puff of wind lifts the corner of a blanket. Standing, I am nearly as tall as my mother's dreamboat boyfriend, Michel Claudel, who kneels to clasp a gold necklace around my mother's throat. She lifts her hair from her shoulders, as if posing or in the middle of a stretch.

And then we're sheathed in white-hot light. It blasts through my brain, sizzles through the metal zipper of my Levi's, leaps across the picnic basket to Claudel's watch, and takes a sharp detour into my mother's birthday necklace.

She gets the worst of it. The light is trapped inside her, racing wildly from spleen to kidney, frantic for a way out. When it finally dissipates, hardly enough time has passed for one of us to blink, but the damage is done. We collapse onto the mountain and fade to black.

When I woke up, everything was white. White from the ceiling to the floor, white on everything in between. White clothes moved all around me: even the smell was white, crisp and clean, a smell that held you captive. In my memory the only thing that wasn't white was the stained-glass window, at my feet, of Jesus Christ, a cross on his shoulder, a single white glass tear on his cheek.

My heart was throbbing inside my skull. I touched the top of my head and found a hairless patch of flesh. It was like touching someone else's skin: I could only feel the touching with my fingers.

My mother was lying in a bed next to mine, under a starched white sheet, with a tube coming out of her mouth. Her hands rested at her sides as if she'd already died and been entombed forever on the top of a stone casket. I turned to Jesus Christ for help, but he was having his own problems.

Claudel was talking to a fat bald man in a white coat, and when he heard me scream, he came running.

"*On y va*," I said. Let's get out of here.

Claudel sat beside me on the bed and held my hand, and for a minute I had the feeling he could make everything right.

"*Bientôt*," he said. "We are in a hospital. In Briançon."

Briançon. I knew where that was. The day before our picnic, we had taken the train from Paris to this tiny town at the foot of the French Alps to celebrate my mother's birthday. Some celebration.

Claudel put his hand softly on my forehead and told me what had happened. Not long after the accident, a troop of French Boy Scouts had come upon us lying in the meadow and turned us into a merit-badge assignment. They'd made stretchers out of branches, tied us to them, and dragged us all the way down the mountain to the Catholic nuns' hospital.

The nuns had wrapped Claudel's wrist where the lightning had galvanized his Piaget watch and burned off the hair and skin. They put salve on the sore at the top of my head and on the burn on my stomach, which stretched across my belly like a broken bridge over a tiny canyon. As the days drew on, it grew into puffy reddened blisters. My mother remained the same.

After a few weeks, Claudel took me back with him to Paris, where I helped him put our sunny apartment into boxes, and we closed the tall wooden shutters so no more daylight could get in.

My mother stayed behind, unmoving under her sheet, and one day a coffin arrived on the train and we drove it in a long procession of cars to the cemetery, where I threw a handful of musty brown dirt on her grave.

Claudel packed all my clothes in one big suitcase, and the next thing I knew I was living in America with a man I'd never even heard of, who'd been married to my mother just long enough to contribute a few strands of DNA to my conception. The subject of my mother was strictly *interdit* in his house, and he didn't know how to comfort me when I cried for the life I'd lost. But he'd taken me in when Claudel sent me away, and he raised me with kindness in a small desert town in New Mexico. I suppose I turned out fine, considering.

But after you've been struck by a bolt of lightning, you know something that no one else can understand: there's no place to hide. No matter how good things get or how bad they seem, all of it is subject to a last-minute rewrite. One day you're headed for a *Princess Bride* ending, the next day you're floating on a fragment of the *Titanic*. You always know that even in the middle of a picnic, death can reach out at you from behind a cloud.

I didn't come here to tell you
how it's going to end. I came to tell
you how it's going to begin.

Laurence Fishburne, in *The Matrix*

1

LOS ANGELES
Twenty-five Years Later
Monday, May 5

"He's dead," Draper said into the phone.

I was standing ankle-deep in mud and slime. My sweat-pants were pushed up above my knees, my cell phone pinched between my cheek and shoulder. The smell of rotting leaves was enough to gag a buzzard.

It was the middle of a still and cloudless spring day that held the promise of a miserably hot Los Angeles summer, and I was groveling in my backyard pond, trying to mend what neglect had broken.

My ex-editor, Vince Draper, who had blithely waved good-bye as I retreated from the *LA News* office ten months before, was trying to make nice with me, but already he was on my nerves. He'd called to tell me my replacement had dropped dead in the middle of writing a story. My pond had sprung a slow leak over the pallid

California winter, and I was obsessing about how to pay the mortgage on my house, but at least I wasn't dead.

"Did you hear me, Nat?" Draper said.

I preferred "Natalie," but Draper had changed my name for my movie column byline because he thought a female journalist could get no respect in a company town like LA. What he meant was that a female journalist could get no respect from *him*.

"I did, I heard. It's awful," I said, but to be honest it was hard to muster the proper sympathy for a man I'd never met, who'd taken a job I'd quit, to write a column I'd never read.

Besides, I was busy trying to resuscitate a goldfish. He was about ten inches long, and I'd found him lying belly-up in the mud and muck along with his seven brothers and sisters. Most of my fish were white with orange spots, and I was holding the biggest one, a pushy orange koi I thought of affectionately as the Orange One.

"His father went toe-up from a coronary. Same age, thirty-five."

The Orange One was dead as a doornail. I considered tossing him over the back fence for a raccoon's lunch, but I didn't want to get into a food-chain debate with my conscience. I dropped him into a plastic bag instead.

"He was a freaking triathlete!" Draper said. "Which is sweet news for a guy like me who likes to sit on his ass all day. But damn!" Vince Draper had turned sloth into an art form. I thought of pointing that out to him, but an ex-editor is like an ex-anything in one respect: by the time we parted ways, I'd pretty much exhausted my arsenal of pettiness.

"Draper, I'm so sorry you've lost your guy, I really am. But . . . what is this? I thought you and I had finished our little horse opera."

"Yeah, I know," he said with forced sadness. "But I'm hoping you can give me one more whinny." I knew he thought that would make me laugh, but it didn't. "Okay," he said, "I'm only going to say this once: I apologize for calling you a neophyte. For saying you were useless. And that other thing . . ."

"Spineless."

"Right." When I didn't answer, he let out a little growl of frustration. "Fine. You're a first-rate member of the fourth estate. And okay, you can't expect that I'll agree with everything you say, but I need you on my team."

I stood there in the rancid pond, the mud drying on my hands like cement gloves, and gaped into the phone.

"Come on, I know you can use the money," he said, and I imagined myself dangling at the end of his line. "Look, what're you working on?"

"I'm doing CPR on some goldfish," I said.

"I mean for money."

I was glad I wasn't in Draper's office, where he could see me blush. I'd worked for him for almost three years, which was longer than I'd stayed at either the *Voice* or the *LA Weekly*. But I'd quit because nothing I wrote ever satisfied him. From the day I went to work for his paper, he had poked and prodded me to get the Hard Story, as if there were such a thing as a Hard Story where movie stars were concerned. I was heartless enough as a critic to satisfy his thirst for blood, but when it came to celebrities, he wanted dirt—a glimpse into Candice Bergen's *pain* when Louis Malle died, Nicole Kidman's *shame* at Katie Holmes's pregnancy—and every ounce of dirt I got made it harder for me to hold on to the one thing I wanted most from movies in the first place: quick and affordable transportation elsewhere.

But how can you give yourself over to the ride when you know too much about the driver? How can you lose yourself in *Mr. & Mrs. Smith* when someone in the seat behind you, who's probably read the dirt you dug up yourself, is whispering to her date, "I wish he'd stayed with Jennifer. They were such a cute couple." I wanted to leave actors safely in their gilded cages.

Needless to say, I rarely got what Draper asked for. The last time we'd spoken was when I'd interviewed Julia Roberts and neglected to mention either her smoking habits or the twins. Draper had called me a lot of adjectives that all meant he was about to fire me anyway, so I quit.

At first I wasn't sorry. It wasn't the first time I'd walked out on an impossible employer, and I had a pretty good reputation as a journalist. But freelancing was harder than I'd counted on. I couldn't seem to break out of the celebrity niche. I turned down several movie star interviews for national magazines because I wanted to be clear of entertainment for good. I only made it through the winter because a weapons periodical offered me a small fortune to take shooting lessons and write a ten-thousand-word piece called "The Lady Learns to Love Her Glock." It was a measure of my desperation that I took the job. After it was published, I'd received several proposals of marriage from trigger-happy readers. If any of them had been millionaires, who knows what might have become of my principles.

After that, I'd resolved to take any assignment that came my way that didn't involve firearms. In January I'd written a twelve-page treatise on the history of chocolate for a food magazine. The gas company turned off my heat in February, and it was a good thing I liked popcorn, because I ate it three times a day. And so I put my little house—a generous term for the high-priced shack I'd bought in Studio City—up for sale. It needed a fresh coat of paint, and the missing tiles on the roof would have to be replaced, but I couldn't afford to make the repairs. I'd borrowed on all the equity, and I had no savings.

I tried not to think about it as I picked at a flake of mud at the end of my nose. When I returned to the conversation, Draper was saying, "Here's the thing, Nat. I need you to take the dead guy's place in Cannes."

"Cannes . . . *France*?" I asked.

"No. Cannes, *Burundi*," Draper said. "Of course Cannes, France. I know you don't want to go, but this is a crisis. What have you got against the French, anyway?"

I wasn't about to answer that question for a barracuda like Draper. It was no small feat for an LA film critic to sidestep the Cannes Film Festival for nine years, but somehow I'd managed. For twenty-five years, the whole country had loomed over me, wrapped in memories of my mother and Michel Claudel and the unlucky event that had catapulted me from a happy childhood to a desert life with a melancholy father.

"Nothing," I said.

I thought I felt a sudden breeze lift the hair from the nape of my neck, and instinctively I looked at the sky. A puff of cloud had materialized over the mountain at the edge of the blue expanse I equated with safety, and here I stood, with my feet in water and a wireless phone at my ear.

"We can give you a pile of money this time. National syndication. Very big job."

A pile of money? I looked at my poor little house. Even in its present condition, it wouldn't be long before someone offered to take it off my hands. And then what? The idea of returning to France was terrifying, but it was less threatening than homelessness. And when you're teetering on the edge of an abyss, you grab on to anything that's rooted in solid ground, even if it draws blood.

If I said yes to Draper, there was also the possibility of learning something about my mother. The idea was appealing. Over the years I'd tried everything, from hounding my father to a search for her on Google, but her name on my birth certificate, Kit Conway, was all I had to go on, and the information I'd gleaned about her had barely filled three lines on a legal-sized page: beautiful, hungry for something my father could not provide, a starstruck blonde who'd made a single appearance in a French film whose name I'd never been able to find. That was it. If I actually set foot on French soil, at the very least I could visit her grave.

One thing was certain: if I didn't make some money fast, I'd have to move back to New Mexico to live with my father. Another thirty-one-year-old failure to add to the national statistics.

"Okay," I said to Draper. "Sell me."

Most of the details I already knew. The Cannes Film Festival was Mecca to every entertainment writer in the world. In my nine years of writing about movies, it was the only major festival I'd missed, and it wasn't just that I was queasy about returning to France. Being a journalist at any film festival is like sharing a hot tub with a school of piranhas: everyone snarling for the same piece of meat. Cannes was the longest—eleven days—and the most prestigious festival of all, which meant a lot more piranhas and a whole lot more snarling.

I cut Draper off in midpitch. "When would I have to leave?"

"The ticket is for tomorrow morning."

"That's not even twenty-four hours from now!" I said.

"Well, the festival begins on the seventh, day after tomorrow. And pardon me for asking, Nat, but has your social situation changed in the last year?"

I started to bristle, but he quoted a sum with a lot of zeros in it.

When I didn't argue, he said, "So, good. Do you have a laptop?"

"I don't . . . when it crashed I couldn't—"

"Never mind, you can rent one in the pressroom. And check your e-mail. Daily. You're mine now, and don't forget it. I'll have your ticket waiting."

For a minute I stood with my grimy hands on my hips, fuming at Draper. But the facts were hard to deny: I had no boyfriend who would miss me, no real friends who'd be disappointed if I didn't show up for lunch, not even a dog to farm out to a kennel.

There were my fish, of course, assuming they were still alive. On a whim, I reached into the plastic bag and scooped out the Orange

One. I sent a breath into his mouth the way you blow on hot soup and dropped him into the pail. For almost a minute he lay on his side in the water, and then, in a violent jerk that caused the water to splash against the bucket wall, he regained his balance and fought his way back to life.

I stood staring into the bucket as he moved sluggishly around in circles, apparently unaware that he had nearly come face-to-face with the great Holy Mackerel himself. Life is thirsty, I thought. Give it half a drop to go on and it'll beat death by a mile.

It took about thirty minutes to make the arrangements. I rifled through old purses and piles of paper on my desk looking for my passport and finally found it exactly where I'd hidden it, sitting on top of the kitchen counter in plain sight. Draper had insisted I keep my passport up-to-date in case of a global cinematic emergency, which was apparently what things had come to.

I was maxed out on my credit card, so I called Draper back and asked him to advance me part of my fee so I'd have some cash. I stuffed a change of clothes for the airplane in my big travel purse and threw in the Worst-Case Scenario sack: dental necessities, comb and brush, lotion, deodorant, aspirin, a pouch of tissues, sleeping pills, makeup, and a sandwich-sized plastic bag containing a crisis-only hundred-dollar bill, which I'd never touched in nine years of traveling to movie junkets. In my big suitcase I packed enough of everything to keep me adequately clothed for two weeks, including something for the inevitable studio parties: my all-purpose, high-octane, cleavage-revealing black dress. I considered bringing the bottom half of a swimsuit, since I was headed for the Riviera, but I knew there'd be no time for swimming.

It was ten forty-five when I sat down at my kitchen table and poured myself a glass of wine, and I could see the moon rising over the mountain behind the house. It cut through the asparagus fern hanging over the sink, making the slender leaves look sharp and menacing, and I felt a shiver from one shoulder to the other. I was ready to return to France if it meant holding on to my house. What I wasn't ready for was telling my father I was going. I gulped down my Cabernet and dialed his number.

My father had retired from the Public Health Service two years earlier and was still living a thousand miles away, in the house where I'd spent most of my childhood. We were on friendly terms—since we'd never really grown together, we'd never grown apart—but I hadn't seen him in months.

When he answered, I heard the high-pitched howl of a color man in the background, calling an old football game my father would have forgotten again by the time he fell asleep.

"Hey, Pop," I said.

"I'll be," he said. I could barely hear him over the TV.

"I hope you weren't sleeping."

"Just watchin' a rerun of the Broncos fumbling for the hundredth time," he said. "How you doin', Buff? You employed or you still looking?"

"Well, Pop . . ." I said.

"What?" he shouted at the top of his voice.

"WELL, POP!"

"Well Pop what?"

"Well, Pop, I'm going to France!"

There was a long pause, during which I wished I could take it back. He groaned slightly with the effort of reaching for his remote, and I heard the color man's voice fade to nothing in the background.

"I got a job covering the Cannes Film Festival."

"Covering it with what?" He made this joke every time I got an assignment. "I guess you think that's heaven: movies all day long."

"Right," I said, and waited for what I knew was coming next.

"When you were a little girl, all you wanted was movies-movies-

movies, morning, noon, and night." I mouthed his next words along with him: *"My favorite movie buff."*

I forced a chuckle. "It's a good job for me right now. I'll be gone for almost two weeks."

"That's a long one," he said. "And France . . ." His voice trailed off. I was sure he was gazing longingly at the Broncos, hunting for a quick exit.

"I'll make enough to keep the house for a few more months."

"Oh, come on. If you need money, I've got thousands stashed away. Just ask."

"I know, Pop." I couldn't bear to get caught in this argument. He did have thousands stashed away, but he didn't have hundreds of thousands. He needed every penny he had just to take care of himself.

"But France. Hell, France." I could almost hear him shaking his head. Every conversation we'd ever had about France had ended that way. He'd been so hurt by my mother's desertion, he blamed the whole country. "Hell, France" was code for *End of discussion.*

"Hey, Pop. Can I ask you—"

"It's late, Buff. Shuffle off to dreamland," and the memory of a thousand lonely bedtimes echoed in my ear.

"Pop . . . do you remember where . . . I mean, did they ever tell you the name . . ."

There was a long and deadly silence before he said, "In Paris. In a cemetery near the Vincennes Château." The color man's voice grew louder in the background, and I barely heard him add, "Anything else you want to know, ask the Frenchman."

I could hardly believe my ears. In all the years I'd been with him, my father had never once offered me information about my mother no matter how hard I'd pried, and certainly he'd never mentioned "the Frenchman." I'd asked, but there were never answers. Finally I'd stopped asking.

"Pop, thanks," I said. If I'd been with him, I'd have hugged him—a gesture that would have made him squirm. I waited for him to say something else. When he didn't, I said, "The Broncos still fumbling?"

"Who cares about the Broncos?"

"Well, then, what?"

"The rattler," he said.

"What rattler?"

"What rattler. The rattler in your bedroom."

The rattlesnake had arrived a few months after I came to live with my father, when I was seven and still scared of wiggly things. A gigantic brown diamondback had slithered into our house during a summer storm and ended up in the middle of my room under a towel. I'd frozen where I was standing when I'd picked up the towel, and it started shaking its tail. When my father called to me from the kitchen and I didn't answer, he ran to my room and found me staring eye to eye with the snake. Before it could get itself coiled for the strike, he'd pulled my Superman lamp from the table by my bed, trapped the snake's head with the base of it, and grabbed it at its throat.

In half a second, snake in hand, he was out the back door and running through the cactus and timothy, where he whirled the rattler around his head like a lariat and tossed it into the sage.

"I remember that rattlesnake," I said now, but I knew he wasn't talking about the snake. He was remembering what he'd told me *after* he'd tossed it into the sage. He'd looked down at me with a face so stern I was riveted to his eyes. "In the natural world," he'd said, "everything is exactly where it belongs. The rocks, the animals, the predators, even the lightning falls where it must. Nothing is out of place. So it's easy to know where a snake belongs. The trick for human beings is to figure out where they belong."

My father had lived in Crownpoint, New Mexico, working with the Navajo Indians since he was a young man, and he knew it was exactly where he belonged. But he also knew, from the moment I arrived to live with him, that I wasn't even close to where I was meant to be.

After he hung up, I held the dead receiver in my hand for a long time. Everything was quiet except for the eerie yelping of a pack of coyotes in the hills behind my house. I wished that just once my father and I might have a conversation that wasn't laced with subtext. Still, he'd told me where my mother was buried, and that was a first. And "the Frenchman." He had never spoken the Frenchman's name, but I'd been falling asleep with his memory since I was six years old, and I would never forget it: Michel Claudel.

I put the phone in its cradle and went to my computer. I clicked "Michel Claudel" on my Google bookmarks and a familiar site popped up, of a gallery on the Rue Bagnolet in Paris called Galérie Claudel: Affiches de Marque. There he was again. In some obscure corner of my mind was a memory of my three-year-old self, dragging my mother into Claudel's trendy poster shop, where an expensive print by Paul Klee was hanging in the window. I'd tugged on the sleeve of Claudel's jacket to ask him about the print, which I mistook for a drawing I'd done that very morning. I was too young to have actual memories of those details, but it was the adorable and possibly apocryphal mistake that had brought my mother and Claudel together, and I'd heard it as often as a bedtime story during the years before my mother's death. Months after I arrived in America without him, I was still crying myself to sleep, babbling his name.

So Claudel was still in Paris. I gave myself a moment to roll that around in my head and then turned off the computer. I had one more thing to do before I left.

My garage was just big enough to squeeze a go-cart into, but I'd opted to use it for stuff I couldn't bear to throw away. The far wall was lined with plastic storage containers and cardboard boxes, which my father had driven from his garage to mine when I bought my house. Under two containers marked "Buffy 8th Grade" and "Buffy 7th Grade" was one that said "Buffy High School." I dug under my collection of stuffed movie dogs and took out my old jewelry box.

It was a simple wooden rectangle about the size of a Kleenex box, with two roses carved on the top, and it was the only ladylike gift I'd ever received from my father. One of the hinges was broken, and I opened it carefully.

On the top shelf of the box there was a small autographed photo of Ethan Hawke from *Gattaca,* which I'd bought off the Internet, and about a hundred earrings, scattered and tangled and indistinguishable from one another. The bottom level was lined with black velvet, and lying facedown under some silver bracelets was a three-by-five-inch color photograph. The picture had been carefully laminated, but not before it had already faded with age and been chipped in places the way photographs get when they're carried around in pockets and folded and unfolded too many times.

Holding it in my hands again made me feel the mixture of danger and comfort I'd felt every time I held it since the day I'd discovered it, twenty-four years before, on one of those summer afternoons when a seven-year-old gets so bored she dares for the first time to look through her father's belongings. The picture had been lying in his sock drawer, under a stash of black socks rolled into soft round balls, and the second I saw it I knew it was my mother, even though my memory of her face had faded. I snatched it up without telling my father and hid it in my pillowcase.

Every night after that, when my father said, "Shuffle off to dreamland," I took it out and looked at it before I went to sleep, but it wasn't long before I started to worry that the pillowcase wasn't safe. I wasn't sure what he'd do to me if he found out I'd stolen his photograph. I didn't realize then that the worst thing my father was capable of doing was throwing up his hands and saying he didn't know what to do with me.

I looked for a safer place, but good hiding places aren't that easy to find. Even in old movies, when the pirate hid the treasure map, or the bank robbers hid the money, you could always tell how somebody was going to find the loot. But when my time came, I was worse than bad guys in old movies.

I finally hid it between the mattresses of my bed so that even when I slept she would be with me. By the time I was ten, it was bent in two places: across the top rung of the corral fence where my twenty-one-year-old mother was sitting, and through the chest of my father, more than twice her age, who was leaning against the fence next to her.

My mother had pointy eyebrows exactly like mine, and in the picture her blonde hair was wild and wispy in the wind. She was laughing with her head back and her mouth open, just a little. She looked like the one human being in the history of the world who'd been chosen to live forever.

My father had written her name, "KIT CONWAY," in big red letters on the back of the picture, above the date, which was six months before I was born. That meant that in a way, it was also a picture of me. The next day she had flown away to France and taken me with her.

I lived with my mother in Paris for almost seven years. I imagined her reading me stories and teaching me to tie my shoes the way other mothers did. I know she loved movies; she must have taken me to a lot of them, because walking into a movie theater has always felt to me like walking into church.

But isn't it odd the way even the most important things drift from your memory if you're not paying attention? Over the years, I'd see pictures of Paris, of the Eiffel Tower or the Champs-Élysées, and I'd recognize them as places I'd probably been to before. But whatever images I'd had of my mother were eclipsed by the memory of that wooden box disappearing into the earth. All that remained was the photograph.

If my father knew I'd taken that picture, he never let on. One day I took the wrapper off a six-pack of raisins and taped the cellophane around it for protection. When I left Crownpoint for college, I left the picture behind in my broken jewelry box.

Now I realized with some surprise that the stolen photograph of my mother was going with me to France. I took one more look at it and slipped it into the zippered compartment in my suitcase.

A commercial airliner is usually a pretty
safe place to be during a lightning storm,
especially when it's parked on the jetway.

American Meteorological Society

2

Somewhere over the Atlantic

Tuesday, May 6

*B*y noon I was on my way to France, and I couldn't relax. I fidgeted in my seat and fussed with my pillow. I stared at the screen ahead of me without putting on my earphones and watched reporters' mouths move in silence.

Finally I took out the folder of festival information that Draper had sent me. It included a map of Cannes and a list of the movies that were being shown in all the competitions, with exclamation points beside the movies and actors and directors I was commanded to interview: American filmmakers like Quentin Tarantino and Robert Zemeckis, actors like Charlize Theron and Johnny Depp (if I didn't get this one, Draper said, I should not return to America). There was an exclamation point next to German director Wim Wenders's name, and one beside an obscure French producer named Jacques Vidanne, who was making his first appearance at Cannes in twenty-five years.

Vidanne was the only item of festival business that piqued my interest. He'd been a personal hero of mine for many years, since he'd written and produced a stunning little movie called *Aimée,* about a five-year-old trying to cope with her mother's death. For obvious reasons the movie had spoken to me in several different languages, and after that I'd seen all of the films I could find that he had made.

It would almost be worth the bedlam of Cannes to talk to Jacques Vidanne, but my mind refused to absorb the rest of Draper's orders. I was reaching for the latest issue of *Sky Mall* when I realized I was being watched. A man in the last row of the business cabin was peeking at me through the dividing curtain. When I peeked back, he looked away.

I fished a sleeping pill out of my Worst-Case Scenario sack and washed it down with Diet Coke.

The movie was starting in an hour—a sci-fi-action-thriller-time-travel-murder-mystery-romance extravaganza—but luckily the pill kicked in during an in-flight sitcom. I was just beginning to wonder whether anything about France would feel familiar to me when I fell, quite suddenly, to sleep.

I was awakened a short time later by a "Psst!" from business class. The man who'd been staring at me before was leaning through the dividing curtain.

"Nattie?" His smile practically sparkled. I squinted at him in the dim light.

He gave me a high-pitched snigger, the kind of laugh that usually accompanies a nasty practical joke. It was something Leland Dunne—the host of a Canadian TV show called *Celebrity 24/7*— was famous for. I hadn't seen him since the morning of my last press junket the year before, when I'd awakened in a post-coupling panic and left his room without saying good-bye.

"Have you come to apologize?" he said with a grin.

My cheeks burned. "I didn't recognize you. You look so . . . different," I said.

"I know—they blonded me," he chortled, running his fingers through his fine hair, which had once been the color of mouse fur but was now a downy gold. "And look at you—gorgeous as ever." Apparently compelled by my gorgeousness to come closer, he and his dazzling smile crossed the business-class barrier into coach and took the seat next to mine.

Leland Dunne was one of those hip, smooth-talking movie connoisseurs whose natural habitat is entertainment TV. It would be charitable to call him tall, and he was just this side of gaunt, with horn-rimmed glasses that covered his vibrant eyes. He had the effete look of an aristocrat, as if he should be wearing a paisley ascot instead of a black blazer over a black T-shirt, but in spite of his slightly nerdy appearance, women loved him. He was witty and charming, and for almost ten years our interactions had been like boxing practice: he jabbed, I ducked. Eventually he'd slipped under my radar when I was too tired for evasive maneuvers.

Movie junkets are overflowing with males and their opinions, but female critics are harder to come by, so I'd had my pick of available men—along with some who only pretended to be available. I'd tried on a few relationships that lasted as long as the first act of a romantic comedy: in the time it took Hugh Grant to get Julia Roberts into bed in *Notting Hill,* for instance, I was out the door.

"You could have left a note," he said, snapping his seat belt closed.

"Don't," I said. "Just because I can't escape now doesn't mean you can pester me."

"I see." On his palm with an imaginary pen he scribbled *Most memorable night of my life did not happen.* He put the imaginary notebook in his imaginary pocket and looked up at me with a smile. "I heard you quit the biz. So then why are you on this plane, if not to reconcile with me?"

"Bills," I said.

He laughed his nasal laugh. "If only you'd stoop to television, your bills would pay themselves."

I shuddered. There are serious prejudices between print and broadcast journalists. TV journos consider print journos to be snobs who write for other print journos (and are therefore read by a Lilliputian portion of the population). Print journos believe TV journos to be cretins who are worshipped blindly by the lowest common denominator.

Leland had the flash and the easy tongue that was needed for TV, but he was a lot smarter than most of the celebrities he talked to and many of the print journalists who tried to dismiss him.

"I've never seen you in Cannes before," he said.

I shook my head. I was moving in slo-mo, and Leland was on fast-forward.

"Well then, I am available to protect and enlighten you at every turn. I promise you, Cannes is nothing to be trifled with. A quarter million people in a town designed for seventy thousand? Last year the airline lost my luggage and the hotel misplaced our reservation. It rained for six days, my passport was stolen." He heaved a sigh that was almost a groan. "I did nothing for eleven days but watch films in foreign tongues and stick microphones in movie stars' faces." He turned to me for sympathy.

"Bummer," I said. I was just hours from this nightmare.

"Eloquently put. But a man has to eat."

I was about to say *So does a woman* when everyone and everything in the coach cabin was thrown forward. One flight attendant lurched into the lap of a sleeping passenger, who let out a piercing scream and shoved her off. Leland's eyes opened wide, and I looked around the dark cabin at the other passengers, who were rearranging their blankets and nervously asking each other questions.

The captain, trying to reassure his passengers that we were all safe as houses, announced that we were closing in on a less disruptive altitude. I felt the giddy lilt in my stomach that meant we were dropping fast, and peered past Leland through the window. I caught a glimpse of the iridescent ring that encircled the moon just before we dove into a cloud and the plane began to shake as if battling a heavy headwind.

And then, as suddenly as it had begun, the ordeal was over. The engine hummed calmly, and the entire cabin erupted in nervous giggles.

Leland turned to me with the delighted expression of a child at the end of a roller-coaster ride.

My heart was just beginning to slow to its normal pace when it suddenly stopped altogether. A brilliant flash of light exploded before my eyes. I froze in horror. The tip of the wing was enveloped by lightning. It seemed to be alive, the way the flame of a newly lit match appears to pulsate with life, and as I watched, it crept over the wing toward us with radiant fingers.

And then it was gone.

"Whoa!" Leland said. "Did you see that?"

A woman behind me burst into tears as my fingers clamped around the armrests of the seat. I couldn't force breath into my lungs, let alone form words.

"Oh, wow," he said. "You look awful."

Leland punched the flight attendant button on the arm of his seat, and over our heads the captain's voice crackled too loudly.

"Sorry about that, folks," he said. "All of you on the right side of the plane can relax. It's just a little lightning storm, nothing to worry about."

But I knew "a little lightning storm" was always something to worry about. I sat there with my head in my lap, hyperventilating, until the flight attendant appeared at my side and switched off the attendant button.

"Do you need a paper bag?" she asked, visibly annoyed that one of her passengers was preparing to hurl. I shook my head.

"She needs help," Leland shot back.

"Do you need help?" the attendant said to me.

I shook my head again and exhaled, and the attendant turned on her heel and disappeared down the aisle. Leland started to unbuckle his seat belt to stop her, but I touched his arm for him to stay put, embarrassed to have called attention to myself.

There'd been a hundred similar panic episodes in my childhood, when I'd startled at the sound of thunder or nearly fainted at a distant flash of light. Living in New Mexico was a blessing in some ways, because it almost never rained. But in the summer, when the temperatures rose to a hundred and the air was dry and brittle, the distant skies were electrified, and the horizon came alive with light.

My father had tried to calm me when I was little, with an endless stream of cheerful movies on his VCR to take my mind off the sky. He read me books and scientific journals about the nature of lightning and taught me to understand it as a fragment of energy, a natural but savage consequence of an ordered universe. There was comfort in that: if it was nothing but pure untamed energy, then it wasn't the vindictive arm of destruction I thought was always following me.

When I was older, I took myself to movies, escaping into stories about safer lives with happy resolutions. Statistics also helped to steady me: if one person in 576,000 is struck by lightning in a twelve-month period, what were the odds against that same person being struck by lightning twice? The answer, according to a *National Geographic* special I'd seen in high school, was one in nine billion.

But those odds didn't work in a whole planeful of people, with the luminous hand of energy so close I could have reached out the window and laced my fingers through it.

Leland sat with me until the color returned to my cheeks, and when he was confident I was back to normal, he said, "Time for me to return to my people." He planted a kiss on my cheek and scooched out over me. "I'll find you when we get to Paris."

I took another sleeping pill from my purse. I was out cold before another flash could threaten my equilibrium.

The flight attendant woke me with an offer of coffee and a plastic-wrapped breakfast, which I ate with plastic utensils. Before I could rub the sleep from my eyes, I grabbed my big travel purse and headed for the restroom.

Airplane lavatories are no place for grooming: I kept bumping my elbows on the walls, and when I took out the hot pink blouse and black pants I'd brought to change into, they accidentally fell in the wet sink.

As I wrestled with the zipper of my pants, I caught sight of the scar on my stomach. It started about an inch above my belly button and ran four more inches straight down to my pubic bone, with ten tiny lines running across it like half a railroad track headed nowhere.

Anyone with a scar of any substance will tell you that it's as changeable as weather. There are times when it seems ruddier or puffier or thicker than usual. Now, thirty-six thousand feet in the air, I thought I could feel it throbbing, calling to me in a kind of silent wail.

My father had tried to convince me that scars were a beautiful journal that proved a body had participated in life. I didn't buy it. By the time I was ten, I loathed it in private. At sixteen, in my only foray into illuminated foreplay, a charming high school senior had told me it looked like something off of Frankenstein's forehead. That sparked a year of painful whispers behind my back about dead mothers and defective torsos, but it proved to be a very effective way of avoiding intimacy. Throughout adolescence, every time I got turned on, I made sure the lights got turned off.

In time I realized that my father was probably right about scars, and I'd learned to feel fond of mine, the way soldiers and police officers feel fond of theirs—hard-won badges and all that, an outer manifestation of an inner strength. Still, my avoidance of sex with the lights on had become a habit I was too self-conscious to break, and it had been one of the reasons I'd slipped unceremoniously out of Leland Dunne's early morning hotel room.

In the tiny airplane lavatory, I finished changing and tucked away my scar. Over the loudspeaker, the flight attendant admonished us to turn off our electronic devices and return our seats and trays to their upright and locked positions. The business class curtain was drawn by an invisible hand.

As the plane bounced onto the runway, I realized that in minutes I'd be standing in the airport I'd left behind twenty-five years before. I wondered if anything would feel familiar. I could see the vague outline of the Eiffel Tower off in the distance. But only if I squinted.

The basic rule to follow if several people are
struck by lightning is to "save the dead first."
Often lightning victims appear dead but
are in fact in cardiac arrest.

"Meteorological Data," Forensic Meteorological Associates, Inc.

3

Paris, France

Wednesday, May 7

A peculiar two-headed bus drove us from the plane to the airport. When we arrived at the gate and were released into the
main building, I looked around for anything that might jar my
memory. But Charles de Gaulle Airport felt to me like any other
airport in the world: impersonal and noisy, a place you want to exit
as much as you want to enter.

Leland was saving a place for me in the customs line, rehearsing
to be my personal guide to the New World. "Let me see your ticket,"
he said, as I handed my suitcase to an officious attendant, who
marked it and sent it on to Nice.

"What happens when we get there? Do we take a bus to Cannes?
A taxi?"

"Anything that moves," he said. "Then we register at the Palais
and the madness begins."

Arrows on the floor directed us out of the baggage area and into the relative quiet of the connections lounge. I found a small table near a snack kiosk, and Leland bought us two *cafés*. I took a sip and shuddered.

"That'll take some getting used to," I said.

"And watch out, it'll keep you awake for a month," he said. "Do you speak any French?"

"I used to," I said.

"Used to, when?"

"A long time ago. I was born in Paris, but I left when I was little, so French was always an easy A for me in school, but I don't know how I'll be in the real world."

"Cannes is hardly the real world. But you must be happy for an excuse to come to France."

"Well . . . ," I said.

"Have you been back since you left?"

I shook my head.

"Why not?"

"Oh God, Leland, don't ask."

He looked at his watch. "You have a full hour to kill before you board your plane. What else have you got to do besides fascinate me?"

I rolled my eyes.

"Really," he said. "Everyone wants to come to France. In France, passion is a virtue! Cooking is a national pastime! Love is a team sport! *Vive la*—"

"Okay, okay." I gave him a brief summary of my life in France, beginning with being born and ending with being dispatched to America from this very airport by Michel Claudel.

"Did you call the old boyfriend to say you were coming?" he said finally.

"Why would I do that?"

He raised his eyebrows in mock alarm. "Did I miss something? Your whole life began with this guy in Paris, and you don't want to track him down?"

"Cannes, remember?" I said, dabbing coffee from my lips. "I'd like to go to my mother's grave, but—"

"Nattie. Sweetheart. Give him a thrill."

I laughed, but the conversation was making me edgy. Just because I'd Googled Claudel didn't mean I wanted to phone him.

Leland was eying me carefully. "Well, I'll be damned," he said. "You're scared. Impressive, this thing you have about men." He saw me flinch and put up his hand as a gesture of peace. "Sorry. Old issues. Knee-jerk male ego."

"Relax. My editor thinks I'm a coward, and he's a lot nastier than you."

"Now you're hurting *my* feelings." He crossed his arms and sat back in his chair. "You should at least look him up."

"Geez," I said, thinking that this casual bullying technique probably made Leland a very good interviewer.

Fortunately for me, our sixty minutes were up. Leland walked me to my gate, where he was the first to see the bad news.

My plane had been canceled for *problèmes mécaniques.* I tried not to say anything that would identify me as a spoiled American and took my place at the end of a long line of desperate travelers. They all looked exhausted—hair in disarray, shirts wrinkled, makeup smeared in places—and judging by the expressions on their faces, most of them were as grumpy as I was.

"*Toutes mes excuses,*" the pert little representative from Navare Airlines said when I reached the front of the line. "The International Film Festival at Cannes is beginning, and all our flights for the next twenty-four hours are filled."

I leaned my elbows on the counter, trying to think of how to say that the airline had jolly well better get me to Cannes pronto, when *français* suddenly began spilling out of my mouth. *"J'espère que votre compagnie a le bon sens de prévenir une telle difficulté pour les passagers à Cannes—"*

Leland elbowed me proudly.

The attendant replied, "I give you two choices. You may stay tonight at the nearby Hilton at the airline's expense and leave on the first flight of the morning." She read from her computer screen as if it were a script. "Also, you are at liberty to wait at the airport today, hoping for a cancellation."

I stared at her dumbly.

"Of course, you might also like to take the train from the *centre de Paris*," she said, and handed me a schedule of departures from the Gare de Lyon. "Next!"

"Well, well," Leland said. "Paris after all!"

I gave him a dirty look and put my name on the standby list for his plane. To ease the pain of waiting, he bought us each a bottle of Evian about the size of a thimble for four euros apiece. When we returned to his gate, it was time for him to board. He took my hand and laid something in my palm.

"This is for you," he said. "It's a French phone card, in case you find yourself in Paris and the hours stretch into days. You can call information and find him."

"Man, are you pushy," I said.

The lucky travelers who had seats on this flight began to thread into the portal, and we watched them vanish one by one into the tunnel. Before I had time to duck, Leland grabbed me and gave me one of those over-the-top movie kisses that bring breathing to a temporary halt.

"So long, toots," he said, handing the agent his boarding pass. He let out another snort and disappeared into the long cave of the breezeway.

It was ten-thirty when I put my name on the standby list, and in the next three hours, I watched four flights take off for Nice without me. I wandered through the airport, exchanged my emergency hundred-dollar bill for emergency euros, and passed at least a hundred phones without picking up a single one.

My nerves were frazzled, and my foot hurt where the strap of my sandal was attempting to cripple me. I was digging in my purse for the money to pay for a Gruyère sandwich when I found the train schedule I'd gotten from the perky Navare clerk. A train would be departing for Nice late in the evening from the Gare de Lyon. I didn't need a *maison* to fall on my *tête:* Leland was right.

The attendant at the Navare desk returned my ticket and promised to have my bag delivered to the festival office at the Palais des Festivals in Cannes.

"La Gare de Lyon," I told the driver as I slid into the back seat of the taxi.

The Eiffel Tower loomed magically on the horizon, but its mystique was lost on me. The taxi drove through the outskirts of the city, weaving dangerously through a mass of tiny cars—Citroëns, Peugeots, Fiats. Even the occasional van was mini-sized. I was definitely not in America.

The taxi driver, who was so tall his hair touched the black felt on the roof of the cab, asked where I was headed from the Gare de Lyon. I almost told him I couldn't speak French, but I heard myself say *"Au sud, pour le festival de Cannes"* instead. He told me his family lived in Marseilles, and pretty soon the sounds became familiar and I realized we were having an actual conversation.

He was in the middle of a long, sad story about moving his mother to Paris when I glanced at my watch. It was three p.m., which translated to French time as fifteen o'clock. My train departed at nineteen-thirty, which gave me four hours to wander the city and find my mother's grave. That sounded like fate to me.

"*Pardon, monsieur,*" I said to the driver. "Please take me to the Château de Vincennes instead."

The taxi driver scowled at me in his rearview mirror and spun the steering wheel around to make a U-turn.

We'd driven several blocks, past boutiques, fruit stands, and magazine kiosks, when I began to feel queasy about wandering through an unknown graveyard by myself.

"*Monsieur!*" I said. "I've changed my mind. Please take me to the Gare de Lyon."

He slammed on his brakes and put his elbow on the back of the seat. "*Vous devez décider, mad'moiselle.*"

"But I don't know what to do!" I said. "You decide."

"*Avec plaisir,*" he said, and pulled into traffic.

Ten minutes later, I stepped onto the sidewalk and took a deep breath of Paris—and nearly fainted. The air was filled with the unmistakable fragrance of a nearby pâtisserie mixed with the street perfume of diesel fuel. A memory flashed in my head of descending the four flights of stairs from my mother's apartment to buy brioches for breakfast.

I tried to hold on to the memory, but the trouble with memories is that they come and go when they want to, and this one wanted to go. I launched myself into the stream of pedestrians to follow the aroma. A flock of pigeons flew off a roof above me, and a cat meowed hungrily at them from a balcony over my head.

I was thinking that even the cat's meow had a French purr to it when I came upon the pâtisserie. The wall behind the counter had loaves of bread sticking out of four separate bins: short fat loaves, medium-length *baguettes* for sandwiches, skinny *ficelles* a yard long, and *flutes* as thin as cigars. In the glass case was a buttery pile of softball-sized brioches.

I bought one brioche from the sad-eyed teenage girl behind the counter, who wrapped it in a square sheet of waxy paper. It was shaped like a mushroom, with a light brown egg-white glaze over the flaky crust, and inside—cakey ambrosia. I took a bite of it and practically swooned. It was light, foamy, buttery, and rich, and I ate it in four swift bites as I fell into step with a group of chattery schoolchildren crossing the street.

There was a moment when I nearly turned back to the pâtisserie for another brioche, but I looked up and found myself standing in front of a high wrought-iron fence. I felt a flutter of excitement. The fence separated pedestrians from a deep, dry stone moat; an iron plaque announced that the ominous structure on the opposite side of the moat was the dungeon of the Château de Vincennes.

The tower of the château, which looked a little too much like Sleeping Beauty Castle in Disneyland to qualify as an actual historical monument, loomed above the dungeon. I made my way around a crowd of tourists taking pictures of the dungeon and followed the fence around the jagged corner of the moat to the edge of the Vincennes gardens.

And there, just as my father had promised, was a sign carved in gray stone that pointed straight into the forest. It said "Cimetière le Nôtre."

I stood for a moment, staring at the sign, and then set off down the path. The gravel crunched under my feet and I had another sense-memory, of holding Claudel's hand at the head of the procession of mourners that buried my mother. I didn't remember the trees or the path, but I could almost feel the steadiness of Claudel's hand.

The cemetery gate was made of heavy wrought iron, and I gave it a hard push. It opened enough for me to pass through, creaking like hinges in *The Haunting*. Inside the gate, the smell of damp earth filled my nostrils. Thick weeping branches bent over the gravestones, some of them new with legible names and dates chiseled in the stones, others so eroded by the elements that they were nothing more than smooth marble.

I didn't know the first thing about cemeteries—I'd only set foot once in the dusty old white man's graveyard in Crownpoint—so I vowed to read every stone in the Cimetière le Nôtre until I found the one I was looking for.

I'd scrutinized at least a hundred tombstones before the sun began to disappear, and I was hunching closer to the writing, thinking that soon I'd have to read the names by Braille, when I came upon a vase of fresh daisies that had tipped over at the foot of one of the graves. I set it right and glanced at the old headstone on the left, a man who had died in 1891. And the stone on the right . . .

My heart stopped. Even in the dim light, with the sun barely peeking through the trees, I could read my mother's full name:

KATHERINE KITREDGE CONWAY

Née le dix avril

Morte le sept mai

I fell slowly to my knees beside the grave, too stunned to move.

The grass at the foot of the tombstone was wet, and dampness oozed into the fabric of my slacks, so I took some tissues out of my purse and spread them under my knees. I could hear the sound of my own breathing, but the air around me was completely still. I'd never seen her full name before—her nickname "Kit," which my father had written on the back of my stolen picture, could have come from "Katherine" or from her maiden name, "Kitredge"— but those four words, *"Morte le sept mai,"* were engraved in my memory as permanently as they were in this stone. I wanted to cry—for all the years I'd been without my mother, for all the tears she hadn't wiped away, for the confused little girl who'd once thrown dirt into this grave.

I waited for my eyes to fill with tears, but all I felt was cold. The sun was almost gone, and the moisture from the grass was seeping through the tissues into the knees of my pants. I wanted desperately to make this a scene that would matter. Fate had brought me here today—I should at least have tears to offer.

So I thought of conversations I might have had with her and hair I'd been forced to comb myself. I thought of the little girl in Jacques Vidanne's *Aimée,* who had wept when her mother died. Still my eyes were dry, and after a while I began to feel silly, there on my knees. I thought, I'm a disgrace to the fellowship of mourners. I felt suddenly bored with this grave and everything it represented. The sun was gone, and the knees of my pants were soaked. I wanted, I suddenly realized, to be rid of this place.

As I pulled myself up, I lost my balance and grabbed at the grass where my hand had fallen. When I got to my feet, I was holding a handful of long blades of grass. Without a thought about why I was doing it, I wadded the grass in the soggy tissues and stuffed them in my purse.

It was nearly seven o'clock when I found a taxi and headed to the Gare de Lyon. I was tired now, weary from twenty-four hours of travel, but even more exhausted from a lifetime of feeling sorry for myself.

The taxi passed blocks and blocks of small art galleries whose owners were pulling down grates in front of their windows, and I wondered seriously what had become of Michel Claudel. He'd been a young man when he put me on that plane to America. I imagined him now, paunchy and bald, with a French wife and several children. I wasn't the only one who'd grown older.

"Would it be out of the way to take me to the Rue Bagnolet on the way to the train station?" I asked the driver, and I heard the words before I planned to say them.

"*Pas du tout,*" he said. "*Cinq minutes.*"

In five minutes we pulled up across the street from a neat little shop with "Galérie Claudel" in large gold letters above a black awning. A single vintage poster was displayed in the window—a bird balancing on a cognac barrel—and inside I saw several people examining a piece of art on the wall. I couldn't see any of them clearly, but a tall man in a black shirt stood with his back to me, pointing at the picture.

"Shall I wait for you?" the driver said.

I stared into the gallery in amazement. Was one of those people Claudel?

"*Mad'moiselle? Je vous attends ici?*"

"*Non, non,*" I said. "I won't go inside. I am only looking."

I knew from Google that his full name was Michel Paul Claudel—the "Paul" for his art professor father and not the French poet and diplomat Paul Claudel, whom I'd read about in college French classes. The "Michel" was for him, but my mother and I had known him only as Claudel.

"I am pleased to hold my car for you," the taxi man said, nudging me to decide.

I pushed on the handle and the door popped open, but I didn't move. In or out? I asked myself. Until I'd told Leland about Claudel at the airport, I hadn't said his name out loud since my seventh birthday, when I'd asked my father if he'd sent me a present. The look I'd gotten in return had been swollen with such complicated emotion—sadness? anger? an apology?—that I never dared utter it again. What could I possibly have to say to Claudel now?

I pulled the door shut, still staring at the people moving around inside the gallery. "*La gare, s'il vous plaît,*" I said.

Half of Paris seemed to be bustling through the Gare de Lyon, pulling suitcases behind them. The smell of body odor and metallic steam stung in my nostrils.

"*Un billet à Nice. Quai numéro six,*" the clerk at the ticket booth said as I handed her my money. "*Partir le sept mai.*"

I thought I'd misunderstood her. "*Quel date?*" I asked.

"*Le sept mai. Aujourd'hui,*" she said, and looked over my shoulder to the next customer.

I stepped out of line in a daze. Ridiculous as it seemed, I'd never connected May 7 with *le sept mai*, the date I'd seen chiseled into my mother's gravestone. The actual day existed even without a name, but May 7 was harmless: *le sept mai* was a hard slap.

When I reached the quai, it was nineteen-fifteen. Fifteen minutes left, and between me and the train was a large circle of free-standing public telephones. I thought: first Leland with his relentless questions, then the phone card, and now this. I could take a hint.

My hands were so clammy I nearly dropped the receiver, but I called information and asked for the Galérie Claudel. I copied the number onto the corner of my ticket and dialed.

"*Allo, oui?*" said a pleasant woman's voice. "*Galérie Claudel.*"

My tongue felt like a piece of cardboard. "*Michel Claudel, s'il vous plaît.*"

"I am very sorry," she said in French, "Monsieur Claudel has left the gallery. I can give him a message on behalf of . . . ?"

"Natalie Conway," I blurted out.

"You are a client, perhaps?"

"No, not a client. I was once . . ." I stopped. "I knew him . . . a long time ago."

She paused, in case I should care to amplify—an effort at discretion, I guessed.

"*Bon, alors,*" she said. "I will tell him he should expect you to call again?"

I couldn't give her an answer.

"May I ask, madame? Are you American? It is a *soupçon* in your accent."

"Yes," I said. "I'm in France for the festival in Cannes."

"*Ah, bon,*" she said. "I will tell M. Claudel he had a call from his old American friend Natalie Conway. *Au revoir, madame.*"

Before I had time to decide if this was an accurate description of who I was, I heard another earsplitting whistle at Quai #6 and turned to see a man in a navy-blue uniform with his arm out straight, his flat palm signaling no further access to my train. I waved at him frantically, sprinting in his direction. He threw up his hands and lifted his shoulders—a gesture that said *I cannot hold back a train! I am only human.* But he let me pass, and I leapt onto the first car.

I found my seat, next to a round German with a bagful of sausage and bread on his lap. I didn't know if I was out of breath from running or from excitement, but I was out of shape for both.

I sat down and shoved my purse under the seat. The bald German opened a pocketknife, stabbed a slice of sausage, and offered it to me.

"You vill haf hungry?" he asked. I said yes and smiled sweetly, because I always smile sweetly at a man with an open pocketknife. The sausage made my mouth water as I chewed, and my stomach growled.

"You haf ride trains of great speed again?" he asked.

"No," I said. With a sigh of relief, I leaned back with my head against the soft white pillow of the headrest.

The German began a long, mostly incomprehensible lecture about the speedy miracle of the *trains de grande vitesse* as he ate his sausage.

He was still talking when the conductor came through the compartment. Blades of grass from my mother's grave fell out of my purse when I handed him my ticket. They lay on my lap like an accusation: what would it have hurt if I'd stepped out of the taxi and crossed the street to Claudel's gallery? He never would have guessed who I was. I could have pretended to be interested in posters.

I was about to brush the cemetery grass onto the floor when I remembered the plastic sandwich bag that contained my emergency euros. I gathered up the blades and put them in with the money. I could have gotten a glimpse of Claudel. Draper was right: I *was* spineless.

By the time the conductor had moved on to the next car, I was so mad at myself, it took a couple of tries before I could match up the lines of plastic and seal the bag shut.

We have come to visit you
in peace and with goodwill.

Michael Rennie, in *The Day the Earth Stood Still*

4

Cannes, France

Thursday, May 8

Seconds after the taxi dropped me off in the center of Cannes, a man wearing a faded black T-shirt with a huge red tongue on the front engulfed me in a bear hug. I didn't have time to be afraid before he kissed me full on the lips, then released me and poured beer on the top of my head.

As the liquid drizzled down my neck and onto my blouse, he whispered in my ear, "*Êtes-vous heureuse?*" *Are you happy?* Then he licked his lips, kissed me again, and danced away.

I watched, dazed, as the crowd swallowed him up. Beer dripped from my chin onto my poor, abused silk blouse. Was I happy? What a question.

Swarms of people were dancing and drinking in the plaza, as if it were the last night on earth and not just the first night of the festival. My watch said two-fifteen. I could smell the fishy sea-scent drifting in from the Mediterranean.

Another body brushed intimately against my chest, and I realized that if I stayed in that spot, I was going to have a romantic experience whether I wanted one or not. I had to find my hotel.

Over the heads of the revelers, I could see a huge building with a long, wide staircase, and at the top of the stairs, draped over the entrance, was an immense red banner with a simple gold palm branch in the center. This had to be the Palais, where the perky airline clerk had promised to send my bag. I elbowed my way purposefully through the crowd toward it: swimming to safety.

All my fingers and toes were still attached when I arrived at the staircase. I could feel the ominous presence of the nighttime sea; lights from a hundred boats twinkled like fireflies on the water.

I found a row of glass doors on the ground floor of the Palais, and through them I saw living beings moving inside. But the doors were guarded by uniformed Frenchmen who informed me that without credentials I was *interdit,* no matter what kind of baggage was waiting for me inside.

"But I have no clothes!" I said. "*Et je suis* jet-lagged!"

They shook their heads to my reasoned plea. Clearly this was a battle I would have to fight after I'd had some sleep.

There were three taxis waiting at the curb, and I heaved myself into the first one and told the driver the name of my hotel—the Chalet d'Isere. He inched carefully through the crowd into a narrow backstreet where there were no revelers or streetlights, only apartments where saner people, who had to work in four hours to serve the festival, were fast asleep.

The Chalet d'Isere was a small three-story stone hotel at the absolute top of the hill overlooking the port of Cannes. In the dim light of the street lamp, I read the rusted plaque on the wall that described how French author Guy de Maupassant had lived, written, and finally died here in 1893. Through the gate I could see a small flowered patio, which, even at three in the morning, looked like the cover of a book about charming French courtyards. Vines covered the two back walls and stretched over the garden, which was encircled by potted plants. A few fallen bougainvillea flowers lay decoratively on a wrought-iron bench.

I pushed the doorbell, and in the back of the house, a light came on. A disheveled woman poked her head out the door.

"*Oui?*" She was rubbing her eyes with her knuckles.

"*Bonjour, madame!* I mean . . . *bon soir!*" I said cheerfully, as if I routinely knocked on people's doors at three in the morning. "*Je m'appelle Nattie Conway. Je suis en retard.*" I thought it appropriate that the French phrase for "I am late" sounds so similar to the English one for "I am retarded."

The woman, whose name was Madame Vigny, wrapped the belt of her pretty maroon negligee around her waist. Against what appeared to be her better judgment, since I'd arrived without luggage, she let me in and led me up to my room—a tiny space on the third floor, at the top of a tightly coiled staircase. The stairway was so steep that any questions I had about Guy de Maupassant's demise were answered: he had no doubt been climbing these very stairs to his attic apartment when his heart gave out on him and he tumbled down the steep spiral, coming to his eternal rest beside a potted plant in the charming flowered courtyard.

"Breakfast will be served in the garden whenever you like, mademoiselle." Madame Vigny gave a great yawn.

"Can you tell me when the first press screening for the festival begins?"

"Everyone in Cannes knows the schedule for the festival," she said wearily. "We are all its captives for the next two weeks. The first movie is at eight-thirty in the Grande Salle des Lumières." Five hours from now.

I arranged for her to wake me at seven-thirty, and she handed me a heavy four-inch skeleton key, gave a tug to the sash of her negligee, and disappeared down the stairs.

My *atelier* was about as big as the average walk-in closet. It had a low-sloped ceiling and one large window looking out onto neighboring rooftops. Next to the window was a wardrobe with one hanger and four shelves, where I hoped to put my clothes should they someday materialize.

In one corner of the room was a portable plastic shower booth, and next to it were a sink and a toilet. I had to bend down several inches to see myself in the mirror over the sink. Draper had spared no expense.

The window was a large double-door arrangement that unlocked by lifting a heavy iron bar to free one window from the other. As I drew the bar up I felt another strange sense-memory of having opened windows like these before: struggling to lift the heavy bar, being too small, and watching bigger hands than mine manipulate the iron rod. The stuffy little room drank in the night air.

At the bottom of my purse I found the clothes I'd changed out of in the airplane bathroom. The pants and blouse looked better than the ones I was wearing, so I gave them the lonely hanger. For ten minutes I let the water in the tiny shower booth rinse away my travel woes, then climbed naked into the soft bed and stared up at the tiny faded baskets of flowers on the wall. The wallpaper looked as old as Guy de Maupassant.

I switched off the little lamp on the table by the bed and gazed at the moon through the window. In less than five hours I'd begin watching movies and talking to as many filmmakers as I could find, trying to identify some kind of trend that would make this festival different from any other before it. At the same time, I'd be looking for gossip—had Orlando Bloom learned any tips about gaining weight from Robert De Niro? Why had Johnny Depp decided to become a director?—so I could put together one story a day to share the festival with readers in America. The hardest part would be coming up with something original, something that would not appear in every other paper in the world. Just the thought of it made me short of breath.

I watched the half-moon disappear behind a cloud. For the first time since I'd left Paris the night before, I thought about all that had happened in the past two days: the lightning that hit the plane, the conversation with Leland, the Cimetière le Nôtre, the man in Claudel's gallery.

The roughness of the sheets was unbearable against my skin. I threw the covers off and lay with the cool breeze floating through the window. In a minute I'd be cold, but for now it felt like a caress.

Madame Vigny's loud voice woke me at seven-thirty.

"*Mademoiselle! Levez-vous!*" I leapt from the bed, stark naked, and hid behind the door as I opened it a crack, but she wasn't there. Her voice seemed to fill the room, and it was a minute before I realized it was coming through a square plastic box on the wall beside the bed. I should have known she wouldn't climb three flights of stairs just to wake me up.

"*Mademoiselle? Levez-vous!*"

I stretched across the bed and pushed the button by the speaker. "Yes! Thank you! I'm awake!"

"Awake" was a bit of an overstatement, but I thought of my poor little house and splashed water on my face. My hair, which usually fell just below my shoulders, had gone in strange directions during the night, and I pulled it back in a ponytail with a silver barrette. I was dressed by seven-fifty in the black blouse and pants I'd worn to the airport in Los Angeles.

Breakfast was a half baguette with strawberry jam and café au lait. I shared a table with two Frenchmen and an Italian filmmaker from Naples, scarfed down as much as I could swallow in ten minutes, and headed down the hill. The air smelled fresh. It had begun to drizzle during the night, and a heavy mist hung over the city. I knew there was no danger of electrical activity with this kind of weather—my father always said I was more likely to be smothered by clouds like these than struck by lightning—and I was grateful for the rain: by the time the other journalists reached the harbor, their hair would look as bad as mine.

The crowd along the Croisette had thinned in the last five hours, and the aura of celebration had been replaced by the fevered hum of the business of movies: begging for tickets to see them, standing in line for them, buying them, selling them, arguing about them. The only thing I knew from the materials Draper had given me was that there was one place I'd better get familiar with right away: the Palais des Festivals, that immense building at the edge of the water where the guards had spurned me six hours before.

The building was as big as the Getty Museum. It had two magnificent staircases, which were the sort of wide, endless steps you'd expect Drew Barrymore to come running down in *Ever After,* dropping a glass slipper on the way to her stretch pumpkin.

I could see the biggest staircase from the Croisette, covered in red carpet. At eight in the morning, the streets were already littered with the Cannes edition of *Daily Variety* and the front page of *Le Figaro,* with last night's pictures of Brad Pitt, dressed in a magnificent lacy black tuxedo. Charlize Theron was also prominently displayed in a silvery floor-length gown that looked like something she had grown instead of purchased.

I'd been exhausted since the moment I woke up, and as I approached the main entrance to the Palais the same two unbending Frenchmen in blue uniforms refused to let me in without press credentials.

I clenched my teeth in frustration. I needed to get into the Palais to *get* my credentials.

"Impossible. *Pas de certification, pas d'entrée!*" The guards crossed their arms haughtily and shook their heads. I thanked them as unpleasantly as I could, although there's something about the word *merci* that sounds nice—you have to smile to say it—and when they turned their backs to check someone else's ID, I snuck in behind them. I asked a dozen people for directions to the press-room, but everyone seemed as lost as I was, and what interested me more than the whereabouts of my credentials was the whereabouts of my suitcase.

I decided to start at the bottom and work my way up. The base-ment was a cavernous space for small films from small countries to set up their displays, surrounded by confusing hallways where tele-vision crews could park their equipment.

A kindhearted Japanese man from a company called Imamura gave me directions to the credentials table on the third floor and handed me a large white canvas bag with the name of Imamura's entry, *Inu to Nekko,* a black cat and dog printed, nose to nose, on one side. The man bowed to me, and I bowed back, and he bowed again. I stuffed my purse into the *Inu to Nekko* bag and started up a huge marble stairway to the third floor. And suddenly I understood why this was called the Great Hall of Festivals.

I was standing at the bottom of a four-story hall whose ceiling was so high I was tempted to yodel just to hear the echo. Posters as tall as movie screens lined the walls, a chronicle of the winners of the Palme d'Or—the grand award of the festival—and as I stepped onto the long escalator that carried me upward, I passed *Pulp Fic-tion, The Piano,* and *Adieu, Ma Concubine.*

At the top of the first level I stopped to admire the poster of *La Panthère,* which had been written and produced by Jacques Vidanne twenty years before. I wondered where I could start to set up an interview with him.

I reached the top of the next level and knew I was in the right place. Hundreds of temporary mailboxes were lined up against a wall and, swarming like bees around a honeycomb, journalists were removing their plastic-coated press credentials from around their necks and using the cards as keys to open their boxes.

One of the mailboxes had been left open, and I poked my nose into it and asked the person on the other side where to go for credentials.

"*En bas,*" he said. "Next to the casino." Reaching through the box, he shoved my nose aside and closed the door.

Finding your way at a film festival is always frustrating, but I wondered how journalists did it in Cannes if they didn't speak French.

Around a corner from the mailboxes, I found a doorway marked "Jack's," where another uniformed guard gave me directions to a tent located *outside* the Palais. Growling in frustration, I retraced my steps—down the escalator, out the door past the imperious guards, and around the corner of the Palais des Festivals to the palais des credentials. At last.

A sassy little French girl at the A–L table asked for my name, and another, even younger girl with a platinum buzz cut handed me my credentials. Draper had taken care of everything: my name, photograph, and affiliation with the wire service were laminated onto a pink card with a small yellow dot in the corner. I asked the sassy one what the yellow dot meant.

"*Mais c'est évident!*" she said. "Without a yellow dot, you are only on the same level with the other Pink Cards!"

I shrugged my shoulders.

"With a yellow dot, you may be admitted to the front of the line at all movies, behind only the festival journalists with White Cards! You will be admitted before journalists with the Pink Cards or the Blue Cards."

"And before, even worse, the Yellow Cards!" said the girl with the platinum buzz.

The poor peons with Yellow Cards, I thought—forced to gather up the cinematic crumbs left behind by the Whites and Pinks and Blues.

So now I was legal. And, apparently, privileged. I had to find my suitcase, and I thought I'd find some clues to its whereabouts back in my mailbox.

My mailbox was stuffed with pictures and production notes from movies being screened during the first twenty-four hours of the festival. There were five invitations, including a request from New Line for my presence at a luncheon that day at the Café Cinématique for their Quentin Tarantino movie *Bloodbath.*

There was also a mountain of publicity paperwork, and at the bottom of the mountain was a Swatch watch with a picture of Bruce Willis and *The Last Orb* on the face. And two personal notes. One was a phoned-in message from Vince Draper, demanding that I call him immediately. Here we go again, I thought. But he couldn't possibly be disappointed in me already. My first scheduled story was today. I tossed his note in the trash.

The other one was from Leland Dunne:

> Nattie—
> If you're reading this, you have triumphed over providence. Well done. I'll be in Jack's at 11:00 this morning. How I long to see you!
> Yours, Leland

I took Leland's flowery rhetoric with about a tablespoon of salt, but it was nice to know I was a blip on someone's radar.

It was nine forty-five. I'd missed the eight-thirty movie searching for my credentials, and since I was covering the festival for print and didn't have my own computer, I still needed to register in the pressroom, which, according to the map of the Palais, was on the fourth floor. I stuffed the mound of mail into the *Inu to Nekko* bag the Japanese man had given me.

I found the pressroom at the top of a fourth flight of stairs that seemed to be paper-clipped to the roof of the building. It was barely a room: a small square space with twenty computers on four long tightly spaced tables. A dozen journalists were already hunched over terminals, staring out windows at the rain on the harbor below and scratching their heads—all of them, no doubt, as desperate as I would soon be to create clever and informative stories to send to their papers and magazines. A wiry Frenchwoman in a flowered blouse handed me an orange card with my personal wireless connection number on it.

"*Pas nécessaire,*" I said. "I don't have my own computer."

"*Pas de problème!*" she said in a lilting singsong. "We will open an account for you to install yourself at a terminal at any time of the day or night, and send your column to anywhere in the world." She made it sound like magic.

I gave her my maxed-out credit card as a guarantee and she turned to her own computer to record my name. As she leaned over to copy the numbers, I saw it! Almost hidden under a desk, behind the legs of a man in blue jeans, was my suitcase—my ratty old navy-blue, clothing-stuffed, wheel-rolling canvas suitcase with "20th Century Fox" painted on the side (a junket gift I couldn't bear to part with) had never looked so good. I nearly hugged it.

Fully registered, I wheeled my bag to the ladies' *toilette* and spent the next twenty minutes changing clothes and making myself presentable. I put on some comfortable shoes, a red skirt, and a clingy black T-shirt. When I returned to the pressroom, the woman in the flowered blouse agreed to keep my bag until I was ready to return to my hotel. I thanked her a thousand times. Things were looking up.

Fortified by clean clothes and yellow-dotted good fortune, I headed for Jack's, which, I discovered, was a dimly lit lounge where only credentialed print journalists were permitted to venture. As if designed by a junior techie to look like a sleazy bar in *Days of Wine and Roses,* it was packed with black faux-leather booths and low stools around small black tables. It felt like walking into another chamber of the beehive, where a great cacophonous buzz of journalists were speaking a dozen different languages and shuffling notes and schedules in the near-darkness, struggling to read by the light of a single flickering candle in the center of each table.

I entered the bar cautiously, but I was no more than four steps into the room when I heard Leland's nasal high-pitched laugh. I followed the sound of it across the bar and found him sitting in a booth surrounded—as usual—by two stunning blondes.

"Well, look at this!" he said when he saw me. "Another lamb to prime for the slaughter." He sniggered through his nose, and the blondes laughed giddily at his wily wit. He introduced me all around—they were both from a Swedish magazine, and I noticed with compassion that they had Blue Cards. Leland had a yellow-dotted Pink Card dangling from a string around his neck, just like mine. It hadn't taken me long to buy into the class system.

"Let me guess," he said to me now, taking his arm from the back of one of the Swedes' seats and reaching across her lap to remove a pile of papers so I could sit down. "You've slept for about four hours. You're completely lost. You don't know whether you're coming or going, and you're famished. Come rest your exquisite derrière on our Naugahyde and tell us your sad story."

I thought about Leland in the airport in Paris, eager for every word I had to tell about Claudel and about my life in France, and in a flash of clarity I understood the secret of his success with women: he operated on the assumption that nothing is more irresistible to a woman than a man who listens to her. So he pretended to want to know everything we were thinking. He asked us questions, he responded with concern and enthusiasm to the answers, and he laughed at anything approaching amusing. As I slid into his booth, I wanted to tell him I was on to him. But what I wanted more than that was to have someone laugh at my jokes and listen to me and respond with concern and enthusiasm. I was putty in his hands.

He leaned across the table to give me a kiss, soft and sexy, right on the mouth. I wiped my lips discreetly with the tips of my fingers and slid into the booth.

"Thanks for the note," I said when I got myself settled.

"When did you get here?"

"This morning at about dawn on the train. I'm moving on one cylinder. You all look like you're popping on all six."

One of the Swedes swung her head to Leland. The other scooted out of the booth and headed for the bar.

"Do you know what day it is?" Leland said. My face must have been blank in response, because he added, "It's Thursday, Nattie. Don't worry. It'll take a few days to get fully conscious. In case you wondered, they opened the festival last night with *The Last Orb*."

"And . . . ?" I asked.

"It has pieces from most of the sci-fi movies you've seen in the last ten years, so you didn't miss a thing. Did you get your *The Last Orb* Swatch watch?"

I nodded.

"That was the invitation to the big gala afterward. They built a five-million-dollar tent for the occasion, and you had to show the watch to be admitted. Just another party."

"What else?" I asked. "I got a schedule for today in my box, but I haven't had time to figure it out."

"Okay," he said, eager to share his vast knowledge of the festival. He removed his arm from around the Swede and leaned on the table so he could see me. "The big films in competition are premiered at night for all the glitterati in the Grande Salle des Lumières, and the next morning we see them there at eight-thirty—asleep or not. Then we go straight to the press conference across the hall, ask a few questions, and then we push and shove our way into an eleven-thirty screening, unless . . . you're going to the *Bloodbath* luncheon?"

I nodded.

"Me, too. I'm doing print for a British rag. Anyway, then you see whatever you can squeeze in before the seven-thirty *séance*—that means 'screening' in French, as if you didn't know—of the next entry. You know that drill. Then as many interviews as you can

stand. I got some great stuff from Bruce Willis at the press conference this morning that I'll be happy to give you."

"What'd he say?" I asked. The other Swede returned to the table,
carrying three plastic cups of black coffee and two cups of a mysterious red liquid, which turned out to be the only two beverages
available at Jack's.

"Thanks, gorgeous," Leland said. I assumed she blushed in the
dim light. "I have the quotes on my computer. How often do you
have to file?"

"Once a day," I said.

"I'll give them to you after lunch."

Had I been fully rested, I would have been suspicious at such
charity, but all I said was, "Thanks."

Leland cackled. "Wait till you hear what I want in return."
Everyone laughed, girlish giggles.

"I was afraid of that," I said. "What?"

"Later." He looked at his watch. "It's Café Cinématique time."
He began to gather his things. We all slid out of the booth, and
Leland kissed the blondes tenderly on their lovely mouths.

Leland and I walked down the long staircase and out into a soft
Mediterranean wind. The drizzle had stopped, but the sun was a
long way off.

"I thought this was the land of the topless bikini," I said.

"It is. You should go down to the beach and see what this wind
does to nipples."

"Eww," I said.

We walked across the Croisette together, and when we hit the
square, he asked, "You have your bearings now?"

"Sort of," I said without conviction.

"Okay." He turned me around so I was looking at the wide stairway that faced the square. It was this side of the Palais where I'd
caught my taxi the night before.

With his hands still on my shoulders, he stepped up against my back and said softly in my ear, "That stairway leads to the *Salle Debussy*—*salle* means 'hall,' of course, but here it means 'theater.' And you know who Claude Debussy was . . ."

I turned my head and did a "give me a break" thing with my eyebrows.

"Okay, Miss Smarty Pants. So the Debussy is where you'll see all the movies for the Certain Regard, the second level of competition." He pointed to the great red-carpeted stairway on the left, where I'd come into the Palais a few hours before. "But tomorrow morning you'll climb that stairway to the Salle des Lumières to see the first-level movies in competition for the Palme d'Or. I suppose I don't have to telegraph to you what Salle des Lumières means."

"Hall of Lights for one thing," I said indulgently.

"You see, this is what I love about having superior intelligence." He gave me a smug little grin. "You're only half right. '*Lumière*' does means 'light,' but remember the cinématographe? In 1895? First public screening of a film?"

"The Lumières!" I said. "Auguste and Louis Lumière. The brothers who invented film."

"I've always thought it was one of those mind-boggling coincidences, that their name is the word for 'light,' as if . . ."

He moved closer so I felt the brush of his cheek against my ear.

". . . as if destiny had anointed them at birth for its lofty purpose."

I thought for a moment. "Did you read that in an ad or something?"

"Nope," he whispered, "I just made it up."

I tilted my head away from him so I could concentrate on the Palais. From this angle, it looked like a haphazard collection of big, angled boxes, arranged around an even larger box in the center. It was four stories high, and remarkable only for its size and the fact that there wasn't a single window on two of its walls.

Leland leaned in closer and whispered, as if he were telling me a secret, "It's a fabulous building, isn't it?" His natural seductive style was beginning to make me nervous, but I was too disoriented to tell him to bug off. Plus, there was no denying I needed his help.

"Fabulous," I said with forced enthusiasm.

"They replaced the original in 1982," Leland cooed, "because Cannes had become the biggest and the best. It has a dozen screening rooms under one roof. The Lumières' theater is the biggest projection room in the civilized world."

"Which would suggest its being the biggest in the world," I said, stepping away from the purr of his voice in my ear.

He laughed through his nose. "Very cute. There's a cute little twenty-five-seat theater in there just for you cute people, called the Salle Bory, where you can see films in the minor competitions, if you have any spare time, which you won't."

He grabbed my hand and led me across the square to the spot where I'd arrived the night before. "You'll love the theaters, Nattie. Nothing like your local cineplex. No cup racks, no Raisinets squished into the floor. Ooh. Your hands are like ice! I'll give them a rub when we get to the restaurant."

"I'm toasty, Leland, thanks," I said, pulling my hand from his to pretend I was scratching my nose.

"Anyway, just wait until you sit in those chairs. They're designed to equalize the movie experience for everyone." He stopped and patted my cheek. "Of course, they can't do anything about the fact that we're all exhausted. I could buy one of those fancy yachts if I had a dollar for every reel I've slept through here in the last nine years."

When we arrived on the other side of the plaza he took my hand again and began to rub it between his palms. The Cinématique looked like any of the other French cafés around the plaza except that it had an ultra-cool logo of a film strip and an American diner emblazoned above the door. A dozen tables were set up outside in hopes of better weather, their surfaces gathering small pools of water.

We stepped into the line of journalists who were waiting to be admitted. Most of them were talking on cell phones.

"I'm assuming you haven't seen the movie we're going to be talking to these people about," Leland said. The hand massage he was giving me was restoring my circulation.

"I haven't seen anything yet."

A young woman with a deep tan and a skimpy halter top walked by, talking on her cell phone, but she still managed to smile at Leland. He smiled at her breasts and then regained his composure.

"It's an antiwar film—a new leaf for Tarantino. About journalists in a war-torn Middle Eastern country. A little boy, lots of carnage, true story—a passionate, informative, intelligent film."

"In other words, no one will see it."

"Absolutely no one, no matter what we say."

We stood in silence, temporarily depressed by the shallowness of the moviegoing public.

"Precisely why I escaped," I said.

"Damned ineffective retreat, if you ask me."

"Apparently I'll do anything for money."

He chortled loudly. God, I was funny.

A New Line agent waved to us, and we were ushered into the diner, where a section of four large round tables had been set up for us. Between courses, in round-robin fashion, one *Bloodbath* star at a time sat down at our table to answer our questions, which we asked while dipping celery hearts into tasteless raspberry vinaigrette. It was odd for me to do interviews without having seen the movie, but New Line was making allowances for travel-nightmare refugees like me. The revolving-celebrity seating arrangement and the terrible food alone would make a good story.

At 1:50, armed with enough gossip and information for a decent story, we headed back to the Palais, with Leland in grouchy digestive silence. By the time we'd crossed the square, he'd apparently made peace with New Line's cuisine.

"Get out your writing implements." He fished through his shoulder bag for his computer and, balancing it on the flat of his hand, booted up the Bruce Willis press conference. "No more transcribing. My producer feeds all my interviews into this bad boy." He pushed a button and the interview appeared in jerky digital on the monitor.

I wrote as fast as I could, but there was only one quote I needed.

> **Leland Dunne:** Bruce Bruce Bruce. Whassup here?
> I assume no one held a gun to your head to get you to
> come back to this kind of formula action movie, with
> pyrotechnics and T&A as your main characters. We all
> thought you'd retired from all that.

> **Bruce Willis:** Leland Leland Leland. These days most
> people in the world don't read anymore. They need to
> get their stimulation somewhere. I'm only too happy
> to provide it for them.

"Yowza," I said when it was over.

"Didn't I say it was worth its weight?"

I closed my notebook. "Okay. What is it I have to do in exchange?"

He closed his computer and shoved his glasses up the bridge of his nose with his middle finger. "I happen to know you got an embossed invitation to the gala for Johnny Depp's movie tonight."

I rummaged through the papers in my *Inu to Nekko* bag and found a big envelope with a piece of velvety white cardboard inside, laced with gold writing.

"This is spooky," I said. "You have eyes everywhere. Here." I handed him the invitation.

He looked at it carefully. "It's for two people."

"I'm way too tired to go anywhere tonight. Just take it. You can go with one of the Swedes."

"I want to go with you. You speak better English."

I shook the invitation at him until he took it. "Go for the Swedes. I wouldn't be admitted to one of those balls, anyway. My black dress and some excruciating sandals are as fancy as I brought."

He raised an eyebrow. "That short little black thing I used to see you in at parties, with all the cleavage?"

I felt myself blush. My junket wardrobe hadn't been updated since *Steamboat Willy*.

"You could wear that dress to a coronation and be taken for the queen, lover. I will personally buy you some costume jewels."

Oh brother, I thought as I threw the bag over my shoulder. "That's sweet, but it starts at one in the morning. I'll be dead by then."

"Go back to your room after the seven-thirty movie and sleep. That's what everybody does. I'll come and get you."

I thought for a minute. I'd missed the movie and the press conference because I'd spent the morning hunting for credentials, and I needed what Leland had to offer. I knew I was making a deal with the devil, but the devil had kept his end of the bargain. I had to keep mine.

"Oh well, why not?" I said. "I can't get any more tired than I feel right now. But my hotel is on top of the hill." I started walking, and he put his hand through my arm. "You'll never find it."

"I'll take a cab," he said.

"I don't get it. Why do you want to go to this thing so badly?"

"Obviously you've never been to a studio gala." When I didn't deny it, he said, "Well, you have to do it at least once."

"It's more than that," I said suspiciously. "Why do I think there's a woman in this somewhere?"

"Am I that transparent? Okay, she's Canadian. Long, leggy, but not for me. I'm doing a story for a German magazine." He stopped walking and, taking me by the shoulders, turned me to face him, to show me he was serious. "She's a body double. *The* body double, for all the big, beautiful, modest actresses. The perfect body."

"What does she look like?" I asked. "I mean above the neck."

"I have no idea," Leland said, lifting his shoulders and his eyebrows simultaneously. "No one knows—that's the story! 'Unidentified Heavenly Body' is what I'm calling it. Her publicist is Tricia Knight. She'll let me talk to her tomorrow, with*out* a photographer. No pictures. But she'll be at the gala tonight, and now"—he waved the invitation in the air—"so will I. You couldn't count high enough to what the Germans are paying me for this."

"Help. I'm in a bad World War II movie," I said.

"You're not the only one who'll do anything for money."

I wanted to see the three o'clock screening of a French movie called *Pauline et Paul,* and Leland needed to get back to his cubicle to tape his Bruce Willis story. He gave me a soft, wet good-bye kiss, which I intercepted deftly with my cheek, and left me with a promise to pick me up in a taxi at one in the morning, bearing jewels.

A wide line of several hundred people had spread out across the stairway of the Salle Debussy theater, and I flashed my Pink Card and said, *"Pardonnez-moi,"* through a sea of resentful Blues and Yellows. As I squeezed to the front, my bag slipped off my shoulder and papers spilled out. The crowd was so tightly packed that the papers never reached the ground, but an Asian woman who was crammed in next to me helped gather them.

"Merci," I said sincerely. *"Il y a tant de monde." So many people.*

"You speak French," she said in French. "But you're American, aren't you?"

"Does it show?"

"It's on your card," she said, nodding at my credentials.

I looked at her Pink yellow-dotted card. She was Korean, and in the forty-some minutes we had to wait for the doors to open,

I learned that she'd been living in Paris for eighteen months, covering movies for a Korean newspaper in Seoul. Her name was something unpronounceable, so we agreed on Marie. She was divorced, or anyway she didn't have a husband, and she had one daughter, a four-year-old whom she'd left in Seoul with her mother because she couldn't afford to have her in France. She hadn't seen her in almost a year. It was unimaginable to me, and I said so.

"We do what we have to do, *n'est-ce pas?*" she said without an ounce of self-pity.

After nearly an hour, we were admitted to the Salle Debussy. I was dazzled by its immense size and elegance. It was blanketed in red velvet, from the walls to the curtains to the seats, and for the festival opening, the stage itself had been decorated with enough flowers for a movie star's wedding. As the lights went down, a public announcement asked us, in French and then in English, to silence our cell phones for the duration of the screening.

The curtains finally opened, revealing a screen that was easily twice the size of any screen I'd ever seen before. One thousand people were suddenly silent. Reverent even. Some were there for the sheer pleasure of the cinema, but all were serious about movies—or at least serious about the jobs that had sent them here.

At Cannes, I was soon to learn, all French films have English subtitles. Films in any other language are subtitled in French. The movie was a charming political love story about three working-class couples who'd all been beaten down by the menial work they were lucky to find.

It was a terrific movie, at least the parts I saw. I fell asleep twice and was awakened both times by audience laughter. I was pretty sure I'd seen most of it, but the seats were soft and friendly, and I was exhausted. At the end, there was a brief dedication to the workers of the world. The movie got a ten-minute standing ovation.

"Does this happen after every movie?" I asked Marie over the noise of the applause.

"Not like this," she said, "but this crowd leans farther to the left than audiences you may have encountered before. Cannes is crazy for the proletariat."

I laughed, but it amazed me that the festival judges and journalists and even people down in the movie marketplace could hope to make sense of the variety of cultures and languages and political perspectives that must be represented by these films.

There was another surge of applause as the director, producer, and all the stars came onto the stage. Each of them spoke for a minute—the usual "I'm so grateful" and "I've never enjoyed working on a film so much." They spoke fast, but I understood most of what they said, because it was the standard opening-night lovefest that actors and directors always engage in for the benefit of the public: "He was brilliant . . . she was exquisite . . . the shoot was a dream . . . we had a marvelous time. . . ." For all we would ever know, they'd fought like tigers from the moment the cameras started to roll.

As we waited for our row to empty, Marie said, "I can tell it was your first day at the festival. Did you sleep well?"

I shrugged. "How did it end?"

"They're all still poor, but finally they celebrate everything."

"Happily, then."

"I suppose."

"But nothing had changed for them."

She shook her head. "That's the best kind of happy ending, isn't it? When it's not because they've inherited money, or won the game, or had their blindness taken away. I like to see how people figure out a way to be happy in spite of everything. It's practically heroic."

We started to sidestep toward the aisle and I said, "So it's not just Americans who love movies with happy endings."

"Even Koreans like happy endings." She paused before stepping into the flow of aisle traffic. "So much can happen in a real person's life. A happy ending depends on where you stop the story."

It was five-thirty when we left the theater, and pouring rain. I said good-bye to my new Korean friend and found a *tabac* across from the Palais, where I bought a Snickers bar *(un Sneeker)* and a five-euro *parapluie,* which wasn't much help in the downpour. There were puddles on the sidewalks, and the curbs were overflowing with water. I had to get back to the Palais to write something to send to Draper, so I splashed across to the main entrance on my way to the pressroom.

The anxious crowd of fans Leland had warned me about had already gathered in front of the Palais. The buzz was that British actor Edward Fox, president of the jury committee for the festival awards, would be arriving with Diane Wiest, Paul Auster, Tim Burton, Michael Ondaatje, and the other jurists. The crowd would have a long, wet wait. It was five forty-five, and none of the stars would arrive until eight-fifteen. They would get out of limousines that had driven them a block and a half from the Majestic Hotel and climb the high staircase while the crowds cheered and whistled and admired their clothes. However long it took, the crowd would wait and wait and wait some more.

I elbowed my way through a horde of people and hiked up to the pressroom. Draper would want an overview of the festival's opening day for my first column, so I sat down with serious intentions. I tried a dozen openers, most of them variations on this theme: "The International Cannes Film Festival got under way today. . . ." But everything I wrote was threatening to put me to sleep.

"The tingle of last night's opening ceremonies is still in the air. . . ." I began again. But any tingling I might have felt from the crowd downstairs had been drowned by the deluge. I stared at the Willis quotes I'd gotten from Leland. I looked at the notes I'd taken at the New Line luncheon. And then I started to write:

May 8, Cannes, France.
It's raining in Cannes, and there isn't a bare breast in sight. . . .

There, that felt better. It was the real story, through my haze of sleep deprivation and hunger, and there'd be plenty of time for serious journalism in the next ten days. For the moment Draper would have to be satisfied with my gut reactions to the first twenty-four hours. I described the scene that everyone who comes to Cannes hopes to encounter: sunny days and topless beaches, and why even rain can't dull the experience.

. . . It may sound melodramatic to say that movie actors are worshipped by the public, but tell that to the crowd I've just sloshed through today, many who have journeyed thousands of miles to Cannes, hoping to come face-to-face with celebrity.

It isn't because movie stars are more beautiful (necessarily), or more intelligent (certainly), or more valuable to the future of the planet than the average human being. It has to do with something sociologist Joseph Campbell said: that we idolize movie actors because they exist in many places at the same time—which is the condition of a god. We're helpless to resist their power: it's in our DNA. If we find ourselves within a fifty-foot radius of one of them, we are—ipso facto—temporary residents of Olympus.

This is why film festivals have the patina of glamour, because the number of movie actors per square foot is staggeringly high. There is a constant air of possibility, of impending rapture when, at any moment, a star might pop out of a limo or step out from behind a tree and we will find ourselves basking in his (or her) aura.

But beneath the shiny surface, film festivals are nothing more than trade fairs for the movie business, and the Cannes

International Festival du Film is the ultimate trade fair for the global movie industry. Moviemakers and actors both famous and unknown gather along this elegant strip of the French Riviera to observe or engage in the seven deadly sins (especially gluttony, lust, greed, and envy) and to sell their movies to studios and journalists.

The Cannes Film Festival began in 1939 as a protest against Mussolini's film festival in Venice. It was interrupted temporarily by World War II, after which it resumed with great fanfare and was held every year for two weeks in May as a pretty respectable festival. . . .

I moved on to last night's premiere and threw in Willis's pessimistic quote about the nonreading public, with a description of Charlize Theron's serpentine dress of the night before. I added a note to Draper to pull a wire photo of Brad Pitt on the Palais steps and pressed the "send" button. Presto: in seconds my column would be in Draper's hard drive.

At the last minute I remembered my promise to check my e-mail. There were two anonymous invitations for various pathways to sexual bliss and an *urgent* message from Draper, saying I was to file no later than eleven-thirty LA time *or else*. Having sent him my story only seconds before—fully three and a half minutes before the deadline—I wrote him back that all was right in the universe and logged off the computer.

When I came out of the pressroom, it was eight-thirty. I grabbed my suitcase and went to the third floor—the *troisième,* as it was called even by non-French-speakers—for a coffee at Jack's, but it was now completely empty, and I was slapped in the face by a heavy loneliness: film festival ennui. Something about the frenetic busyness of people rushing to movies and eagerly trading their impressions gives you the feeling that other people are having more fun than you are, that you're constantly making the wrong choices for your editor, missing the right scene, and at Cannes that feeling is amplified a thousand times by the glimmer and glamour of the Riviera.

I was also beat. I wished I'd had the good sense to tell Leland to go to the gala alone.

I left Jack's without waiting for coffee and stopped at my mailbox on the way out of the Palais. It was stuffed with schedules and press kits and more invitations to press luncheons. I could do interviews all day long and never have time for movies. It was while I was reading a publicist's announcement that Kenneth Branagh would be available for interviews about *Faust* that I realized all of the invitations were for English-language movies, which included the Wim Wenders film. If I wanted an interview with Jacques Vidanne, I'd have to make a special request of his studio. I made a mental note to find his company the next day, shoved the papers in my bag, and left the Palais.

When I came out into the open air, it was still raining hard and I was starving, but between me and the possibility of food on the other side of the Croisette was an expanding throng of fans and photographers, crushed against police barricades. They were hiding from the rain under umbrellas and newspapers, waiting for the limousines to arrive and for Johnny Depp to emerge on his way to the premiere of his movie *The Brave.*

I couldn't possibly wade through this crowd, even to scavenge for food. I took out my *Sneeker* and munched on it as I hiked up the hill to the hotel. When I got to my room, I dropped my suitcase and my heavy bag on the floor and collapsed across the bed. It would be the last peaceful sleep I'd have while I was in France.

Fasten your seat belts,
it's going to be a bumpy night.

Bette Davis, in *All About Eve*

5

Cannes, France

Just after midnight
Friday, May 9

 ven before I opened my eyes, I knew I wasn't alone. I could feel the heat of another body and a slight tilt to the cheap mattress. Soft fingers lifted a strand of hair from my face and smoothed it behind my ear.

The overhead light was on, and my nose was flush against the ancient wallpaper. I had a moment of groggy panic about where I was, and willed my eyes to open as I rolled over onto my back.

"I came into the yard with the couple across the hall," Leland Dunne said in a whisper. "The door was open."

"Mmmm," I said, still muddled.

He moved his hand softly over my forehead, following the line of my eyebrows with his finger. "I love the arch of your brows, Nattie. Did I ever tell you that? Sexy, sharp curves. I've never seen eyebrows like yours on a woman. It's like you're excited all the time."

I opened one of my eyes and looked at him warily. I wasn't about to be sweet-talked by Leland Dunne. "Not on your life," I said. "Off my bed."

"Oh, all right," he said. "Can you wake up?"

"I'm awake enough," I said.

"I'll wait till you're upright. Then I'll go out and sit on the stairs while you put on your black dress. I found it in your suitcase." He was still whispering. "It's almost one. How long did you sleep?"

I fought hard to remember. "Nine-thirty," I said out of the part of my mouth that was fully awake.

"Almost four hours. You could run a marathon! Rise and shine, sweetheart. I've brought you jewels."

He dangled a gaudy plastic diamond necklace above me. He was handsomely dressed in a shiny black tuxedo that only had a couple of deep wrinkles on the arms to show for its long voyage in his suitcase.

"Up! Up!" he said, sticking the jewels in his pocket. I stood unsteadily, and he pointed me to my dress and shoes. I was too foggy to protest. "Can you do this by yourself? You want me to help?"

"Go away," I yawned, shoving him out the door. I staggered to the bathroom alcove and looked at myself in the mirror. My hair had formed one of those bizarre pompadour things that happen when you fall asleep with abandon, but I brushed it straight back and wadded it into a big black clasp. It almost looked like I'd done it that way on purpose.

I put on the dress and gave a perfunctory nudge to fluff up my breasts, since cleavage was the main attraction. I took the emergency euros out of their grassy plastic pouch: I knew Leland well enough to be prepared to take care of myself.

He was sitting on the top stair when I emerged, leaning his back against the wall. "Ooh-la-la," he said. He stood up to put the gaudy necklace around my neck. "I wish they were diamonds."

"Just so I don't look like a hooker."

"Only a little," he said.

The rain had stopped, and the sweet fertile smell of a departed downpour filled the night. The streetlamp flickered on and off and the wet cobblestones glistened in the moonlight. The taxi had been waiting for a long time, and we drove for an hour into the hills above Cannes. I hoped the Germans were paying Leland enough to cover the fare.

The gala was being held in a magnificent old château, complete with a moat, a drawbridge, and torches on either side of the grand doorway. Two uniformed guards stood at the entrance, stopping everyone who went in, checking invitations.

"*Pas d'appareil photo!*" one of them said. Leland and I shook our heads.

"Why no cameras?" Leland asked. "Isn't this all about publicity?"

The guards looked at one another and made insolent-American faces.

"Because, *monsieur*, each country has an exclusive. Only one. If your name is not on the list, you may not take pictures. *Allez-y!*" he said, pointing us through the doors.

In the great hall, loud rock and roll came from a band in one corner and beautiful people shimmered shoulder to shoulder from one end of the room to the other.

"This is the only place you'll see movie stars on the loose while you're in Cannes," Leland said into my ear as we stepped into the hall. "The fans mob anyone with a familiar face the second they hit the Croisette, so the stars stay in their hotel rooms like prisoners for most of the festival. When they come out into the open, they're working, just like us."

A few heads turned our way as we entered, then quickly returned to more promising conversation when they realized we were Nobody.

I expected to see Johnny Depp near the front door, since this gala was for his movie, but if he was there, I missed him. There were lots of familiar American faces—Ashley Judd, Billy Bob Thornton, Melanie Griffith—all of them engrossed in conversation but glancing up whenever a camera flash went off.

Leland took my hand to guide me through the crowd. Cameron Diaz brushed past me, smelling like gardenias. I kept looking at the floor to keep my feet from ending up under someone's heel, but I glanced up from time to time to see if there was anyone I knew or even recognized.

Leland let go of my hand to forage for drinks, and I had three conversations in rapid succession: with a Frenchwoman from *Le Figaro* in Paris, with an entertainment journalist from Amsterdam, and with a TV reviewer from Seattle. I nodded as each of them reminded me of the movies I ought to have seen.

Eventually, Leland spotted Nancy Sheldon, the studio exec who'd sent me the invitation, and he grabbed my hand, elbowing his way in her direction for a token embrace.

"*Quel bash!*" she shouted with a smile.

"How was the screening of *The Brave*?" Leland asked loudly.

"Boos, hisses, a witch hunt," she said before she floated away in another direction. That explained why Depp was nowhere in sight.

"Poor Johnny," Leland said.

"Why poor Johnny?"

"Because you can't imagine how nasty people here can get when they don't like a movie. They feel the director has betrayed them, that if the movie doesn't work, the whole cinematic world has been duped."

"Oh, come on." I said. "Aren't most audiences like that? If you pay your money—"

"I'm not exaggerating, Nattie. Any expression of disappointment you've seen at other festivals, especially in America—that's like a tea party. They're all so freaking erudite here, promoting real 'films.' " He made quotation marks on either side of his head. "But they're the same learned film scholars who cheered and applauded last night for that abominable *The Last Orb*. Wait and see." He took my hand and led me into the crowd.

"How can Depp show his face in public after something like that?" I asked as we moved along.

"My guess is, he can't. Not unless he's made of Teflon. I'll bet a thousand euros he won't show tonight. Or maybe even tomorrow. You have a one-on-one with him?"

I nodded.

"Don't count on it."

It made me sad for Johnny Depp, who had always been generous and polite to me in interviews. A little sloppy, maybe, and you always wondered when was the last time he'd washed his hair, but he tried to take the ridiculous interview process seriously, and he deserved some respect just for putting himself on the line as a director.

None of those boos and hisses were evident in the gala crowd, however. No matter how bad the movie had been, there was shrill laughter coming from all directions, and two sets of shoulders away from me, a man in a tux was twisting with three women in long black gowns.

"Do European filmmakers ever come to galas for American movies?" I shouted to Leland, thinking I might stumble upon Jacques Vidanne and have a high-volume conversation with him.

"I doubt they'd come for this one," he said, "especially if the movie is as bad as Nancy said it was."

The band started to play an old Beatles tune and a section of beautiful people began to bounce up and down.

I was not in the mood to party. I was in the mood to sleep. I leaned in to Leland's ear and said, "I hate this. Take me home."

"Nonsense!" he shouted back, and pulled me through another morass of tuxedoed and sequined bodies. The room was so dark and big and crowded, it felt like a brownout at a shopping mall, and everyone seemed to be only half interested in the person they were talking to.

"Where will you find your heavenly body?" I asked him. I had to shout straight into his ear so he could hear me.

"I don't know!" he shouted back. "I don't even know what color hair she has. Just look for a perfect body."

"That narrows it down," I said dryly. A glance in every direction was a feast for the eyes: flawless bodies everywhere. We were looking for a perfect needle in a haystack of perfect needles.

We'd wandered through the crowd until we'd circled the entire hall when I spied a massive table of food along one wall and pulled Leland toward it. I might have expected to be served sliced truffles en brochette or mini-soufflés d'escargots, since we were in the heart of the French countryside, but the American film company was serving food that would feel at home at a cocktail party in Kansas. We piled our plates high with cold shrimp and drippy, deep-fat-fried cheese balls.

I was on my third cheese ball when someone tapped me on the shoulder and a television camera light blinded me.

"See here!" a voice said from behind the lights. I recognized the voice from my junket days. It belonged to a trendy VH1 DJ named Steve something, and he stepped out from behind the light and said, "Let's take a break from the evening's star-studded vapidness and speak to a humble journalist—Nattie Conway from the US of A. Ms. Conway, perhaps you can give us an idea of how the festival is going so far?" He shoved a microphone in my face.

I wiped the grease off my mouth daintily with a tiny napkin and said, "I've been here exactly"—I looked at my watch—"twenty-three hours and fifteen minutes, but I'd have to say it's going well. I've seen two movies and spoken to some actors. And I've eaten a lot of cheese balls."

"Is the festival everything you expected?" he asked.

"Well, I haven't seen as many breasts as I'd hoped," I said.

The light on the camera jiggled up and down. "Turn it off, she's useless," Steve said to his cameraman. He shook my hand and said he was glad I was back on the circuit.

"You must be the American exclusive," I said, but there was a roar of applause from the center of the room and I looked around to see what it was. When I turned back, Steve was gone. I had no time to feel abandoned because the crowd cheered again, and Leland grabbed my arm and pulled. "Over there!" he shouted excitedly.

As we squeezed into the crowd I saw his hand dive into the pocket of his tuxedo jacket, which I noticed for the first time was bulging suspiciously.

A dozen men had formed a circle around one of the tables, and all of them were dressed like Leland, in slick black tuxedos. They tossed questions at a girl who was sitting on the edge of the table, balancing her stiletto on the end of her big toe. When the shoe slipped off her toe and fell to the floor, she squealed and threw her head back. She appeared to be in her late twenties. Her long legs were crossed, and the slit at the side of her short white dress crept seductively up her thigh.

She had a pug-nosed, round-cheeked look. I would never have described her face as pretty, but I could tell it would have been more attractive had it not been loose and droopy-eyed from some kind of inebriant—marijuana maybe. Alcohol definitely.

"What kind of actresses use a body double?" one of the tuxedos asked in a thick French accent.

"Okay," the girl said, as if explaining something to a child. "Sandra Bullock. Julia Roberts. Madonna. It's trendy, see? They think it's beneath 'em to show their own nudity." She shook her finger sloppily at the crowd, which had increased by a factor of ten—all of them men.

"Why do they choose your body?" another accented voice tossed into the circle.

"What d'ya think?" she said, her eyes at half-mast. "No cuts or moles or scars or blemishes! It's perfect!" She raised both hands in the air in drunken triumph.

I squeezed Leland's hand, but he was way ahead of me. "What's your name?" he asked, elbowing between two of the tuxes in the inner circle.

"Naomi," she spat, lifting her head to Leland. "Naomi Paul." The spitting threw her slightly off balance, and she had to grab the edge of the table with both hands to steady herself.

On the other side of the room the band began playing "Twist and Shout." Naomi ran her hands sensuously up along her waist and over her breasts, flinging her arms in the air above her and throwing her head back.

"I wanna *dance!*" she shrieked. Somewhere in the ring of tuxedos someone started to clap. Just one man at first, and then another, until the entire circle of men was clapping in unison. Naomi pushed herself from the table and kicked off her other shoe.

She began to move her hips slowly with the rhythm of the band, and it was easy to see what all the fuss was about. She was fairly tall, about my height, and her arms were sinewy and smooth, strong without being muscular, and there wasn't a freckle or scar to be seen.

Her dress was a piece of seamless white satin, held up by a single string of rhinestones over each shoulder, and the satin stuck to her like Saran Wrap. Under it, the curves of her breasts and hips were breathtaking. She was not much of a dancer, especially in this condition, but that hardly mattered to her enthusiastic fans. They whistled and clapped to the music as she built up to a serious bump and grind.

It was beginning to feel like a scene from *The Accused*. More tuxedos splintered from the crowd and joined the circle, some clapping, some swaying. I was forced to sway along with them, until two men from the inner ring suddenly stepped in and lifted Naomi like a ballet dancer onto the table. Another moved the candelabra to the floor.

Naomi didn't miss a beat. She continued her dance, seemingly only half conscious of where she was and how many people were watching her. The band finished "Twist and Shout" and began playing "I Feel Good."

Naomi slipped her thumbs under her rhinestone straps. The dress raised several inches, revealing the crotch-triangle of her white lace thong. The inner circle, now at least thirty strong, had closed in on the table, clapping in time, catcalling to her, egging her on. Across the table a camera light came on, and I saw Steve from VH1 wrap his hand over the lens before the light went out.

Aroused by the attention, Naomi snapped the straps so hard they broke, in perfect time to the music. A sick feeling began in my stomach as I looked around me. For a moment the men stopped clapping and gaped, as Naomi's dress slipped slowly, sensationally, to her feet. The lace of her thong didn't cover much, and she wasn't wearing a bra.

She opened her eyes sleepily and looked around her. The music seemed a million miles away. *So this is it,* the crowd said to itself. *So this is the body that's paid to show things real actresses refuse to show.*

I looked at the fifty or so women gathered around the table with me and realized there were not enough exercise machines in the world to make our own figures look like that. This body was one in a million.

Naomi hooked the dress on the toes of her right foot and flung it into the crowd. Someone whistled.

I might have walked away in disgust had it not been for Leland, who pulled out a compact silver camera that had been the mysterious bulge in his jacket. He pointed the camera at Naomi, and I realized why he'd dragged me out of bed at one in the morning.

I felt the dizzy rush of adrenaline that accompanies sudden

anger. These photographs would earn Leland an unspeakable amount of money, precisely because he'd been forbidden to take them. Naomi Paul would open a magazine in a month or so and see these drunken pictures of herself, and I was furious that Leland had made me his accomplice.

. Without stopping to think, I elbowed my way into the tuxedo circle. I shoved through the men until I reached Leland, who was edging his way in for a close-up.

"Give me your jacket!" I shouted at him.

"Why?" he said, as Naomi teased with her thumbs in the string of her panties. I grabbed Leland's tuxedo jacket by the shiny lapels and yanked. He was too startled to protest, and I shoved past him.

It might have been the sight of another woman among her admirers, or perhaps she was beginning to sober up, but Naomi Paul stopped suddenly and stood in the middle of the table with both hands over her mouth, her arms hiding her naked breasts. I helped her off the table and wrapped Leland's jacket around her shoulders.

By the time her feet were on the floor, the tuxedos had turned away, searching for new excitement. Her dubious moment of glory had passed.

Naomi took hold of my arm, and we walked slowly through the crowd. Leland caught up to us at the door.

"Don't worry about your jacket. You'll get it back," I said, and Naomi and I walked out of the hall. We were halfway across the drawbridge when I heard Leland's voice behind us.

"For Christ's sake, Nattie! Hold up!"

We didn't stop, but he caught up with us and his finger was looped through the sling-back heels of Naomi's shoes. He handed them to me as we moved toward the moat.

"Where are you taking her?"

"None of your business!" I said, guiding her along. "Where *am* I taking you?" I added softly to Naomi.

"To Mashure V'don's boat, I guess." She staggered slightly and wrapped Leland's jacket tightly around her.

I turned to Leland with a smug look that said "See?" The three of us walked in icy silence to the head of the line of taxis that were waiting in front of the château. I opened the door for Naomi, and she climbed in.

"You're not using those pictures, Leland."

"I sure as hell am!" he said. "What did you think, I just wanted to get a look at her?"

"I wasn't thinking." I got into the taxi and slammed the door. Leland didn't move. I rolled the window down and unclasped the necklace from around my neck. "Here." I dropped it into the palm of his hand and held out my own hand, waiting for the film.

He looked me straight in the eye and shook his head.

I pulled my empty hand into the taxi. "Fine. But if you use those pictures before you get her permission, I'll sue you myself. *Allez-y!*" I said to the driver, and the tires dug into the gravel as we drove away.

As the taxi wound around the curves and down the hill on the road back to Cannes, Naomi turned into a lethargic chatterbox. She told the driver to take us to a specific quai in the harbor at Cannes; she was cold, she said, even though she'd grown up in a freezing part of Canada—as if there were other temperature zones in Canada—and she wondered whose jacket she was wearing.

"A friend of mine loaned it to you."

"French, right?" she asked.

"No," I said. "Canadian, like you."

"Huh. 'Cuz the French are *beyond* fabulous as a people."

"Yes, they are," I said.

She considered my reponse for a moment and then said, "Most of the French people are awfully short."

75

I tried not to laugh. She had come to the gala with a French producer whom she'd met at a prefestival party. He had been *beyond* fabulous to her, and she'd been staying on his yacht, which was merely fabulous, since Tuesday.

Naomi Paul was hoping to break into movies as a real actress, and she thought she'd have a chance if she started in Europe. I shifted awkwardly in the taxi seat: I'd heard this story before—my mother had left my father with the same stars in her eyes.

"I didn't, like, sleep with him or anything," she said sloppily, and immediately I assumed that she did. But she added, "I mean, probably I would have, he was so nice to me, except he told me he had a kind of, like, wife, and I don't go for that."

"Was he at the gala, when, you know . . . ?"

"Oh God!" she moaned, hiding her face in her hands. "Did I really . . . ?" I waited while she dragged herself through her table dance at the party. She started to cry, and I scooted over next to her and put my arm around her.

"If it's any consolation, I'm pretty sure no one noticed your face."

"Ha!" she said bitterly from behind her hands. "I hate myself, I hate what I do, I hate men, I hate movies, I hate cameras, I hate white wine, I hate red wine, I hate—"

"You could start all over again," I interrupted. "And this time you could wear all your clothes. No one would have any idea who you were."

She bit her lower lip as she considered the possibility.

"Yeah," she said, looking groggily out the window at the passing trees—mere shadows in the darkness. "But, like, what do I do right now? My publicist is going to kill me to death!"

"I can't give you advice, Naomi," I said finally. "For one thing, I don't know anything about you. And who knows what I'd be doing if I had a body like yours?" That was the awful truth. I couldn't imagine what it would be like to have a body that was perfect by movie-star standards. Mine wasn't even in the ballpark of my own standards.

As the taxi careened around a corner on the steep downward slope, Naomi flopped against me. "But the thing is, if you want to be more than a body double, you have to stop thinking of yourself as just a body. Take some acting classes. Live a normal life for a while." I had no idea if she was sober enough to hear me.

She gazed out the window as the moon disappeared behind the clouds, and nothing but the taxi's headlights gave a hint about where we were. "Thank God he'd left the party," she said with a shudder.

"Who?" I asked.

"Mashurc V'don. He stayed, you know, and talked to people for a while. But his movie's in one of those competitions, so he has to do a conference thing, with the press." She sat up as straight as she could and brushed off the satin lapels of Leland's jacket. "I was kind of hoping he'd give me a chance, y'know, but if anybody tells him about . . . Boy, what a mess."

"Why did this guy leave you at the party? That sounds pretty rude to me."

"Oh no, he's, like, a French gentleman or something. My publicist told him she'd get me home, so he left a little after the party started. He said he was receiving company on his yacht, but I could stay there as long as I wanted."

Through the half-open windows came the fishy aroma of the sea. There were at least fifty ships anchored on this side of the harbor, and Naomi pointed proudly to the yacht where she was staying. It was hard to miss, easily the largest of all, with lights stretching end to end like a luxury liner.

"There's, like, a boat-taxi that can take me there. It's free, or anyway Mashure V'don pays for it. You wanna come with me? I can give you that man's jacket when I get there, and the boat guy can bring you back."

"I don't think so, Naomi. It's after three in the—"

"How will I get this jacket back to your friend if you don't come with me? Please?" There was a whiny tone to her voice that made me think this was the way she usually got what she wanted. It worked.

I paid the cab fare, which took almost half of my emergency euros, and Naomi announced to the boat driver that she had arrived and was ready to return to the yacht.

When he'd seated us at the front of the boat, he spoke into a handset to make sure Naomi was expected.

"*Monsieur Vidanne?*" he said. "*Je vous appelle.*"

My head whipped around so fast it hurt. "*Monsieur Vidanne?*"

"Uh-huh," Naomi said. "Jock V'don, I told you."

In the next moment we were idling noisily next to Jacques Vidanne's elegant craft. We bounced against the hull of the bigger boat for a minute, before a short bald man in a white bathrobe appeared on deck. He nodded at the driver and greeted Naomi. I couldn't believe my eyes.

"*Bienvenue,* my leetle friend," Vidanne said to Naomi, Charles Boyer in terrycloth.

"*Boneswar,* Jock," she called back. "I hope it's okay that I brought a friend, to show her the yacht? Just a teensy little look?" She squinched up her nose and made the "teensy" sign with her thumb and forefinger.

Vidanne laughed agreeably, an older man titillated by the audacious confidence of a sexy young woman.

"Were you sleeping?" Naomi asked as we stepped onto the yacht. She gave him an affectionate kiss on each cheek.

"Not at all," he said with a thick French accent. "Ze 'elicopter was late."

He looked curiously at Naomi, apparently noticing for the first time that she was wearing a tuxedo jacket and carrying her shoes.

Naomi looked to me for help, and I stuck out my hand to him. "*Monsieur Vidanne, je m'appelle Natalie Conway.* I'm a journalist from the United States, and I am so delighted to meet you because I want to say that your film *Aimée* made an enormous impact on me, and I have always wanted to speak to . . ."

He turned to face me as I rattled on in the best French I could muster, still offering my hand, which he glanced at fleetingly and ignored.

"*Mes excuses, mademoiselle,*" he interrupted. "*Vôtre nom . . . ?*"

"Natalie Conway," I said. "Naomi had some difficulty at the gala, and she wanted to give me the jacket so I could return it to—"

He was staring at me, his hands hanging limply at his sides. I looked at Naomi. She shrugged. It was an awkward moment, and I had no idea what I'd said to upset him.

"Okay, listen, Nattie," Naomi said at last. "I'll just go and change so I can give you the jacket." And she headed for the downstairs cabins. At the top of the stairs she bumped into a tall woman with a scrawny ponytail that stuck out of the back of her head like a tuft of pine needles.

"Oh, 'scuse!" Naomi said, and vanished into the bowels of the yacht.

The woman turned to Vidanne and said, "Madame would like to come up— " She stopped when she saw me and squinted, as if trying to get me in focus.

"It would be inconvenient at this time," he said. His jaw was clenched so tightly I could see the muscles in his neck.

Suddenly he clapped his hands, and the woman, still staring at me over her shoulder, hurried down the stairs.

Vidanne stepped toward me and put his hand firmly on my shoulder, guiding me toward the boat-taxi. "It is very late," he said. "In only a matter of hours we all must work, *n'est-ce pas?*"

"*Oui, monsieur, pardon,*" I said, embarrassed to have made some unknown faux pas.

"*Ne vous en faites pas,*" he said with an artificial laugh. *Don't worry about it.*

In one swift motion, he had me at the ladder, hovering over me as I climbed down into the boat. Over the noise of the motor, he said, *"Vous parlez toujours un français impeccable."*

"Pardon?" I shouted back, but he waved the boatman away.

I didn't have time to protest. The driver reached over to adjust his headlight, and for an instant the beam swept to the right, just barely illuminating the letters ". . . LAIR" on the side of the yacht. He gunned the engine, and as we sped toward shore, I watched Vidanne grow smaller and smaller. Naomi's perfect little form joined his on the deck. She lifted Leland's jacket in the air and waved. A second later the two of them were enveloped by the night, and all I could see of the yacht was the string of lights from stem to stern.

"Monsieur," I said to the driver as he helped me onto the pier, "did you hear what Monsieur Vidanne said when we were leaving his yacht?"

He shrugged, slipping a rope around the cement pylon. *"Que vous parlez toujours un français impeccable."* He tied the rope in a complicated knot.

"Toujours?" I asked.

"That's what he said." And he descended into the cabin of his boat.

I stood on the pier and stared after him. *Toujours?* Always? I *always* speak impeccable French—what was that supposed to mean? But there were two meanings for the word *toujours,* weren't there? "Always" and "still."

Either way, everything about our encounter was odd. How would Jacques Vidanne know I used to speak French? And why had he been in such a hurry to get me off his boat? It was practically rude. All I'd done was praise his film. Maybe I'd come on a little too strong, but he'd even refused to shake my hand! What sort of Frenchman refuses to shake a woman's hand? The whole thing made me so mad I shouted down toward the cabin.

The door flew open and the driver, shirtless, poked his head out, not bothering to mask his annoyance.

"*Je m'excuse,*" I said. "Can you take me back to the boat of Jacques Vidanne?"

"Not without his permission."

"Please!" I said as he was closing the door. "Could you call the boat for me?"

"Not tonight!" he shouted. "*Demain!*" And the sound of the slamming door shook the boat.

"*Bon,*" I said to the empty deck. The last thing I wanted to do was come back in the morning. Maybe I was overreacting. Six hours' sleep in forty-eight hours is not enough for sanity.

I saw the Palais off in the distance, but was too far away to hear the sounds of celebration in the square. I started down the Croisette, and I'd been walking for ten minutes when a taxi pulled up to the curb. The driver opened the door, looking as tired as I felt.

When I got to my tiny attic room, I went straight to the little mirror above the sink and stared at my own face. My makeup had faded completely. I had heavy bags under my eyes, and wisps of hair had escaped from my impromptu 'do and had frizzed around my face. I wasn't exactly a prize, but I wasn't revolting enough to offend a famous French movie mogul.

It was a tribute to my stellar interpersonal skills that I'd managed to get myself banished by the one man at this festival I was looking forward to meeting. How could I possibly get an interview with him now?

I was just clearheaded enough to register that the big hand and the little hand were both pointing at three. I splashed ice-cold water on my face. I hadn't managed to get one single thing right since I'd left LA. Even Leland's jacket was still on Vidanne's boat.

A bolt from the blue is more than just a figure of speech. Lightning bolts can on occasion jump 10 or more miles from their parent cloud and appear to strike in a region having blue skies overhead.

Wisconsin Department of Health and Family Services

6

Cannes, France

Friday, May 9

The telephone's ring was so shrill I nearly fell out of bed.

"*Oui?*" I said. My voice sounded like a bullfrog's.

"I was worried you dropped dead."

"Draper?" I rolled over on my back and closed my eyes. "Oh, brother."

"I left a message for you to call me."

I punched the button that lit up my watch: seven after four. "You can't imagine the trouble I've had already. My plane was canceled, I had to take a late train from Paris, so I missed—"

"What can I do about that? *Nada.* You're there to do the job. Just do it."

"But I sent you the story. Didn't you get it?"

"Pure pedantry." I could almost hear his spittle hit the receiver. "Nobody wants to *learn* something in a piece about movies."

I covered my eyes with the back of my hand.

"Get me the glitter and glam and can the sophistry," he said. "Write that a hundred times on the blackboard so you don't forget it. And by the way, you only gave me seven hundred and ninety-two words. We need eight hundred, remember? I can't use it if it's not long enough."

My throat tightened. Just like that the old panic was back. "Okay, I get it about the column. But your note was before I'd even written the column. So why did you want me to call you?"

"Before the column I wanted the column! Also I wanted you to see the violence movie. The Wenders thing. You can't not see it, I need a review of it ASAP."

"I was planning—"

"Don't argue with me about this, I'm paying you too much money. It's opening here tomorrow. Your today."

My head hurt. "Draper, it's four in the morning."

"Then go to sleep," he said, and he hung up.

I slammed the phone in its cradle and lay back in bed, concentrating all my energy on being mad at Draper. This was exactly why I'd quit in the first place. I knew he wouldn't give me half of what he'd promised if what I sent him strayed minutely from his narrow definition of perfection.

And then the image of me being forced off the yacht an hour ago muscled its way into my head. A crashing wave of humiliation hit me: Vidanne would never talk to me now, even if he did think I spoke impeccable French. Still? Always? The words bounced around in my foggy brain.

It didn't take long before my anger had shifted to Leland. If he hadn't dragged me to the gala, none of this would have happened.

I had to get back to that boat. But before that I had to get some sleep or the next day was going to be a nightmare. I rolled over and wrapped a pillow around my head.

By the time I finally rolled out of bed, the focus of my anger had boiled down to Vidanne. I set off for the Palais with only one thought: to return to his boat and get back to the Palais in time to catch the morning screening of *The Brave*. I cleaned the pile of press kits and invitations out of my mailbox and took a cab to the dock where I'd given up on the shirtless boatman in the middle of the night.

The water-taxi bumped against the dock as I approached, and I knocked on the bow. It wasn't long before an angry head poked through the door, with hair matted and eyes bleary from lack of sleep.

"*Bonjour, monsieur!*" I said, trying to duplicate the melodic singsong that the French affect to mask their impatience. "Remember me? From last night? I need to return to Vidanne's boat."

"You again!" He slammed the door and shouted from inside, "*Fichez le camp!*" which, roughly translated, I took to mean *Get off my land!* I knocked again and he burst out of the door, jabbing his arms into a wrinkled navy-blue jacket and wearing only his underwear.

My knees began to shake, but before he could speak I said, "I know how tired you are. I am also tired, but it's very urgent for me to speak again to Monsieur Vidanne."

The thing I'd learned about Frenchmen from French movies is that they are, for the most part, eminently responsive to even the clumsiest feminine charm. They love women, and they love especially to help women. All I had going for me now was that I was helpless and female, and I could tell that a decision was brewing in his sleep-addled head.

"*Eh bien,*" he said finally, and picked up the hand-speaker on the boat's control panel. "Hello, this is Gaspar at the pier for Monsieur Vidanne. Speak!"

I glanced at my watch. It was eight-fifteen. Depp's movie would be starting in fifteen minutes, but I was going to find Vidanne even if it meant missing it altogether.

"*Monsieur Vidanne? Parlez.*" He switched off the speaker, squinted in the direction of the sea, and turned to a small bulletin board beside the controls. Then he disappeared into his cabin and reappeared a minute later, fully dressed and buckling his belt.

"*Monsieur!*" I called out as he turned over the motor. "May I come with you?"

He gunned the engine. "*Oui, oui,*" he said. "Why not? *Montez.*"

We sped off toward the horizon, and as we approached the ships, the boat slowed, floating silently through the huge and imposing forms around us, flags waving from their rear railings and fabulous names stenciled on their hulls: *La Victoire, Pigale de Paris, Erotique, Le Délice.*

Gaspar slowed his boat and drove in a wide circle around a red buoy, staring at it as if he thought it should speak to him.

"Is this where Vidanne's yacht was anchored?" I asked.

He nodded, frowning. "They should always inform me of their departure."

"Monsieur Vidanne is gone?" I said. He nodded again and then turned away from the buoy and into the garden of yachts.

"Who do these boats belong to, Monsieur Gaspar?" I asked.

"Men with money," he said matter-of-factly. "Some of the moviemakers stay at big hotels like the Majestic or the Carlton. Those rooms cost ten thousand euros a night. But these guys, even the ones who rent the smaller yachts, they're so wealthy, they don't even eat in Cannes. When they go ashore, it is over there." He pointed into the distance on the other side of Cannes, where the shoreline curved around the harbor, to the Cap d'Antibes. "They don't mingle with the festival *bourgeoisie* unless they have to."

He maneuvered around a dinghy and pointed us slowly back to the pier.

"Is it strange that Monsieur Vidanne would leave before his film is presented?" I said.

Gaspar eyed me suspiciously. "Who are you?"

"I . . . I'm here to cover the festival for a newspaper in the United States."

"What were you doing with Vidanne last night?" he asked. "You came with the young lady in the tuxedo, *n'est-ce pas*?"

"Yes," I said.

"She was wearing a white dress at the beginning of the evening when I brought her to shore."

I nodded, and he gave me a conspiratorial wink—he hadn't even been at the gala and still he was part of Naomi's audience.

"Monsieur Vidanne asked you to leave," he said.

"Yes," I said, feeling my face redden. "I don't know why."

He studied me for so long I began to feel self-conscious. Then he furrowed his brow, the picture of understanding. "*C'est évident.* Three women already on board. Four would have signaled disaster."

I tried to smile.

"Are you returning to the Palais?" he said. "I can easily drop you at the pier nearby."

"That would be very kind."

As we approached the pier, I said to Gaspar, "Did you meet the other women on the yacht?"

"Besides the young lady who lost her dress? There was a maid with silly hair, and a woman in a long velvet *capuchon*."

"A *capuchon*?" I said.

"A vestige from the seventeenth century. It means 'cloak,' like this." He tossed his right hand over his left shoulder and drew both hands forward over his head. "The Capuchin monks used to cover themselves in supplication under those heavy hooded capes."

"Did you see her?"

He chuckled. "Of course not. She was wearing a *capuchon*."

"Was she a movie star, do you think?"

"*Je pense que non*," he said. The boat veered hard to the right as he pulled up next to the jetty. He offered me his hand to help me out of the boat. "And you, *mad'moiselle?*"

"Me?" I almost burst out laughing. "No, no, I only write about movies." I took his hand and stepped onto the pier. "Thank you, Monsieur Gaspar."

I reached the top of the steps at the Palais at nearly nine o'clock and snuck quietly into the back of the theater for the last half of *The Brave.*

The ending of the movie was slow and ponderous, with a grubby, long-haired Depp as a poverty-stricken Native American who makes a snuff film in exchange for money to feed his family. I'd missed too much to understand how bad it really was, and my mind wandered to Vidanne. He was in Cannes with a movie in competition; the producers of all the movies were listed in the festival program, but mine was on the bed at my hotel where I'd dumped it last night. I'd have to borrow one from Leland.

Leland! My heart sank. It wasn't likely that he and I would be on speaking terms today, even if I had his jacket. I'd have to find another program. Not to mention another friend.

The audience around me exploded in a chorus of boos. The curtains were closing, the lights came up, and wads of paper flew through the air and onto the stage.

"Snuff out the director!" someone from the front shouted in French.

"For this I missed my coffee?" a Spanish woman grumbled across the aisle.

People were shouting in at least ten languages, and all of them were furious. Leland had been right. These were the same people who had stood and applauded for ten minutes the day before, but now they were like an angry mob. The hisses continued for several minutes, and I wondered if Depp would dare to come out onstage the way the filmmakers had done for *Pauline et Paul*. He didn't, and I couldn't blame him.

I slipped out of the theater as the booing tapered off, hoping to find a festival program at the American Pavilion, a huge white tent at the foot of the grand stairway. The pavilion was teeming with Americans. Inside, critics were shoving each other into the post office area to the right and toward the information table on the left. I could smell coffee drifting in from the back of the tent, and I elbowed my way through the crowd to the source. It was a tiny makeshift café, with a window for buying the basics: coffee and croissants. The second I stepped through the archway, I was accosted by a tiny redhead, who leapt out of her seat and dragged me to a chair.

"Coffee?" she asked, sticking her hand out for me to shake.

"I . . . sure," I said. She whirred away like a little hummingbird, and the VH1 DJ Steve, who'd pointed his camera at me at the gala, sat down beside me.

"That was my cameraman. Person," he said. "She's just a stringer. My real guy's plane— Never mind, you don't want to hear. Anyway, you're her hero."

"I am? Why?"

"Last night. You made her day when you rescued that girl from her striptease. The body double, right? Did you know her?"

"No, I'd never seen her before. But look, I have to be at the *The Brave* press conference in"—I looked at my watch—"ten minutes. Do you have a program for the festival? The big one they put in our boxes, with all the films listed?"

He took the program out of his pack. "What are you looking for?"

"A movie I don't know the name of. Jacques Vidanne produced it."

"The French guy? Should we be covering it? We don't have anything till eleven-thirty. Damn!" Festival paranoia, a classic case.

A loud whistle pierced the clamor of the café, and Steve's cameraperson started waving to him to come help her.

He made an exasperated face. "Save the table."

The program was filled with ads, testimonials, biographies, and exactly what I was looking for: a list of the films in competition, with summaries for all of them.

The director, cinematographer, and primary cast were listed along with the studios themselves, but no producers or screenwriters were included. Of the fifty-five productions in the competitions combined, only ten were French, and all of them were based in Paris. I had no idea which one was Vidanne's movie, since I never pay attention to the names of production companies, which come and go like mirages even in America. I was scribbling the studio names and numbers when Steve and the little redhead returned to the table.

The redhead was Shawn, a petite person with skinny arms that poked out of a tight green VH1 T-shirt. She looked just about strong enough to carry a cup of coffee across a room.

"Was that you last night behind the camera at the gala?" I asked her.

She nodded. "What . . . a . . . way . . . to see . . . a party!" she said.

"I never thought of that. It must be weird to experience everything through a lens. As if you're not really there."

"That . . . is . . . exactly . . . it!" she said, wide-eyed and dazzled at my powers of perception. "Wow!"

I looked at Steve. He smiled and shrugged.

"You don't look big enough to carry one of those gargantuan video cameras," I said.

"But YOU! You . . . were amazing! How you . . . rescued . . . that . . . girl!" She laid her open palm on her chest and bit her lower lip. I thought she was going to cry.

"Well . . . ," I said uncomfortably.

"Her . . . publicist . . . Man! . . . I'd like to . . . wring . . . her . . . neck!" Shawn slapped her palm on the table and the salt and pepper shakers rattled in their tiny tray.

"Her publicist?" I asked.

"Tricia Knight, you know her," Steve said. "She's the one who always hangs around the interview rooms at junkets and tells you what you can and can't ask her clients. She kept bringing drinks to the body double all night. It was almost like she was trying to get her drunk."

"No kidding," I said. "Did people know who she was?"

He laughed. "Sure, everyone knew she was the body double. It's probably the first time she's been out in public like that. And I'll bet money that Knight knew she'd flip out with all the attention. You can't pay for publicity like that," he said.

"It . . . was . . . appalling!" Shawn added.

"Did you get any of it on tape?" I asked.

Shawn started to answer, but mercifully Steve interrupted her.

"At first I told her to turn off the camera," he said. "So sleazy. But then I realized everyone in the room with a camera was zooming in on her. And, God help me, it'll make a great story. We'll have to use fog patches to cover the good parts, but . . ." He trailed off, and the silence hung in the air.

"What a business, huh?" I said. Even seedier than I'd remembered. If Tricia Knight had staged the whole scene as a photo op, Leland had just been playing into her hand. And so had I.

I looked at my watch. "Five minutes." I said, standing up to go. "Thanks for the coffee and the program."

Shawn actually stood up with me and shook my hand. "You are . . . SO . . . cool!" she said.

I ran as fast as I could run with a hot cup of coffee back to the Palais. The press conference was on the *troisième,* in a small windowless room that was packed with journalists. I found an empty seat at the back, between a black-haired woman from MTV in Jordan and a row of TV cameras. A long panel had been set up at the front of the room, with a wall-sized poster of the festival banner behind it.

The door opened, and the line of filmmakers filed in, led by Iggy Pop, who had apparently scored the film. He was followed by the three producers and, finally, by Depp.

Depp looked like a dream. He was dressed in a black suit over a black shirt, and his hair was short and clean. The mediator, a Turkish-French critic named Henri Behar who was reputed to be conversant in all civilized languages, opened the discussion by asking Depp how he was feeling.

"A vat of hot oil looks pretty good right now," he said.

The room erupted in laughter, and the mood was set. He was so gracious that no one wanted to attack. He volunteered the story of how he'd found the novel and cowritten the script with his brother, and then fielded some softball questions about being a rookie director.

The Jordanian woman next to me took the portable microphone and asked Iggy Pop if he'd seen the movie before he wrote the music or after.

"Before," Iggy said, and in the front row, Leland raised his hand and asked the question to which everyone wanted an answer.

"This is for Mr. Depp," he said. "I don't think anyone in the world—and in this room we have representatives from just about everywhere—would disagree that compared to other actors, you've been very brave in following your own authentic vision in the movies you've made. How does *The Brave*, which may or may not see the dark of a theater again, fit into your vision?"

Depp gave a little laugh and leaned into his mike with a long, articulate answer about real courage and the plight of the American Indian, which I hoped some of the critics who'd hissed and thrown wads of paper could understand. His movie may have been a disappointment, but he was a class act.

When the press conference was over, it took ten minutes for all of us to ooze out of the room. I came into the hall, and Leland was talking to the Swedes next to the mailboxes. He stared at me as I walked by. I stared back. Neither of us spoke.

A new pile of invitations and press kits awaited me in my mailbox, along with the daily deluge. There was a note that my one-on-one with Depp had been canceled, but I was happy to have the hour free—I wanted to call the French production companies I'd gotten from Steve's program. For my column, I thought I could piece together something interesting about *The Brave* and the press conference and the gala. Eventually I'd have to get myself down to the beach to check out the scene, but for the moment I had work to do.

I bought a ham sandwich and a Coke in the café on the second floor and finished them on my way to the pressroom. The room was noisy with clicking computer keys and all the computers were taken, so I put my name on the waiting list and went down to the bank of telephones at the foot of the stairs.

There were ten French movie companies on the list, and, armed with my phone card, I started from the top. A pleasant female voice answered after two rings.

"Yes, hello. I'm . . . calling from Cannes. . . ." I said.

"*Oui, madame,*" she said. "But you have called Gaumont Pictures in Paris. Everyone from our bureau is in Cannes to promote *The Last Orb.*"

"Yes, but I'm calling . . . to ask . . ." I'd been speaking pretty good French for the last two days, but I was surprised to find myself stumbling over the simplest words. "Can you tell me, is Gaumont the studio that released the Jacques Vidanne film that is appearing at the festival? I am a great admirer of his, but I'm afraid I don't—"

"Where are you from, madame?"

"I'm a journalist from the United States," I said.

"Oh, the United States!" she said in English. "That explains it. I have been to the United States many times. Always to California."

"To Los Angeles?" I asked.

"Always. Is there another city in California?"

We both laughed. "You speak very good English," I added.

"It is useful for me to speak English. France is the birthplace of cinema, you know, but even the French must admit that the cinema is alive today because of America."

"That's generous," I said.

"In any case, *ne vous en faites pas*. It is normal for strangers to be unfamiliar with foreign studios, especially that of Monsieur Vidanne, who is notoriously absent from public view even in France. But you will certainly find a publicity representative for his studio at the festival."

"*His* studio?" I said.

"*Mais bien sûr*. He is a producer only occasionally of his own *scenarios*. More notably he is the *propriétaire* of the Éclair Studios in Paris."

"*Éclair?*" I asked, remembering the letters I'd seen in the early morning, accidentally illuminated on the side of the yacht by Gaspar's spotlight: "—LAIR." I looked quickly through the list of companies. There it was: Éclair, for a film called *Le Vol*.

"Madame?" I asked. "This is a . . . very silly question. But your English is so good. Perhaps you can tell me. What is the meaning of the word 'éclair'? It's not just the name of a French pastry, is it?"

"Oh, no. The pastry was given the name because it comes and goes so quickly."

"Yes, it does," I said.

"Translated to English, the word 'éclair' means 'flash of lightning.'"

It was like being kicked in the stomach.

I mumbled a thank-you and hung up.

Éclair productions. What a coincidence. "Éclair" was a perfect name for a company devoted to capturing light and transforming it into moving images. The poetry of it was not lost on me. But what did it mean to Jacques Vidanne?

Beside the wall of windows overlooking the water, I found an empty bench and slumped onto it. I didn't know what to do. Something told me I should leave this alone, that I should go back to the pressroom and write my column and forget I'd ever heard of Vidanne or his company. But I couldn't do it. If he knew that I'd spoken French as a child, I had the feeling he knew something more about me, and I wanted to know what.

I rifled through my bag and found the broad festival calendar. *Le Vol*, the movie Vidanne had brought to the festival, was being screened for competition in the *Un Certain Regard* category at two-thirty on Monday afternoon.

Through the glass, as if it were coming from my head, I heard a deep bellow from a ship announcing its arrival in the harbor. The sky and the sea were an uninterrupted blue, but on the northern edge of the horizon a cloud was forming, and I felt the familiar anxiety creep over me. The expectation of bad weather was as unsettling as the information I'd just learned about Jacques Vidanne, and there was nothing I could do about either. My only recourse was to get on with the job I'd come here to do.

I wandered down the stairs to the Salle Debussy to watch a melancholy French film called *Mimi et Yvonne,* about a beautiful Gypsy who saves the life of a rich banker and his young daughter. For a while it looked as if the three of them might ride off into the sunset together, but it deteriorated into the inevitable catastrophic finale. I cried without stopping through the entire second half.

When the movie was over, I came out of the theater into warmth and sunshine. The front of the Palais was packed with fans, already straining the barricades for the arrival of Orlando Bloom and Andie MacDowell for the evening premiere of *Face of Peace.* I walked onto the Croisette, along the footpath in front of the American Pavilion and past a monstrous TV screen that was playing archaeological footage of Bette Davis and Cary Grant from Cannes festivals long past. And then I let myself be swept up in the flow of people strolling languidly beside the beach and talking importantly into cell phones.

The sun was glistening off the Mediterranean, and the beach was littered with sunbathers—men and women wearing nothing but skimpy bikini bottoms. I felt like a professional voyeur, which in fact I was, looking out on a sea of breasts: big breasts, little breasts, rounded breasts, cone-shaped breasts.

I shouldered my way onto the beach through a crowd of oglers, put my sandals in my bag, and burrowed my feet in the sand. It was still wet from the rain, but it felt warm and sensuous under my feet. With my toes totally buried, I took in the scene around me and almost laughed out loud.

A six-foot yellow banana walked toward me, arm in arm with a pineapple as round as a sumo wrestler. The "DOLE" logo was stuck on the front of their costumes, and both of them wore greenish leggings and white Mickey Mouse gloves on their hands. Every few feet they stopped and posed for cameras, as if they'd been hired by central casting.

Cameras were everywhere. Up and down the beach, clusters of reporters and photographers were huddled in small crowds, snapping pictures and laughing.

A few feet from the narrow pier that jutted out from the Croisette, I saw a blonde woman, barely five feet tall, who must have weighed at least 250 pounds in her bare feet, wearing only a bandanna bikini bottom. Her body was covered with tattoos—a vein-blue dolphin arched gracefully over one shoulder, and a red-and-black-striped tiger covered the other. Her breasts were the *pièces de résistance,* tattooed with two preposterous daisies, her erect nipples popping out in the center of each flower like the knotted ends of two big balloons. She smiled as she moved from one grotesque posture to another, her enormous round breasts flopping sloppily. Pictures snapped with each new pose.

I was thinking how degrading the scene was for everyone involved when I realized that I was gawking right along with everyone else and having a wonderful time. This was just part of the entertainment.

"Are you an actress?" one of the reporters asked the woman in French. She smiled broadly in response, showing a mouthful of dirty teeth.

"What's your name?" someone else asked, and she turned to him with her hand lifted behind her head in a voluptuous posture.

The crowd laughed, and she laughed, too—she was in on the joke—and I heard a nasal chuckle amid the laughter. I looked across the circle of onlookers and saw Leland Dunne. Our eyes locked for a long moment, and he jerked his head in the direction of the Croisette in an apparent invitation for me to join him.

One of the gawkers reached out to touch the woman's left daisy. She saw the hand coming and swatted it away as if it were a gnat. The crowd laughed again as the gawker cradled his wounded hand. Leland had not moved his eyes from me.

I shrugged and joined him next to a massive poster of Clint Eastwood's *The President's Assassin.*

I didn't know whether I wanted him to apologize to me or—if Steve had been right about Naomi's publicist—if I should apologize to him.

He reached into the pocket of his pants and pulled out a roll of film, offering it to me on his open palm. His face was set in a resigned smile.

"I'll trade you for my jacket," he said.

"I don't have it. But you'll get it back. I'll buy you another one if I have to." I pointed to the film in his hand. "And that is none of my business, Leland. I thought it was last night, but today I can see that it's your business with Naomi."

He paused for a second and then put the film back in his pocket. "I was an ass. I admit it. I wish I could prove to you what a compassionate, humane, gentlemanly icon of—"

"You could have leveled with me," I said. "That would've been a start."

"I should have," he agreed. "But what would you have done if I'd told you? Refused my jewels, no doubt."

"No doubt. You could have gone alone. I didn't want to go in the first place."

Leland leaned one shoulder against the poster, next to Eastwood's chin. "But that's the heart of it, Nattie, my sweet. I wanted to go with you. I told you that from the beginning. All my vitals sprang to attention when I found you on the plane."

I brushed a piece of sand from the blister on my heel. "So what if you wanted me to go with you? You've got the Swedes. You've always got a million women hanging on you."

"Why don't I have you hanging on me?" he asked. I looked at his eyes for a clue that he was messing with me, but it seemed to be an honest question, so I considered it honestly.

"Well, I admit that you're smart and witty. And charming."

He shivered. "Oooh, worse and worse."

I smiled, a little embarrassed. "But the thing about you charming men is that you're indiscriminant. Every woman is just as fascinating to you as every other woman. It's freaky."

"For a discriminating woman like yourself, you mean."

"Right."

"Well, if you don't mind my saying so, you're so damned discriminating, you discriminate yourself right out of having any fun at all, and that's freaky, too."

"Ouch."

"I'd feel better if I thought there was *someone* you were having fun with," he said.

"Wait a minute," I said, shoving him on the shoulder so he lost his balance and had to reposition himself against Eastwood's chin. "When you say 'having fun' you don't mean 'having fun.' You mean having sex!"

"I mean not disappearing the moment someone tries to get close to you."

I forced myself to look at him, but I was afraid I was going to cry.

"I think the whole idea of really connecting with someone scares you," he said.

"*You* scare me."

"Why?"

"Because I wouldn't . . . *it* wouldn't mean anything to you."

"How can you know that?" he shouted. "You walked out on me before I even woke up!"

The gawkers who'd been gawking at the woman with daisy breasts turned in our direction and gawked at us. We gawked back. The woman reclaimed their attention by shimmying her shoulders so that her daisies fluttered in the breeze. I bet she didn't have men telling her she never had any fun.

Leland and I stared at the crowd for several minutes before I said, "You're just dangerous for me. I don't expect you to understand."

"I'm dangerous?" he said, feigning disbelief. "Look at me! I can barely lift my own laptop!"

I laughed. "You know what I mean."

He leaned into me and whispered in my ear, "I'm harmless."

"No," I said, "you're hopeless." We both managed a smile, and I felt some of the animosity from the night before evaporate. What remained was the edgy frustration of knowing Leland and I would never quite be on the same wavelength.

He cocked his head to the side and smiled, as if he were looking at me through a window.

"I feel a little better," I said. "This will be a long festival if we aren't friends."

"Friends for sure," he said. "But when you're ready for more, I'm your man."

"Hopeless!" I hitched my bag over my shoulder. "C'mon. I have to get back to the pressroom to write my story."

"I can't go back with you. I have my interview with Naomi Paul in five minutes."

I stopped in my tracks. My mind began to race. Naomi Paul was a thread that could lead me to Vidanne. I raised my eyebrows and sauntered slowly back to Leland, trying not to look as excited as I felt.

"You still want to make it up to me? The thing last night?"

Leland raised his right hand. "I swear. What can I do that won't land me in a French jail?"

"Let me come with you."

He frowned. "Do I look like a chump?"

"Just for a few minutes." I held up my own palm as a promise. "Okay, just for a minute. Thirty seconds! I won't even mention last night. You can negotiate with her about the pictures." He held his frown. "Or *not* negotiate about the pictures. I'll be gone, I swear on my passport. I just want to ask her a couple of questions."

He cocked his head a little and said, "And then we're square?"

"We're square."

"What a deal," he said. He took my hand, and we started toward the Croisette. "I don't suppose these questions will be about the pictures?"

"If you only knew, Leland, what an insignificant part of the night those pictures turned out to be."

The rush of cars on the Croisette was intense, and it took most of Leland's remaining five minutes to get to the other side. I looked up and saw an enormous billboard of *The Simpsons* directly in front of the Majestic, and it seemed to me the essence of Cannes: low-rent and luxury, all in the same line of vision.

A steady stream of vehicles, Peugeot sedans and stretch limousines alike, pulled up to the ornate glass doors of the hotel and deposited their charges, then swept around the circle and rejoined the stream on the Croisette while a throng of fans waited, hoping for a glimpse of celebrity.

The Majestic—where Gaspar had said some of the rooms cost ten thousand euros a night—was old and red-carpet elegant on the inside and lined with huge Greek and Egyptian statues, which I barely had time to appreciate as Leland whizzed us through the foyer. The restaurant was a big airy room with immense chandeliers and red velvet furniture. The sound of silverware on china made my stomach growl.

A long line of people was waiting to be seated. Leland went to the head of the line to give his name to the maître d' but was interrupted when Tricia Knight stepped in front of his podium.

"Leland Dunne! Right on time, as you always always are."

Leland laughed his nasal laugh and said, "I never never am on time, Tricia, but thanks for the vote of confidence. You know Nattie Conway, don't you?"

Tricia turned her head in my direction, and in a moment her eyes followed.

"I do know Nattie Conway. I sure do," she said.

She was a handsome woman with a head of thick black hair that always looked as perfectly coiffed as a wig, and I'd never seen her in anything but the sleek black pantsuit she was wearing now. She put her hands on her narrow hips and said, "But I haven't seen you in ages, Nattie. Ages!"

"I saw you last night, Tricia," I said. "At the gala."

"No, really?" She gave me a nasty little grin and then turned abruptly to take Leland by the hand. She tossed a cold farewell at me over her shoulder. "Just wonderful to see you!"

I watched her lead Leland to a table outside, where I could see Naomi sitting primly under a big yellow umbrella. Tricia would certainly expect me to have the good breeding to fade gracefully into the background, but I wasn't about to miss this opportunity. I watched discreetly through the tinted windows that separated the indoor restaurant from the patio as Leland took Naomi's hand, kissed it, and sat down next to her. Ever the charmer.

Tricia Knight patted her watch, squeezed Leland fondly on the shoulders with both hands, and left them alone. When she was out of sight, I walked quickly through the restaurant to the patio. Naomi looked up from her conversation with Leland to give me a big smile.

"Hi!" she said, waving with both hands. She motioned for me to join them. "Nettie, right?"

"Close enough," I said, sitting down at the table.

"See?" she said with a giggle, using her hand to shield our little secret from Leland. "I wasn't *that* drunk." Then she turned to Leland. "I went home from a party with her last night." Leland nodded sagely, as if this were news to him.

She ran her fingers through her long blonde hair, and I noticed that she was much prettier than I'd thought the night before. She was wearing almost no makeup, and her shiny hair fell softly at her shoulders. In anticipation of her new career, she'd put on an almost prissy white lace sundress that covered her shoulders and gathered into a dainty collar.

"Naomi," I said, "I was wondering if you knew where I could find Jacques Vidanne."

She shrugged and rearranged herself in her chair so she was facing me, girl to girl. "On his yacht, I guess."

"Do you know where it is?"

"Nope." She shook her head and frowned prettily. "He took me to the Hôtel du Cap. Have you been there? It's over on the Cap d'Antibes, and it's—"

"Mmm-hmm, I've heard it's beautiful." I glanced over at Leland, who appeared to be having trouble following the conversation. "When did he take you there?"

"This morning. Re-e-e-ally early, like six or something. I was so-o-o tired, were you?"

"I was, too. But—"

"He got a room for me that is *beyond* fabulous. It has a balcony and a garden, and there are three really gargantuan rooms, and every room has its own television."

"Why do you think he took you to the hotel? Didn't he invite you to stay on his yacht during the festival?"

I saw Tricia Knight at the restaurant door, whispering to a waiter and pointing at our table. Naomi was thinking hard. "I think 'cause his wife or whatever she was ... *Madame* ... had arrived." She singled out a strand of her hair and was twirling it around her index finger when she remembered Leland. "Hey, wait. Do you know . . . I'm sorry, what's your name—from Canada, right?"

"Leland Dunne. Nettie, is it?" he said, offering me his hand.

"Mr. Dunne," I said with a smile. "Well, I'm sorry to interrupt your interview. I'll leave you both to be brilliant."

"Oh, too bad," Naomi said.

"Yes, too bad," said Leland.

"It's been a pleasure." I stood up to leave. "So if Monsieur Vidanne calls you, could you find out how I can contact him? Would that be a problem?"

"Gee, no. You were just so great to take me home and everything. And hey!" She took my hand and pulled me close so she could whisper in my ear. "I still have that man's jacket."

"Perhaps he'll find you," I said, glancing at Leland. "And if you hear from Vidanne, leave a message in the pressroom, okay?" And I hugged her good-bye.

I let Leland kiss the back of my hand before I left the restaurant.

Just outside the foyer was a small sign on the wall next to the concierge desk that said "WARNER BROTHERS," with an arrow pointing around the corner. As I noted the location for Warner's press luncheon on Wednesday, it occurred to me that there might be more production companies in this hotel.

The concierge was having a heated discussion in German, and I waited for a lull. Finally she covered the mouthpiece with her hand and whispered, *"Oui, madame?"*

I whispered back that I was trying to find the Éclair Studio's hospitality suite.

She whispered "Five-six-zero" over the mouthpiece and returned to her phone call. I took off around the corner, looking for the elevators.

In the hallway of the fifth floor, which was more narrow and spartan than I'd have predicted from the hotel's lavish exterior, I followed the numbers to a small room with one enormous wall that someone had decorated magnificently with the Mediterranean Sea. Boxes were piled along another wall, and a square table had been set up as a desk in front of the picture window. Along the wall to the right was a bigger table with sandwiches and pastries and cups for tea and coffee.

I heard a toilet flush, and a pretty young man came out of the bathroom, patting the crotch of his pants.

"I wanted to ask about your movie, *Le Vol*," I said.

He flipped through a pile of papers on his desk and handed me a single sheet that gave a brief summary of the plot to *Le Vol*.

"It's the story of an airplane mechanic who crashes alone in the Sahara Desert and finds a boy who teaches him the secret of life."

"It sounds like *The Little Prince*," I said.

"Yes, precisely! But you are American, yes? Do not confuse it with the American movie. This is authentic."

"Luckily, I never saw the inauthentic version. But I'm so happy to know about this one. I intend to see it on Monday, definitely. It's one of my favorite books. Very popular in America, did you know that?"

"But of course I knew that, mad'moiselle," he said. "Until the little wizard books, *The Little Prince* was the third most-read book in the world."

I grimaced at my ignorance and wondered what the first two were. He handed me a press kit with a stylized drawing of a simple biplane on the front and a star above the horizon. I was flipping through the pictures inside when two journalists wearing baseball caps and credentials around their necks walked into the suite.

"We need a schedule," one of them said irritably in a crisp English accent. "Who will be at the Tuesday luncheon?"

"The film's stars," the Éclair rep said, "Jean-Paul Tournat and Philippe Couronne, will be there, and the director, Edgar Loos." He glanced at the list on the desk in front of him and added, "Also the producer, Jacques Vidanne, will attend the luncheon."

Suddenly I was all ears. The Brits grabbed the schedules, said a hasty *au revoir,* and left the suite. I stood still, trying to think what to do next.

"You're having a luncheon for *Le Vol*?" I asked the man.

"Yes, mad'moiselle. On Tuesday. But we have invited no journalists from the United States. It is a very small picture."

"But eventually the movie will be released in America, *n'est-ce pas*? Is there any chance at all that I could join the luncheon? I could promise to eat my lunch before I come, if food is a consideration."

He laughed.

"Really, I would be so grateful to be included."

"I'm sure there will be room for someone like you"—he nodded at my yellow dot—"who is so interested in the movie."

I gave him my information and agreed to call if I didn't hear from him. Three more journalists came into the suite, and he offered me food and coffee. While he organized papers and placated the journalists, I ate three tiny pastries. Who knew when I'd find desserts like this again for free: custard-filled tarts with sliced kiwi and strawberries arranged to look like flowers?

"Thank you again," I said to the man as I patted my mouth with a linen napkin. I was on my way out the door, but I turned back to him. "Can you tell me how long Éclair has been in operation?" I asked.

He looked up from his papers. "Oh yes. This Cannes is an important festival for Éclair. We have been in force exactly twenty-five years this autumn."

I stood stock-still as the man looked back down at his papers indifferently. "You will find a studio history in your press kit. And a list of all our films. We have had a distinguished twenty-five years, I promise you."

"I'm sure you have," I said. "I hope to hear from you about the luncheon."

"Of course," he said. "*Au revoir.*"

I turned the corner into the hall and pulled the press kit out of my bag. It was in French but identical to the ones for American movies: it included several glossy black-and-white photos of *Le Vol*, along with a dozen pages of production notes. They gave mini-biographies of the actors and all the filmmakers, and there was a whole page devoted to Saint-Exupéry's life. The bio on Vidanne was six lines long: he had begun his career as a pure *auteur*, writing, directing, and producing his first film, *Zeitgeist*, which had shaken the French consciousness and made his name in the industry.

He had then formed a production company, which had released

eighty-seven pictures in twenty-five years. Eight of them were written and produced by Vidanne, and since I moved to LA I'd seen all of those except *Zeitgeist,* which I'd tried to find for years.

Vidanne had never directed another movie after *Zeitgeist.* That was very strange by moviemaking standards. As the head of a studio, he could be involved in every film that was produced under the Éclair banner, but film is a director's medium: the director has creative power in the production of a film; the producer's job is basically to make sure the bills are paid. Actors and producers say so often that they hope someday to direct, it's a filmmaker's joke.

It wasn't surprising that I hadn't known Vidanne owned an entire studio. In the credits for his films he was always listed as *scénariste:* screenwriter. He was often included in the lists of producers, but even actors sometimes share production billing. And I rarely registered the long chronicle of production companies at the beginning of even American movies. But it was odd that after twenty-five years *Zeitgeist,* the film that transformed this man's career, was still unavailable on DVD or video.

I left the hotel in a daze. Vidanne had built a studio named "Lightning," just one summer after lightning had changed my life. Fifteen years later, he'd made a movie that meant so much to me, it had spawned my own personal Jacques Vidanne festival. Was it sheer coincidence that he'd chosen "Éclair"? I didn't believe in signs—no one who's been struck by lightning wants to believe in signs—but how could I ignore this one? My only hope for answers was to sit across from him and ask him myself. And that brought me right back to where I'd begun: after my unwitting faux pas, he would never agree to an interview.

It was nearly six o'clock when I got myself moving down the Croisette, and the sun was edging its way toward the western horizon. All of the human energy in Cannes seemed to be pooling together at the steps of the Palais. The limousines wouldn't begin to arrive for another hour and a half, and the temperature was dropping with every fading sunbeam, but the crowd seemed to be growing bigger and more impassioned, as if the very fact that they were waiting made what they were waiting for worth waiting for.

I took a detour up one of the back streets and cut over to the plaza, entering the Palais from the back. I reached the pressroom with just enough time to write my column before I caught Wim Wenders's *Face of Peace,* the film Draper had ordered me to see. I found a computer, and a nasty little e-mail from Draper:

> *YES to glitter and glam*
> *NO to sophistry*
> *800 words or nothing.*

I deleted it and got to work.

CANNES, Friday—May 9. The sun is shining on the celebration of the world's most famous festival, bringing with it a mother lode of mammaries. A brood of bosoms. A network of nipples. What would be more difficult than selling refrigerators in Alaska? Selling breast implants in Cannes.

The fact that I didn't delete the paragraph the moment it hit the screen made me question my journalistic integrity, but Draper would love it. I wrote about the brutal reception Johnny Depp had gotten for *The Brave,* what he'd said in the press conference about his desire to help the American Indians. I wrote about *Mimi and Yvonne,* the crowds, the yachts in the harbor, the mob at the Majestic Hotel, the ubiquitous cell phone.

I offered an observation on France's love-hate relationship with American movies, and I was finishing up with a description of the sensuous performance by a nameless starlet on a tabletop at the gala when the image of Naomi stuck in my head. Perfect Naomi:

pretty, blonde, trying to start a new career, and vulnerable to the easy power of a man like Jacques Vidanne.

The cursor was blinking on the word "starlet." It was such a cliché: the aging producer and the beautiful young actress—the perfect symbiosis, like egrets and water buffalo. But it hadn't felt like that kind of arrangement to me. I couldn't remember the details of my conversation with Naomi in the taxi, but she'd been pretty convincing when she said she hadn't slept with him. Still, he certainly hadn't treated me with the same kind of deference he'd shown to Naomi. What kind of man *was* he, really?

I sent the column to Draper and then went to Google. I'd Googled Vidanne plenty of times before, looking for details about his movies, but none of the sites in English went much deeper than the press notes I'd just read—it was part of what made him mysterious that he never spoke about his personal life.

There were twelve pages of links to Jacques Vidanne, most of them in French, which presented a bit of a problem for me. Since I hadn't learned to read French as a little girl, reading it as an adult hadn't come as easily, so I'd never gotten very far with any of those sites. This time I had to try harder.

Le site officiel de Jacques Vidanne looked like a pretty good place to start. His picture filled the left side of the page—he was dressed in a white jacket instead of white terrycloth, but it was the same bald head I'd seen on the boat the night before.

Below the photo was a more personal biography—his birth to dairy farmers in the mountain town of Corte on the island of Corsica, his solitary childhood. At age seventeen he'd moved to Paris, where he'd seen his first movie and fallen in love with cinema; he began taking odd jobs on various films; twenty years later, he wrote, directed, and produced the seminal *Zeitgeist*.

I decided to start at the beginning. I Googled *Zeitgeist*. Ten pages came up, from psychology journals to advanced marketing techniques. " 'Zeitgeist' is German for 'the spirit of the age,' " one site advertised. At the bottom of the second page I found *"Zeitgeist: a film by Jacques Vidanne."* It was an independent film site, with instructions for ordering hard-to-find films. Even this site was unable to order *Zeitgeist,* but "Production Details" flashed on the right side of the screen. I clicked on it. The movie's site came up, with the usual postage-stamp-sized photo of the publicity one-sheet. It was too small to make out the details. Under the photo were the standard production notes:

Director: Jacques Vidanne
Genre: (Drama)
Screenwriter: Jacques Vidanne
Tag line: She was the spirit of her generation
Plot outline: In sunny Marseilles, a sexy peasant girl loves a
    young man but marries his father.

I scrolled down through the reviews—all of them in French—to the cast list. There were only six characters.

Isabelle: Lynette Hamilton
Gregoire Janus: Claude Evelain
Josette: Katherine Kitredge
Thierry Janus: Paul Dubois
Cousin Henri: Jules Gassner
Cousine Marie: Elaine Moselle

At first I didn't see it, but then my hands froze over the keyboard. It was the name I'd seen chiseled into the stone at my mother's grave: her maiden name.

I felt the tinny taste of adrenaline on my tongue. Images flooded my head, of standing on his boat, of his refusal to take my hand, of being rushed down the ladder before I had a chance to ask him questions. When he heard my name, had he known at once that I was her daughter?

I stared at the cast list until my eyes began to hurt, and then shut off the computer and stared at the empty screen. I had a million questions for this man, but unless I heard from Naomi or happened to stumble upon him, I wouldn't be able to talk to him until Tuesday. I couldn't wait that long.

I grabbed my bag of papers and notes and invitations and headed down the stairs to the bank of phones I'd used in the afternoon. A woman answered after one ring, with the same lilting French voice I'd heard two days before.

"Michel Claudel, *s'il vous plaît*," I said.

"I am sorry, but you have only just missed him," she said.

"Could you give him a message?"

"*Mais oui.* On behalf of whom?"

Here goes, I thought. I gave her my name and the number at the hotel.

"And the message?" she asked.

I wondered what message I could leave that would persuade him to return my call. What if he didn't even remember me? "*Je . . . je . . . ,*" I stammered. "*Je veux seulement lui demander une question—*"

"A question on what subject, madame?"

"On the subject," I said, "of my mother."

There are only four questions of value in life:
What is sacred? Of what is the spirit made?
What is worth living for? What is worth dying for?
The answer to each is the same. . . .

Johnny Depp, in *Don Juan de Marco*

7

Cannes, France

Saturday, May 10

I was showing my Pink badge to the guards at the Salle des Lumières and swallowing the last bite of my morning baguette when Marie of the unpronounceable Korean name called to me from the front row of the third balcony. I climbed the short stairway and joined her. She looked exhausted. She'd seen six movies the previous day (only one of them worth remembering) and had written three articles (only one of them worth reading), which she'd finished at three in the morning.

I'd barely had the energy to drag myself to the Wim Wenders movie the night before, and all I remembered about the review I'd sent to Draper was that it contained precisely eight hundred words. It was clear that half of Cannes was passing me by, and I felt the inevitable film festival panic that I was missing out on essential movies and stories that were vital to the future of cinema.

This morning's screening was a modern French road picture called *Western*, about a Russian and a Spaniard traveling across France in search of love. It was a charming movie, and it got a wild ten-minute standing ovation at the end.

Marie was off to write something about a Japanese film she'd seen at midnight, and we said good-bye at our mailboxes. I stuffed everything from my box into my newly emptied bag. I was thinking that there was just enough time to stop in at Jack's for a cup of coffee before the *Western* press conference when I noticed among the printed pamphlets and glossy movie materials a small piece of pale blue paper.

"Conway: pressroom. Message," it said. It was written in precise French script, the old-fashioned kind of penmanship that was the result of strict professors slapping wooden pointers on young knuckles when the curves of their *m*'s were imperfect.

A message in the pressroom? I felt a new twinge of panic: Draper, dissatisfied again with the columns I'd written. Too pedantic. Too short. Too something else. And then I realized I hadn't given my father any information in case of emergency. How else could he track me down but to call the press office?

I headed to the fourth floor, and on my way up the last flight of stairs, I tried to calculate how much money Draper would be likely to pay me for the work I'd done so far. I'd be lucky if there were two zeros involved. I envisioned the roof crumbling in on my little house in the canyon.

The computers were all in use, and the tiny pressroom was packed with frantic reporters. Behind the counter, three women and one man were taking names for wait lists and trying to accommodate the nervous crowd of journalists. When it was my turn, the man at the desk flipped through a box of alphabetized messages and pulled out another piece of blue paper.

"It says 'Unable to enter the Palais.'" The man looked at me and shook his head. "'Would like you to meet at the Café Promenade, next to the Café Cinématique. For lunch,' it says."

"Who is this message from? And did they leave a time?"

"Frankly I do not know," he said as someone nudged me out of line.

I looked at the note, relieved that it couldn't be Draper or my father. Maybe it was from Naomi, with info about where I could find Vidanne. She had no credentials to enter the Palais. There was nothing I could do but wait until noon.

The *Western* press conference began five minutes later. The room was nearly empty, and I understood why: this one was conducted entirely in French. I was curious to see whether the questions and answers would sound more intelligent.

They didn't. Someone from Italy asked the Spanish star if he'd always known how to walk on his hands or if he'd learned how expressly for the movie. He had always known how. There were questions about the difficulty of lighting on locations where the sun is always hidden, and whether the theme of the movie was betrayal or forgiveness. I could understand, but I couldn't concentrate on the answers.

When I left the press conference the sun was burning hot directly overhead. The Wim Wenders luncheon would begin in forty-five minutes, but if Naomi could point me in Vidanne's direction, Wenders would have to lunch without me.

I squeezed through the crowd on the Croisette and crossed the square. A sprightly white-haired man in a Hawaiian shirt and Panama hat who looked like Maurice Chevalier on vacation was singing "La Vie en Rose," karaoke-style, from a microphone connected to a little yellow Isetta car, parked outside of the Cinématique. His singing voice was no better than Chevalier's had been, but he was grinning from one oversized ear to the other.

When I walked into the Café Promenade, the maître d' asked if he could find me a table, and I told him I was meeting someone.

"Under what name?" he said.

"I don't know, precisely," I said.

"*Oui, madame,*" he said with a patronizing grin. "*Par ici.*" He motioned grandly toward the back of the restaurant, and I followed.

The tables were all draped with white linen, as even the shabbiest restaurants in France seem to be, and there were tall red flowers in vases in the center of each one. All of the chairs were full, and the smell of garlic grew as we neared the kitchen. Then the waiter stopped suddenly and stepped aside, to give me a full view of a man sitting alone at a table in the farthest corner of the restaurant. When the man saw me, his face broke out in a smile. He pushed the table away from him and stood up slowly.

I knew immediately who he was. I had last seen him twenty-five years ago, at Charles de Gaulle Airport, through a torrent of tears.

Michel Claudel's smile was radiant. He was dressed in a gray suit and blue shirt, the collar open and casual. His hair was thick, and graying only at the temples, and his eyes were riveted on me. The fingers of one hand rested expectantly on the edge of the table, apparently uncertain whether to advance toward me or to retreat into his pocket. He was as handsome now as he'd been in my childhood memories.

Out of the corner of my eye, I saw the waiter pull the table out to allow him to step around it, so we stood several feet apart, facing one another.

A thousand nights I'd fallen asleep imagining this scene. I'd thought of it while I was riding my bicycle, or walking on the mesa, or sitting across from my father at the dinner table. But never once, in all my fantasies, was I a grown woman when I met Claudel again. Always I was six years old, returning to him exactly as I'd left him, kneeling on the hard airport floor to embrace me at my own child's level. In every single daydream, he'd held me as I cried. But now I was not a child, and tears were out of the question. I had no idea what to say.

Apparently, neither did he. He shook his head slowly, and his smile became tentative, afraid to commit itself. We stood looking at each other, until finally Claudel fell back on his ingrained French manners. He took an awkward step toward me, so I had to tilt my head back to see his face close up, and put his hands gently on my shoulders. He leaned over and gave me a *bise*—a little kiss—on one cheek and then the other. My hands were still at my sides, one of them wrapped fiercely around the cloth handle of my bag, the other in a limp fist.

He stepped back and looked at me, from the top of my casually combed hair to the tips of my uncomfortable black sandals. And then his eyes rolled over me again from feet to head. There was nothing sexual or provocative about his gaze: he was looking at me as if I were a forgotten painting he'd come across in a closet, something he was delighted to find again but barely recognized. Again he shook his head slowly, and his smile grew and was no longer conscious of itself. I felt his hand on my elbow as he motioned toward the table, but I didn't move one way or the other, and he waited.

I wasn't sure I could handle this. Part of me wanted to throw my arms around him and hide my face in his blue shirt. And part of me wanted to walk right out of the restaurant, back to the numbing delirium of endless movies.

The functioning part of me said, *"Bonjour, Claudel,"* and it came out so soft and hesitant, I could barely hear it myself.

"Natalie," he said in three distinct syllables. His smile had vanished. Clearly he hadn't been sure how this would go, and it looked as if it might be heading in a bad direction.

The waiter was still standing patiently with his hands on the back of my chair. I sat in the chair, and he pushed it forward, shook open my napkin, and laid it on my lap.

"*A boire, madame?*" he asked.

I didn't respond, and Claudel pointed to his own glass of white wine and held up one finger. Then he gave the waiter a French nod that seemed to say *Go now, and return when the bloodletting has ceased.*

I set my bag on the floor and sat back with my hands in my lap. Claudel eyed me nervously.

One thing I'd always feared about myself was that I was a woman without social delicacy. Growing up without a mother to observe in awkward moments had left me feeling tongue-tied and clumsy in most situations that required grace. I'd watched enough Michelle Pfeiffer movies to recognize the easy submission that makes a proper female proper, and had even tried to duplicate it. But I was afraid there was an edge to me that I was always struggling to soften. I tried for softness now, without much luck.

"*Vous avez bien reçue ma communication,*" I said. *You got my message.* But I used the formal "*vous*" form, more out of nervousness than respect, and I sounded like a secretary opening a business meeting.

"I did," he said, and his smile was genuine. "And you called me Wednesday." He used the familiar "*tu.*" He was having none of my formality. "My assistant said your French was nearly *sans accent,* the kind that only comes from speaking French as a child. But you left none of your information."

"I was only in Paris for a few hours. I wasn't sure I wanted to talk to you," I said, and immediately regretted it.

He nodded and touched his water glass. I needed desperately to be softer. He couldn't possibly know why I'd called him. He was obviously here because he was curious to know what I had become, and I realized with a jolt that I wasn't sure of that myself. I flailed around in my head for help, but all I came up with was dating advice from an old movie, to Debra Winger in *Cannery Row:* Do everything slowly. So I lifted my water glass in slow motion and brought it to my mouth. The coldness of it felt good on my lips. I took a slow sip and slowly put the glass back on the table.

"I wasn't sure you'd remember me. Such a long time." That was better. "I didn't know if I'd recognize you. . . ."

"It's changed, my face, but not as much as yours," he said.

For a second, I was afraid he was going to tell me I'd grown into a beautiful young woman, or that I reminded him of my mother, or some other flattering platitude. But he didn't. He squinted slightly, as if he were seeing me from a great distance.

"What were you doing in Paris?" he asked.

"I went to the cemetery."

He nodded. "Twenty-five years. And it was *le sept mai.*"

"It was an accident," I said. "My plane to Cannes was canceled, and I was stranded. I didn't plan to go. It was so green." I took another slow sip of my water. "Have you ever been there? You know, since?"

"Yes, of course. At first I went rather frequently. Now only once every ten or twenty years," he said with a little laugh.

"Why go at all? I mean, I am expected, *comme il faut*. But you?"

The edges of his mouth turned up slightly. "It was a cataclysmic event for me, as it was for you." He added, "But I have a life now, if that's what you are wondering."

I lowered my eyes, blushing. That was exactly what I was wondering.

The waiter, apparently sensing that blood would not flow after all, came to our table with a glass of white wine, which he put in front of me, and disappeared. I looked at the wine for a second—

it was so pale that it almost looked like water—and took a big gulp. And coughed. It was stronger, or less innocent, or it had more bouquet than I'd expected, but it tasted better going down than it did coming out of my nose. I patted my face with my linen napkin and tried to regain my dignity.

"What kind of life?" I asked from behind my napkin. "Do you . . . do you have a family?" He shook his head.

"I have a business. And I have had several . . . satisfying relationships with women. A marriage. A divorce. But no, I have no children." He looked across the table at me. "Why are you here, in Cannes?" he asked suddenly. "Do you work in movies?"

For the first time since I'd walked into the restaurant, I almost felt myself relax, and I realized that from the moment I'd seen him sitting in the corner, I'd expected Claudel to fill in all the gaps, to answer all the questions that had haunted me for the last twenty-five years. But there was no way to step back into the past without validating the present. Michel Claudel and I didn't know each other. We were just two people who had survived a bad accident a long time ago. If I wanted answers from him, I had to let him make my acquaintance first.

"Not exactly," I said. "I'm a journalist. I used to write about movies for a newspaper syndicate, but now I'm working free . . . um . . ." I searched for the French word for "freelance." "*Libre-lancette?*" I said.

He smiled patiently. "*Journaliste indépendente.*"

"Exactly. I'm here to cover the festival."

"And how are you finding it, the festival?"

"Frustrating," I said. "I love watching movies, and there are so many available here, it's heaven. But it's also hell, because I'm so tired and rushed that I can't stay awake for them or even begin to see them all. It's like sitting at a table that's piled with food and being too full to eat it."

"I've spoken to journalists about the festival before," he said.

"They never seem happy to be here because they're so busy. How is it you have time to lunch with me?"

"Frankly, I don't," I said, tapping the face of my watch. It was almost one. "I have a press luncheon that starts in five minutes, for a Wim Wenders movie I saw last night at midnight."

"*Face of Peace,* yes?" he asked. "How did you like it?"

"It was wonderful," I said. He nodded. His chin was resting in his palm, and I was feeling slightly short of breath, sitting across from him, but I had the feeling he just wanted to hear me talk, so I did. "The movie was brave and important, I thought, and it tried to say something no one dares to say in movies, about our taste for brutality and who's responsible for it. And . . . they hated it! The audience hated every minute of it! They started booing even before it was over. They stomped their feet. It was a horrible display of . . ."

"Manners?" he said.

"No, it was . . ."

"Disrespect?" he suggested.

"No!" I said, too loudly. I was working myself into a frenzy over this audience response, and I didn't know why. "It was just mean!" I used the word "*vicieux,*" which was a little stronger than I meant, but it was all I could think of. "And now I have to go to this luncheon but I don't want to go, because . . . here you are!" I gave him a sad smile that he answered with a happy one. "But if I don't go to the luncheon, I won't have anything to write about today, and that's why I came to Cannes. Except that suddenly everything else seems so unimportant. . . ." I looked at Claudel and realized with horror that my eyes had started to sting, and I could feel the awful humiliation of being about to cry and not having the strength to stop myself. I'd been waiting all my life for this lunch, and I was making a mess of it. "I have to write my column this afternoon, but seeing you like this, I can't think clearly . . . and I have something important to ask you, Claudel. . . . I need to know . . ." My eyes began to fill with tears, and I set my jaw and willed them dry.

Claudel reached over the table to touch me, but decided not to and pulled his hand back. A tear spilled out of one of my eyes, and I wiped it away. I couldn't even look at him.

"You're under no obligation to stay in this restaurant, Natalie," he said softly. "If you have work to do, you must do it. For me, it was a miracle only to get your message."

"It was?" I said, and wiped away another tear.

"*Me voici!*" he said, with his palms open. "You must believe your eyes. When I received your message last night, I did everything I could do to come to you. Do you think I'm going to return to Paris this afternoon? That after twenty-five years I should share a glass of wine with you and then send us back to our lives"—he snapped his fingers—"*comme ça?*"

Another tear streamed out of my eye, and I wiped it away, hoping he hadn't noticed. And then another one, and another. I couldn't stop them. I could only try not to blubber while they fell. Claudel sat calmly on the other side of the table, as if dining with a woman in tears were a regular *déjeuner* experience for him. He waited until I was breathing normally, and then he reached over and put his hand on mine.

"This has nothing to do with movies, or fatigue, or Wim Wenders, you know?"

I nodded, but my tears continued to fall.

"Let me try something," he said. He signaled to the waiter for the check and sat back with his arms folded. "Perhaps if I talk about myself, I can bore you so completely that even your tears will dry." I sniffled loudly, and he reached into his coat pocket and gave me his handkerchief. A handkerchief! I couldn't remember the last time I'd seen a man with a handkerchief. New tears spilled from my eyes.

Claudel leaned his elbows on the table and said, "Here is the shape of my life: I live in the country outside of Paris, but I keep an apartment near my gallery in the city. I still have the gallery in Paris, do you remember? Ah, but you did remember, because you found the number."

I nodded and sniffled again.

"But perhaps you do not know that I now have three galleries altogether." He held up three fingers, and I gave a perfunctory response with my eyebrows—I vaguely remembered seeing the other galleries when I'd Googled him—and wiped my nose. He continued, watching me carefully, but reciting as if he were giving information to a reporter.

"I also have a gallery in Lyon. And I have another one here in Cannes, off the Croisette. I'll take you there if you'd like to see it."

"All posters?" I asked. My nose was stuffy, but my composure was on the mend.

"Yes, posters. Although we prefer to call them 'artistic reproductions.' " He laughed. "Each gallery is somewhat different from the others. In Paris, all the tourists want prints of Toulouse-Lautrec. In Lyon, the real connoisseurs want Mucha or the Impressionists. Here in Cannes, everyone wants to buy old movie posters. You would be surprised how much money people will pay for a sheet of paper someone had to scrape off the wall seventy-five years ago." He shrugged. "*En tout cas,* it is a concept that has made me very comfortable, so I should not make fun of it."

The waiter materialized with the check, and Claudel took two notes out of his wallet and laid them on the small plate. He reached across the table to lay his hand on mine.

"If we leave now, you will arrive in time to have salad with Mr. Wenders."

I nodded, but my head was foggy with the effort of not crying, and I couldn't think properly.

"When will you finish with your work?" he asked.

"I don't know. Late." I took a deep breath and reached into my bag for the day's schedule. "After the luncheon, I have to see an American movie called *The Blackout* and go to the press conference afterward. And then I have to write my column. Since today is Saturday, there's nothing scheduled that I have to see tonight for interviews tomorrow. But I'm sure I won't be finished before ten." I looked at Claudel and felt my eyes burn again.

He laughed softly. "Then we will have dinner late tonight. I cannot write your article, or go with you to the interviews. But I can come to the movies, if you like."

"You can?" I said. "But you don't have credentials—how can you get tickets? There are huge crowds of people standing around outside trying to buy—"

"*T'en fais pas*," he said with a smile. *Don't worry.* "It will take some time, but—you know what they call *l'art de l'ombre*?"

"Shadow art?" I said in English.

"Exactly. Shadow artists are those who write about other people's art—like you—or make money from it—like me. We can't pretend to be the real artists, can we? We survive only in their shadow. But they need us. We are their most reliable connection to the public."

"It's a depressing thought," I said.

"Not so depressing, because it gives us the possibility of obtaining tickets to movies when the public cannot. You see?"

He put his napkin on the table, next to his empty wineglass.

"So let us postpone our meal. I can drive you to your luncheon, wherever it is."

"It's just off the Croisette, on the beach across from the Carlton. But you have a car?"

"The gallery keeps a car. They came to meet me in Nice when the train arrived. No flights available, of course."

"When did you leave?" I asked.

"Late last night," he said. "I thought I could be here before you left for the Palais, but I arrived too late."

I was astounded. He must have left the moment he got my message.

"My car is parked at the gallery, which is just around the corner."

I patted my nose one more time with his handkerchief and offered him the unsightly ball of fabric.

"I don't suppose you want this back," I said.

He laughed and shook his head. "I am famous for my generosity."

We left the Café Promenade and walked briskly to Claudel's car, which was parked directly in front of the Galérie d'Affiches du Cinéma. On the sidewalk in front of the gallery, there were posters everywhere: posters lying flat on two long tables, posters rolled into tubes, and posters standing at attention in boxes. The doors to the gallery were wide open, and Claudel waved to a young woman inside.

"*Je reviens!*" he said.

We lurched into traffic, in front of a small delivery truck, and he turned immediately onto the Croisette and drove for a few blocks before he stopped for a red light.

"Do you know Jacques Vidanne?" I said.

His eyes opened wide. "Naturally I know him. He is an important French producer of many films."

"I know that, but do you know him personally?"

Even moving slowly through traffic, we were in front of the Carlton in a few minutes, and he pulled to the curb. He gazed through the windshield toward the beach. An enormous inflated balloon of a naked woman was floating upright in the water fifty or sixty yards from shore, bulbous vinyl arms on top of her head and black vinyl hair resting on cream-colored vinyl shoulders. She was so incongruous to the tropical elegance of the beachfront, not to mention my conversation with Claudel, that I couldn't pull my eyes from her.

"My mother knew him, didn't she?"

There—I had mentioned my mother.

"Why do you ask me this question?"

"Because I met him myself. On Thursday night."

His jaw was set hard. "So he has come to present a movie."

"A movie called *Le Vol*," I said. "A new version of *The Little Prince*."

He let out a derisive sound. "Your mother was an actress in a movie he directed," he said. "An important movie of his career."

"*Zeitgeist*," I said.

"You've seen it?" He sounded surprised.

"No," I said. "I've never been able to find it. And I didn't know she was part of the cast until yesterday."

"That is understandable. No one, not even in France, has seen it since its first release."

"Why not?"

"Vidanne imagined himself an iconoclast, you see? *Zeitgeist* was a small, avant-garde film—in America you call them 'independent' movies, I think—which had great meaning to young people. But it enraged the general public. For a small period of time in Paris, *Zeitgeist* was a popular topic for heated debate—our favorite pastime." He grinned. "So Vidanne pulled the film from theaters, and to this day he has refused to release it to video. Only a handful of copies—"

Suddenly there was a loud knock on the top of the car. We nearly jumped out of our seats.

"*Allez-y!*" a voice shouted. "This is not a parking place!" He was dressed in a gendarme's uniform all the way to his waist, but his navy-blue shorts gave him the appearance of an oversized schoolboy.

Claudel rolled down his window and shouted back, "Yes, yes! All my excuses! We are discussing the essence of life!"

"*Ah, bon,*" the policeman said, as if this were a worthy excuse for breaking the law. "But the demonstration is arriving. You must move out of traffic or we'll have World War Three!"

Claudel and I looked over our shoulders through the rear window. We could see a swarm of people marching arm in arm up the Croisette.

"Demonstrations," Claudel said to me. "Our second favorite pastime." He turned to the policeman. "Two minutes."

The policeman hiked up his short pants and nodded again in agreement, then returned to his beat, waving cars around us on the Croisette. Claudel turned to me, his face serious.

"Today Vidanne is a powerful man in the French movie industry. But twenty-five years ago, he was nobody. He made this one movie, and your mother was its star. Not the starring role, but she had something . . ." His mind wandered off, and I watched him watching her in his memory.

"Were you together when she made the movie?" I asked, and for some reason it felt as if I were inquiring about some intimate item of his clothing.

"Yes. We had been together for nearly two years. You were there, too, Natalie, but perhaps too young to remember. After the movie, he wanted her to continue working with him."

"Wasn't that what she wanted?"

Claudel's eyes narrowed as he stared out the front window. "The reality was not what she thought it would be. She loved the fuss they made over her afterward, but the tedium of day-to-day filmmaking was not . . . amusing. And she had money. She had no need to work. She was toying with the idea of accepting his offer when . . ." He didn't need to finish. I knew he was talking about the mountain.

He looked through the window at the policeman, who was frantically defending our right to stop in the middle of the Croisette. "You know what he named his production studio?" Claudel asked.

"Éclair," I said.

He nodded. "That should tell you something. He was obsessed with her."

I felt a chill run up my back.

"I'm surprised you don't remember him, Natalie. In the months before the accident he was a prominent figure in our lives. Wherever we went, he was there, always in his white suit. He was the reason we went all the way to Briançon to celebrate her birthday, so we could be alone. But even there, he found us. It made *la chair de poule.*"

"The flesh of a hen?"

"When something makes the hair on your skin stand up."

The policeman stepped off the curb and pounded on the top of the car again. In the side mirror I could see the demonstrators advancing, but I couldn't tell whether they were closer or farther away than they appeared.

"*C'est tout!*" he shouted. He moved the tips of his fingers back and forth at his throat. Claudel lifted his sun visor and waved at the policeman.

"*Bon.* Tonight. I will meet you at ten in front of the Café Promenade." In one movement he reached across my lap to open the door and gave me a *bise* on each cheek. "I'm sorry this is so hurried, Natalie. Is Wim Wenders so important?"

For a moment I was tempted to forget Wim Wenders and his movie. But I had nothing else to write about today, and Draper would end our deal in a heartbeat if I didn't file. I had to do the luncheon.

"I'm afraid so." I stepped out of the car and closed the door. The policeman waved his stick at me as Claudel pulled slowly into traffic.

I watched his car disappear into the automotive flow of the Croisette and had to force myself to move from the spot where he'd left me. A cool breeze from the sea drifted my way, and between the palm trees in the distance I saw the naked-woman balloon bouncing on the waves. What a crazy place, I thought. Easy to get crazy right along with it.

A small sign with *FACE OF PEACE* in block letters rested on an easel by the stairway to the restaurant. It was a casual beachfront establishment, the kind where cheap seafood was probably served to tourists who came to relax and sit in the sun during the other eleven and a half months of the year. With the festival's arrival, the place had turned posh: white canvas tents had been raised from the back door of the restaurant along the beach, and five round tables had been set up in the sand.

Waiters were serving crêpes smothered in mushroom sauce as I took an empty chair at Orlando Bloom's table, where a German, two Frenchwomen, and someone from *Newsweek* magazine were already seated. Bloom's hair was short and black, and he was dressed in an unironed red-and-white-checked oxford shirt that made him look like a pizza delivery boy.

The woman next to me asked Bloom a serious question about the film industry's preoccupation with violence, which he answered seriously. But I knew Draper would be more interested in the tattoo on the inside of his right forearm.

"Is that the tattoo you got with the cast of *Lord of the Rings* in New Zealand?" I said.

Bloom nodded and rolled up his shirtsleeve to show us the flowery symbol. "It means 'nine' in Elvish." The German leaned over my plate to get a good look.

"Is that your only tattoo?" I asked, as if I didn't know that he had another one, just below his navel.

He grinned at me. "I do have another. It's a lovely tribal sun design, but I can't show it to you without undressing."

Everyone laughed and thanked him, and he moved to the next table. Wim Wenders took his seat and when he was asked about violence in the movies, he gave an answer I could see Draper turning into a headline: *Paranoia, America's Number One Export.*

I took more notes, ate my salad, and thought about how much time I'd wasted being afraid of calling Claudel.

Wenders was replaced by Andie MacDowell, who was having a bad hair day. She was tired and whiny and wanted to be elsewhere, and I scribbled *Tired and whiny. I wish she were elsewhere* in my notebook and ate a spoonful of brandied cream. I wanted to be elsewhere, too. Claudel had found me at last, and here I was, listening to movie stars complain about working on the Riviera.

Andie MacDowell responded with a curt no to a German question about her modeling career, and a grumpy yes to a question about violence in America, and I calculated that I had one more movie to see, one more column to write, and then dinner with Claudel.

When the luncheon was over and I was headed back to the Palais, the demonstration had dwindled to a low hum in the distance. Along the Croisette I passed a merry band of policemen gathered around the hood of a police car, pouring wine into glass goblets and eating cheese and baguettes. I was definitely not in Los Angeles.

I made it into the line at the Salle Debussy just as the Blue Cards were being admitted for *The Blackout.* I squeezed ahead of them and endured their sneers, for such is the burden of the elite.

As the lights dimmed a woman sidled into the seat next to me and sat down.

"This is the director who made *Bad Lieutenant*?" she whispered in French. Abel Ferrara's name appeared on the screen.

"Yes," I said.

"Very popular in France," she said. "Sadistic Americans."

The Blackout was dirty neon America at its absolute worst: an amoral actor, drugs, alcohol, seedy sex, you name it. There were boos from the audience before the lights came up, and I was relieved when it was over. Even more relieved that Claudel hadn't made it to the screening.

At the press conference, reporters made the stunning realization that the movie's female star, Claudia Schiffer, was smart. The supermodel spoke fluent French, German, and English, and everything she said in the languages I understood was impressive. Her high-powered American male costars were rubes by comparison.

A gutsy little Frenchman with wire-rimmed glasses asked the director what had possessed him to make a revolting movie like *The Blackout,* and he leaned into the mike and said venomously, "Every year Cannes has to have some afternoon freak show, and this year it's my film." Then he stood up and walked straight out the door. The panel moderator tried to get control of his audience after that, but the press conference was over.

We trailed out of the conference room, and I was thinking about Claudel's concept of *l'art de l'ombre* when I saw Steve from VH1 waving at me.

"Please tell me you saw *East Palace, West Palace,*" he said urgently. "The Zhang Yuan movie?"

"I didn't," I said, what-did-I-miss anxiety slinking up on me from behind. "Why?"

"Oh, well, nothing, it's just today's biggest story. A gigantic movie about gay lovers. The audience went crazy for it, but Zhang can't get here because the Chinese authorities took away his passport." He slapped his forehead. "And I didn't see it because I was at this pile of poo."

I laughed. "Me too, but it's still a story."

I went straight to the pressroom and took the last computer. It was seven p.m. Draper had actually written to thank me for my review of *Face of Peace,* which made me feel like celebrating until I remembered that with Draper you were only as good as your last complete sentence. I had to send him something else in a hurry, but for almost an hour I stared at the monitor, unable to concentrate on anything but Claudel.

It felt so strange to be thinking about him in a concrete way—a wonderful lightness in my whole body that almost felt like happiness. He was everything my seven-year-old mind had dreamed about—funny and kind and attentive. It seemed insane to me that I'd waited so long to contact him.

Enough of that. I had a mortgage to pay: what was I going to write about?

If Draper didn't want pedantry in my stories, I'd give him a historical sidebar and let him tack it on at the bottom like an intellectual Band-Aid. I wrote a paragraph about a starlet named Simone Sylva, who gave the Cannes Film Festival its racy reputation in 1954 when she took off her bikini top and threw her arms around Robert Mitchum.

I was coming to the part where photos of Sylva's breasts on the front page of newpapers around the world made Cannes the festival everyone wanted to cover, when a frantic journalist burst into the pressroom, practically foaming at the mouth about being trapped in the Paris airport for twenty hours with a million other festival revelers.

"Jeez-us H!" he said with a thick Australian accent. He slammed his notes and his mound of mail on one of the tables. "It was like the migration of those monarch butterflies to Mexico or something! Every single actor and director ever spawned in Southern California was trying to get here for that bloody celebration tomorrow, and do you think a peon like me could get a plane?"

"How did you get here, then?" someone said, echoing my thought.

"Jeez-us H!" he said, ignoring the question. "What a nightmare! Francis Ford Coppola, the Coens, Roman Polanski, coming from God knows where, they were all berserk—what's-her-name Spice

Girl was there, for chrissake, screaming about being late because she had to meet Prince Charles in Manchester! And then I was just about to get a plane and they canceled it, because of some bloody helicopter snafu at the airport in Nice!"

I thought of the landing pad that Gaspar had pointed out to me in the harbor. I wondered how many VIPs were important enough, or rich enough, to be helicoptered into Cannes.

"By the time I got on a plane, I wanted to slit my wrists!"

At this point, as far as everyone in the room was concerned, it would have been a relief if he had.

"And now I'm starving," he said. "This is torture!"

The guy next to me looked up from his computer and said, in American English, "Shut up, man! We're working!" The intruder stomped off. We could hear his shoes echoing as he stomped down the stairs.

There was a momentary silence in the pressroom, and then without looking up from her computer, a young Spanish woman said in a lilting voice, "Dees weel be a bad week for heem." Everyone laughed.

I, for one, was grateful to him. He'd given me my lead: "Even celebrities get the blues. . . ." There was Andie MacDowell, who couldn't wait to get out of town and sleep, and all those unhappy campers at the Paris airport. The *Blackout* director's silly tantrum and China's seizing of director Zhang's passport. I ended the story with the naked vinyl woman I'd seen bobbing on the surf. What a town.

When I finished it was only nine-fifteen, so I gathered my notes together from all of the day's interviews and molded them into something catchy about the challenge for directors to make movies of substance. If I'd been writing it myself, it would have read like a soapbox diatribe about hypocritical moviegoers who buy tickets to see violent trash and then complain about how violent and trashy popular movies are. But Wenders had said it better than I could, and in forty minutes I had an extra story that would make even Draper happy.

There was a new mound of mail waiting for me at my mailbox, and I stuffed it into my already bulging bag. On top of the pile was another blue note with two words and a number written in black ink: *Call Naomi.* It was almost ten.

The phone at Naomi's hotel rang three times, then four, and I was expecting a French answering machine to ask me to leave a message when a man's voice said, "Hello?" in English.

"Hello? May I speak with— Oh, they must have given me the wrong room, I'm sorry."

"Well, if it isn't Nat Conway," the man's voice said.

"Who is this?"

"For a movie journalist you have a rotten auditory memory."

"Leland?" I said, incredulous. "Where are you?"

"Stretched out on my little friend's sumptuous king-sized bed. Are you stalking me, or do you want to talk to her?"

The image of the scene in Naomi's room played itself out, fast rewind, in my mind.

"You have *got* to be kidding," I said.

"Ah-ah-ah," he said, with a little nasal laugh that made me want to stick my fingers in his nose. "Don't say anything you'll have to apologize for later."

I took a deep breath. I wasn't sure what I wanted more: to hang up on Leland or talk to Naomi.

"Please," I said politely, "you colossal skunk, may I speak with Naomi?"

"Certainly, doll. And by the way, you're going to love the pictures!"

I held the phone at my ear with one hand and made a fist with the other. I stared down at the white speckled tile under my feet, trying to remind myself that I hadn't thought of Leland Dunne in a full year, and when this week was over I would never have to think of him again.

"Hey, Nattie?" Naomi's voice was clear and upbeat, and I could imagine why.

"Hey back. I got your message. You okay?"

"Oh, yeah," she said, in that dreamy way a person eating ice cream says "yum." "I just called because I wanted you to know I gave Leland back his tuxedo coat." She giggled—a high, tinkling, puppy-whine giggle.

"Oh, goodie," I said. "Anything else?" I wanted this call to end as quickly as possible.

"Hmmm. Oh. Yeah, about Mashure V'don?" she said. "He left me a fabulous good-bye gift here at the hotel. A gold bracelet . . . anyway I think it's gold. Is it gold?" she asked Leland.

"Yes, my little chickadee," Leland answered in the background, "it is definitely gold."

She giggled her puppy whine again. "So, Jock left me a note that he was finishing up some business and then he and Madame were returning home."

"Today?"

"I dunno, I guess. The bellman brought up this box, like, at five or something."

Leland grunted agreement.

"That was all? Are they coming back?"

"Goll, I dunno. He has his movie next week and everything. Prob'ly he'll be back. You want me to let you know if he calls me? He's paying for this room till the end of the festival, he said." She yelped with delight, and I imagined her bathing with Leland in champagne and chocolates.

"Okay. Good. Well, thanks, Naomi. Take care of yourself."

She giggled and hung up.

As I slung my heavy bag over my shoulder and headed to the

Café Promenade, I reminded myself that I was not Naomi Paul's babysitter. It wasn't my place either to warn her about Leland's reputation or to tell her that remaining at the Hôtel du Cap at Vidanne's expense put her in a compromising position.

And then, as if the realization had fallen on my shoulder like a bird dropping, I saw with annoying clarity that whatever dubious designs Leland or Vidanne had on Naomi Paul, she sounded a whole lot happier than I had felt—maybe ever.

I have crossed oceans to find you.

Bela Lugosi, in *Dracula*

8

Cannes, France

Saturday, May 10

*I*t was after ten when I ran past the Café Cinématique. The plaza was already bustling with people, but I saw Claudel standing in front of the Café Promenade, and I stopped in the middle of the crowd to watch him. He was leaning against a lamppost, arms crossed, talking to a tall, dark-haired woman in a skintight black jersey dress. He was wearing the same blue shirt he'd been wearing in the afternoon, and even from a distance he seemed self-assured and dignified. He said something that caused the woman in black to laugh unprettily, her head flopping back in her excessive good humor.

I took a brush from my *Inu to Nekko* bag and ran it through my hair, hoping I didn't look as disheveled as I felt. My black skirt was polyester-tidy, and the lavender blouse I'd put on in the morning . . . well, a couple of wrinkles never hurt anybody.

Claudel's face brightened when he saw me. He straightened up from the lamppost and put out his hand for me to grasp, gave me two *bises,* and then introduced me to the woman in black—a film distributor from Paris whose name I immediately forgot.

"Natalie Conway," he said, watching me closely as I shook her hand, "my very old friend from the United States."

The woman eyed me skeptically—I certainly didn't look like his very old friend. She and Claudel exchanged three *bises* on their cheeks, and she sauntered off in the direction of the Palais. Three *bises,* I thought, remembering the French Rule of Bise from somewhere in my child's memory: The fewer the *bises,* the more intimate the relationship.

The maître d' took us again to a table at the back of the restaurant, where we sat exactly as Claudel had described us: two old friends. If it felt as surreal to him as it felt to me, he didn't let on.

Our lunchtime waiter was still hard at work, and he brought a basket of sliced baguettes and welcomed us warmly. I let Claudel order for me, and he asked for wine and sparkling water.

"And are you content with your article?" he asked.

I started to answer, but then I changed my mind. This was pure small talk—anything Michel Claudel and I talked about would seem insignificant until we'd answered each other's questions.

"Can we go back to where we were when you drove away?" I said.

"Of course," he said. "We have your entire lifetime to cover. It hardly matters to me where we start."

"So I take it you're not friends with Vidanne?"

He laughed bitterly. "Friends? My association with Jacques Vidanne ended twenty-five years ago. And in spite of the devastating circumstances, I confess I felt relieved that his presence had been lifted from my life. No, *chérie.* We are not friends."

"When did you last speak to him?"

"On the last day I spoke to you." A heavy silence fell on us. After a moment, he said, "Do you remember?"

I nodded.

"Tell me," he said, leaning toward me with his forearms on the table, "what you remember."

My mouth went dry, and I wished the waiter would return with our wine.

"I remember . . ." I began, clearing my throat. "I remember in still pictures. I was wearing a pink dress. I remember you let me lock the door to the apartment. And standing on the stairway, holding your hand. Riding in a black car to the Gare de Lyon. The box." I took a breath. "I remember holding your hand in the car, and the trees. The sound of the gravel under the tires. The hole in the ground, the wet smell of that big hole. And holding your hand while I grabbed some dirt and threw it on the box." I had never spoken any of this out loud, and even though I'd had it in my head forever, it sounded oddly unemotional as it came out of my mouth. "But none of it looked familiar when I was at the cemetery on Wednesday."

Claudel nodded.

"I remember you gave me a box of chocolates and put them in my backpack. Is that right? And the stewardess came"—I raised my eyebrows—"and you let go of my hand." I looked at his hands now, folded on the table between us, and my eyes started to sting again.

"Oh yes," I added with a smile. "And you told me not to cry."

We sat like statues, me staring at his hands and fighting back tears and Claudel's eyes fixed on my face, until the waiter finally arrived with a bottle of wine. In spite of our mood, the opening-cork-sniffing-tasting-and-pouring-wine ritual was completed. Claudel told the waiter something about the bouquet while I took a healthy gulp from my glass. This time I didn't cough.

"And you?" I asked.

"I should remember all of it. But my head was jumbled after the accident. It took several weeks to make sense of what had happened. I returned with you to Paris because there was nothing we could do. The nurses, the doctors. It was evident to everyone we were only waiting for the inevitable. So I took you with me back to Paris."

"Was Vidanne in Briançon?" I asked.

Claudel nodded. "He came the day after, when he read our story in *Le Figaro*."

"And he stayed in Briançon, didn't he?"

Claudel looked up from his wineglass without answering. "Where did you encounter him?"

I told him what had happened, from the moment we stepped onto the yacht until I'd been rushed off of it. He swirled his wine absently. "I wasn't sure what had happened. Suddenly I was in the water-taxi headed for shore. The whole thing lasted about two minutes. I might have thought he was just rude, but as I was climbing down the ladder he said I still spoke impeccable French. I couldn't figure how he knew I ever spoke French. And then I found her name in the cast list for *Zeitgeist*."

"He must have recognized you the moment he saw you."

"Do I look so much like her?"

Claudel gave me a sad smile and nodded. "You have *les sourcils circonflexes*," he said.

I almost choked on my wine. *Sourcils circonflexes* was a phrase I'd heard only from Claudel—his little tongue twister about our pointy eyebrows, because they looked like the French circumflex accent, a half-diamond arch above the vowels in words like "hôpital" and "hôtel" that means an *s* was removed from the word centuries ago.

The waiter laid our fillet knives next to our plates and refilled our glasses. From the flat expression on Claudel's face, I had no idea what he was thinking.

I waited for him to say something, but he just stared at me with a kind of fearful fascination. Then he sat forward and shifted his attention to his plate. Without a word, he lifted his napkin from under his forks and took in a great breath, never moving his gaze from his plate.

Like mine, it was a beautiful collage of foodstuffs: a whole trout accompanied by its own personal sachet of lemon, with three small carrots sliced and flayed like fans on one side, and four long slender green beans tied in a bundle with string-thin slices of onion. Shavings of truffles covered the entire plate.

"Claudel?" I said. "Please tell me what you're thinking."

Instead of answering, he shook out his napkin and picked up his knife and fork. "You must give me a moment to digest. We will continue after," he said. *"Bon appétit."*

"Wait—"

"Please." He glanced at my plate. "Do you need help with the bones?"

I was stunned. After the way everything had unraveled since I stood on the deck of Vidanne's boat, how could he expect me to shut down, just to enhance the pleasure of some fish? The French! I thought, with clenched teeth. No wonder wine is so important to French meals. A country of diners unwilling to talk about important matters over food needs all the alcohol it can get.

The waiter deboned the trout for me, and I moved pieces of it from one side of the plate to the other with my fork and drank two glasses of wine. Since my usual alcohol limit is just under a full glass, I was in orbit by the time Claudel's plate was empty.

"Now?" I asked. "Could we finish our conversation now?"

The waiter appeared with a tray of saucers and two small cups of thick espresso, a bowl of sugar cubes, and a third plate with our check on it. Claudel paid again with cash, and the waiter took the plate and disappeared.

Claudel dropped a cube of sugar into his espresso and stirred. I put a cube of sugar in my cup and stirred right back, waiting.

Claudel drank his espresso down in one gulp. I took a tiny sip and my whole body shuddered. There weren't enough sugar cubes in the whole of Cannes to make this drinkable for me.

Claudel smiled woodenly. "*Pardon.* I forgot Americans do not like European espresso." He reached over and took the edge of my saucer between his fingers and began to draw it across the table to him. For some reason, this made me furious. I grabbed the opposite edge of the saucer between my fingers and held it.

"I thought you did not want it."

"I don't!" I said. "I don't want the espresso. But please, answer my question! Do you have any thoughts about everything I just told you?"

He pressed his thumb and forefinger into his eyes and then pulled the espresso toward him, gazing into the little cup so intensely he seemed to be studying the swirl.

I watched, unable to believe he was going to drink a second cup. I wanted to scream. I was afraid I was going to spoil everything if I didn't get out of the restaurant. I scooted my chair back and, as calmly as I could manage, stood up.

"I'm going outside, Claudel. I can't stand this."

I was sure he'd stop me, sure he'd take my hand and ask me to sit down. But he only nodded and brought the little cup to his lips.

When I was outside, I clasped my hands behind my neck in exasperation. What was the matter with me? Why couldn't I get an answer from anyone about anything?

I paced in front of the restaurant for several minutes before I crossed the Croisette and started walking toward the beach, thinking what an idiot I'd been to believe that finding Claudel would make a change in my life. What had made me think he would be any different from my silent, unresponsive father? Or the fickle Leland Dunne? Or Vidanne, for that matter? At least my father had been right about one thing: coming back to France had been a huge mistake.

I stood on the beach looking off into the harbor and thought about the years I'd wasted resenting my father, wishing he were Claudel. But he had been the one who took care of me when Claudel had shipped me off to America. What in God's name had made me think that any amount of money was worth the frustration of coming back to France?

I began to plot my escape. Tomorrow was Sunday. There were no movies I absolutely had to see for interviews, and the festival party was not open to journalists in any case. I could learn everything I needed to send to Draper from press releases and conversations with other journalists. Sunday wasn't officially slated as a day of rest, but I'd stay in my pitiful Chalet d'Isere bed all day long and not come out until Monday morning. Then I'd decide if staying was worth the money.

I was wondering if I could convince Madame Vigny to bring me food when I felt Claudel beside me.

"I'm sorry," he said.

I stiffened. "The least you could have done was to answer me. Tasting your wine and shaking out your napkin and deboning your fish?" I turned to look at him. "You deboned your fish!"

"I'm sorry. I could not answer you."

"Why?" I said.

He grasped the back of his neck, as if he were massaging a sore muscle. "Everything came into my head at once. I did not know what to say to you."

"Is that what you do when you don't know what to say? You don't say anything?"

"Well, yes," he said with a little smile. He looked at his feet and shook his head, visibly trying to control his frustration. "You must listen to me for one second." We were only inches from the smooth wet tide-wash that separated the soft sand from the water, and he sat where he was standing, taking my hand and pulling me gently next to him on the sand.

"I must ask for your patience," he said. "There is a pressure that builds in my head when I am ... shaken. Here." He laid his hand on his forehead. "I am told it happens occasionally to victims of trauma to the brain. You will understand better than anyone that for me its cause is obvious."

My breath caught.

"It subsides, but I must remove myself from the source, focus on a task. Otherwise it evolves into pain and I have a completely new battle to fight."

"I'm so sorry," I said.

"When you told me this afternoon about meeting Vidanne, I was suddenly furious, like an explosion." He blew a puff of air through his lips and shook his head. "After this enormous space of time, he can still enrage me."

"You could have told me. I would have been more patient."

He laughed softly. "Never mind now. If I have some time I always manage. I am perfectly fine again." He reached over and took my hand. "I will tell you what is moving through my mind: Vidanne knew. Even if he did not recognize the similarities in your face, without a doubt when you told him your name, he knew. Of course he would have been surprised—astonished, even—that you should appear on his boat like that. He would have embraced you! He would have welcomed you, her daughter. At the least he would have shown curiosity, would he not? He would have asked, were you the same Natalie Conway he had known as a child? He would have asked, what was your mother's name? There are a thousand questions he would have asked. He should have asked!"

"So why didn't he?"

"I cannot imagine. His impulse to make you disappear is so strange it is nearly an incrimination. A guilty man reveals himself before suspicions have begun to flower. Balzac said that." He rested his forehead in the cradle of his clasped hands, his thumbs fast at his temples. "I would have been happy never to think of him again, I must tell you."

We sat on the sand, silently, for a long time. Off in the distance a horn bellowed. A breeze floated down the beach and kicked up a cloud of leaves that drifted in front of us. I was suddenly so tired I wanted to lie back on the sand and fall asleep.

"Let me take you back to your hotel, *chérie*. It is late."

As we wound our way up the hill to the Chalet d'Isere in the silver Citroën, I listened to the cobbled stone beneath the tires and watched the street-shadows fall on us and then disappear. We stopped at a traffic light, and the red glow was so warm on Claudel's face, I dared to ask him the question that had been bothering me all day.

"You said today that you were happy to hear from me."

He turned to me with a smile. "Much more than happy."

"Well, if you wanted to find me so much, why didn't you call me yourself?"

"I did."

I sat up straight in my seat. "When?"

"On your twenty-first birthday I spoke to your father in Crown-point. I assume he did not tell you."

"No!" I said. "He didn't—"

"Of course," he interrupted. "He would never have told you. This time I only wanted to find your phone number, wherever you were." I could tell by the tightness of his voice that this was a subject that made him angry.

"What do you mean, 'this time'? Had you called before?"

He caught my gaze and held it. "Many times," he said.

I felt cold. "Claudel," I said evenly, "you can't imagine how important it is for you to answer this question. Please tell me, how many times have you spoken to my father?"

He sighed. "*Pendant les années—quelques douzaines.*" *Over the years, several dozen.*

I was astounded. How could Claudel have called me and I never knew? Had I never picked up the phone myself?

"In the first few months, I called every few days," he said, and the memory of it seemed to embarrass him. "I only wanted to be sure that you were well. I had seen for myself the burns on your head and abdomen. And the effects of lightning can be lingering and unpredictable. He assured me that you were in perfect health. But you realize that it began to infuriate him. Even I could see why he would find my attention irritating."

"Did you . . ." I began, but my voice sounded so small I cleared my throat. "Did you ask to speak to me?"

"Every time, and always he responded with a new piece of logic. That it would be confusing for you if you spoke to me. That you were *his* child. That the past was the past. That you deserved a chance at a new life. That if I cared about you at all, I would not call again. And after some time, I began to see that perhaps he was right."

I had no memory of overhearing these calls to my father, but I remembered how timid I'd been about answering his phone. All the years I'd spent wishing that Claudel would come for me, feeling abandoned by him, how could I not have suspected that my father, who wouldn't allow even a mention of my mother, would refuse to let him back into my life?

A memory came to me, of driving at night with my father in New Mexico. I was nine or ten, and the casual intimacy of moving along a moonlit road in a car had made me feel an unaccustomed closeness to him. We'd driven to Albuquerque on a snowy February afternoon to see a movie called *Real Genius,* and he'd suffered through it and finally even enjoyed it. On the long drive back to Crownpoint, we hit a patch of ice on the road. The car swerved for a minute, and when he'd regained control, my father quoted a line from the movie.

"You see, Buff," he said. "This is what happens to water when it gets too cold."

It was as whimsical as anything I'd ever heard him say, and we'd actually laughed out loud together, which I never remembered having happened before. For a moment a door between us opened. We laughed about some other funny lines from the movie, and then for some unknown reason, with that door open, I asked a terrible question.

"What was my mother like?"

And the door slammed shut as quickly as it had opened. He said something I'd heard a hundred times—"You live here now"—and we drove the rest of the way in silence.

Now, driving through the streets of Cannes, I felt myself tense with the memory of many such severed connections, but I heard myself asking the same question.

"Claudel," I said. "Talk to me about my mother."

He didn't flinch. "How? The way she looked?"

"Anything," I said. "I don't know anything about her."

"Not from your father?"

"Never."

He shook his head in bewilderment. "And you never saw *Zeitgeist,* so you have no idea how she moved or spoke."

"Was she graceful?" I asked suddenly. "Did she move like an angel? Was her voice like music?"

"What are you asking me?"

"Just please don't give me all the banalities people tell daughters and sons about their dead mothers."

He frowned. "I see. You are trying to be ironic. It does not work in French, for your information. It comes out biting."

"I'm sorry," I said. "It comes out biting in English, too."

"And I am sorry to disappoint you, but she was rather graceful. She had been a swimmer when she was very young. She liked to ride horses and climb mountains. She moved too fast, and she was always breaking things. Glasses and chairs and fingernails. But she did not care about 'things,' and that alone carried an element of grace."

He stopped at a street sign and shifted slowly into neutral. For a long moment he stared through the window, as if memory had caused a temporary blip in the present, and then he pushed into first.

"I thought it was charming that she always spoke to you as if you were an adult."

"How do you mean?"

"She asked your opinion about everything—about food, about art, about whether a lamp should go here or there."

"Was she serious?"

"Absolutely. And you always had an opinion. She required you to have an opinion. Sometimes you looked at me as if you thought she was a lunatic, and most of the time you did not really know what she was talking about, but you always had an opinion." He smiled at some private thought. "When Mitterand was challenged for the presidency of France, she asked you whether you thought I should vote for him or for Chirac, and you said, in your tiny voice, 'If Chirac is elected president, the nation will crumble!' "

We both laughed at my adorableness.

"Had she coached me to say that?"

"No," he said with a grin. "Possibly someone else."

"You?"

"A mystery." He smiled.

And then we both laughed at Claudel's adorableness. For a few blocks we drove in silent, post-laughter contentment. My head was filled with visions of a small, innocent, precocious Natalie and her graceful tomboy of a mother.

"But," he said suddenly, "before you begin to shuffle through thoughts of how perfect your life might have been if she had lived, you must remember something important about your mother. She left your father without an explanation. You know that, *n'est-ce pas?* Without even an apology. She met him when she was driving through the American Southwest in her shiny red car. She had stepped on a nail or something. Maybe she cut her toe, I can't remember, but she was tired of driving alone. So she went to his hospital for a tetanus shot and accepted his invitation to ride his horses. She must have hit him like *un coup de foudre,*" he said, a thunderbolt. "She appeared; a few days later she married him, and after a month, she left him. He had begun to bore her, that is what she told me, so she simply left. What kind of person does that?"

I thought about it for a moment. Only a selfish person, was the obvious, disappointing answer—an immature person. But honestly, I had to admit, my father wasn't the most exciting man in the world.

"And even if he was a bore," Claudel said as if he'd heard my thoughts, "she never took responsibility for hurting him. She merely sent him the divorce papers, end of story. I've thought about it many times in my life since then. And I believe—you may think I am old-fashioned, but I believe a decent person accepts responsibility for causing pain to others."

I was struck dumb by what Claudel had just said. This view of my mother had never entered my mind. How could it, without memories, without information? It was a strange thing: she was never out of my mind, but by myself I had been unable to piece together even a semblance of her character. Only Claudel could give me a glimpse of the whole picture.

I watched the dashboard lights reflected on his face, and I felt something I'd never felt before in all my life: a connection. This was someone with whom I had something in common. Not DNA, not blood, not legal judgments. But Claudel seemed to be at the end of every line my life had left dangling. And so far he seemed willing to take hold of each of them to gather me up.

———————

A few minutes later we pulled up in front of the Chalet d'Isere. Claudel stopped abruptly at the curb and said, "Is your schedule for tomorrow demanding?"

I decided not to share the fact that I'd planned to stay in bed all day. "Why?"

"I want to take a drive."

"Now? Tonight?"

"Now. There is a place I want to go. I'd like for you to come, too. But only if you wish."

He shut off the engine. "I will wait for you to put some clothes in a valise."

It was almost midnight. I couldn't understand what he was asking me to do.

"There is so much for us to talk about, Natalie. Too much for lunches and dinners."

I stared at him, hating myself for my indecision. Was I afraid to go with him? But what was I afraid of? My hand gripped the door handle so hard it was cutting off the circulation.

"Where do you want to go?" I asked.

He put his hand on my shoulder and smiled, but his eyes were not part of the smile.

"If you have work for tomorrow, you must do it. If you do not, you will have at least three free meals and see a little of France."

"But why won't you tell me?"

"Do you trust me, Natalie?" he said. "That is the question. I can understand why you would not, after so many years. But if you can trust me, hurry upstairs and pack a bag. For two nights."

"For two nights? But tonight is almost over."

"You are right," he said, looking at his watch. "Soon it will be only one night. I'll have you back by Monday morning, in time for your first movie."

I was paralyzed.

"But I don't know what to bring."

"Do you have so much to choose from? Don't worry about clothes, *ma petite*. If you have comfortable shoes, bring them. Other than that, I have a warm coat for you."

"I don't know if—"

"*Voyons.* There is something I must do—with you, if possible. If you are unable to go with me, do not be angry with yourself. Go to bed, sleep. I will find you when I return on Monday, I promise you that."

"Ten minutes," I said. I left my bag on the front seat.

Although only 20 percent of lightning victims are immediately struck dead, many doctors do not understand how to treat the injuries of the other 80 percent who survive a strike. The pathology of lightning, or keraunopathy, is known only to a few specialists.

"Lightning Injuries to Humans in France"
by Dr. Elisabeth Gourbière

9

FRANCE

The High Alps of High Provence

Sunday, May 11

*I*t took less than five minutes to put a dress, some sweatpants, a T-shirt, a nightgown, my comfortable shoes, and a toothbrush into one of Madame Vigny's starched pillowcases and climb into Claudel's car in a jumble of conflicting emotions: I was crazy to agree to travel to some nebulous place with a man I hadn't seen for twenty-five years, but it also sounded like an adventure, and I hadn't had many of those in my life.

For a while I sat nervously in the passenger seat next to him. Occasionally he turned to me and smiled, his face bathed in the eerie light of the dashboard, and I smiled back. I stared out the window, trying to make out the contours of houses and trees, but there was no light anywhere, and everything around us was relegated to imagined shapes. A sliver of moonlight appeared as we made our way through the hills north of Cannes. The trees along the road took on a ghostly glow, and a gradual feeling of comfort descended upon us. Claudel began to talk easily about the events of the afternoon in his gallery. The low hum of the car was hypnotic, and the frenetic events of the day vanished. All that remained was Claudel.

We passed through a small cluster of old stone houses that seemed white in the moonlight, and we didn't speak for so long that when I said his name it seemed to startle him.

"I thought you were sleeping," he said.

"I was just thinking about the miracle of seeing you again."

"Ah," he said softly. "A miracle. More like a pleasant accident."

"Not an accident. I called you, remember?"

"Yes, you did," he said. "But would you have called me if your path had not crossed with Vidanne's?"

"I called you in Paris—"

"And you didn't leave your number or where I could find you. What I'm saying is that perhaps you were not ready to find me again. You said yourself you would not have had the courage."

I couldn't argue with that. "But now I don't know what I was afraid of," I said. "It's strange to be able to say your name out loud."

He smiled. "It is perhaps more strange for me than it is for you," he said. "When you say my name, it is no longer with the voice of a child. You have grown into a woman. You have had a life I can only imagine, but I am the same. Am I not as you remember me?"

I was about to say *Hardly*, but he was what I remembered.

"In any case, I still live in Paris. I still sell posters, I am still the same height, with the same hair." He thought for a moment and then smiled. "All right, perhaps not the same hair. . . ."

He gave a little laugh. "No doubt it is always a surprise to find someone again after many years," he said. "They have continued to live their lives and to change, but in your mind, they have remained the same."

"In your thoughts of me, I was still a child?"

"I suppose, yes. And I was still a young man."

"Then we imagined each other the same."

"Yes?" I could see a faint twinkle in his eyes.

"I used to dream about you at night sometimes. I would let go of the stewardess's hand and run back to you."

"*Ah, non,*" he said sadly. "And then what?"

What I wanted to say was *And then we would return to our little apartment.* Instead I said, "And then I grew up."

I looked out the window, and he gave the back of my neck a squeeze.

It was nearly four in the morning when Claudel woke me with a touch on my elbow.

"Where are we?" I asked. The air was crisp and cold, and the sky was filled with stars.

"Just outside of Briançon," he said, guiding me and my pillow-case to a flowery room that smelled like cinnamon. "Sleep like a kitten," he whispered at the door. He gave me a *bise* on each cheek and disappeared down the hall to his own room. It was almost morning.

At nine-thirty he tapped at my door and I leapt out of bed as if I'd been snoozing on the job.

"Hi!" I said in English. My nightgown was inside out, and the tag was in front. "Are we really in Briançon?"

"*Oui, chérie,*" he said.

I shook my head, bewildered.

"*Voyons,* this will make it easier." He handed me a large cup filled with hot beige liquid. "I will wait downstairs while you dress. And wear comfortable shoes—we have a busy day."

As I heard his footsteps disappear down the hall, I wondered what I'd gotten myself into. The floor felt icy under my bare feet, and I noticed for the first time that I was in a huge wood-paneled room with a big bed and three small windows decorated with white lace curtains. The bathroom had a bidet, which took me a couple of fun-filled minutes to master. Then I brushed my teeth, combed my hair, and put on the sweatpants and T-shirt I'd stuffed into the pillowcase along with my tennis shoes. When I emerged from the hotel, my eyes were still bleary.

Claudel was sitting on a bench reading a map. He handed me a croissant and patted the space beside him. The croissant was warm and soft, and it tasted like melted butter. I took another bite and didn't stop until it was gone. I sipped the coffee.

We were sitting in a leafy courtyard under a huge tree at the foot of a mountain. The tree stretched out over a small garden of wildflowers with tiny blossoms that would cover the ground with color in a few weeks. The air was chilly, and I wrapped my hands around my cup to warm them.

"How long have you been awake?" I asked.

"*Pas longtemps.* Twenty minutes."

I gulped down the rest of the coffee.

"Are you ready?"

"For what? You haven't told me what we're doing here."

"Do you remember this place?"

I looked at the front of the inn. It was more like a cottage than a hotel, with a stone path leading to a wooden front door with rusted cast-iron hinges. Across the path from where we sat was a quaint little table surrounded by wooden chairs. It looked like the kind of place where mice with hats might live. I shook my head.

"It is where we were staying. I have not been back since then."

"Why are we here?" Even as the words came out of my mouth,

it started to make sense: Briançon. Comfortable shoes. The mountain. The last drop of sleep lifted from my brain, and I leapt off the bench.

"What are we doing here?"

"*T'en fais pas,*" he said. Don't worry.

"You're going to make me go up there, aren't you?"

"Sit down, Natalie. Sit down."

"No! You should have told me what you were doing."

"Stop for just a minute and listen. Please."

I folded my arms.

"*Mon dieu,* you've turned into such a prickly thing. Sit."

I sat.

"Thank you," he said in exasperation. "Good. Okay. You deserve to hear what I am thinking." He turned toward me. "I am not blind, Natalie. I see the conflict that is going on inside you. You are happy to see me again, but you are also longing to pick a fight."

"I am *not!*"

He cocked his head to the side and waited for me to get it.

"Now, look. None of this is any easier for me than it is for you. But I will try to make you understand why I believe we must do this." He paused. "I do not know what I expected when I got on the train to find you. I thought I wanted you to know that I have felt your absence in my life for all these years, that there are no days that pass without a thought of you. But I see now that such a disclosure cannot possibly have meaning to you."

"Claudel—" I said.

"*Shht!*" he said with his finger in the air. "Listen to me. Let me tell you this, and then you can talk for the rest of the day." He smiled faintly as he rested his elbows on his knees and clasped his hands together, leaning close to me so I couldn't shake my gaze from his. "I loved your mother. She was my first true affair of the heart, and that is something a man never forgets. But you should know that she was not the end of my emotional life. I have loved two women since then. Good women, who were every bit her equal. And I can tell you honestly that there is not much difference between a love affair that ends because love has died and a love affair that ends because the lover has died. There is mourning and loss either way, and both are the kind of sorrow that a human being who dares to fall in love must learn to endure."

I gulped. I wasn't expecting this.

"But losing you was different. It was . . . an unnecessary loss. Your father did not even know you existed, you see? He did not know your mother was pregnant when she left the United States. There was no reason for him to know, and I did not want to tell him. I wanted to keep you with me. I thought . . . I could give you a good life."

I pulled my eyes from his and looked down at my hands.

"Then why did you tell him?" I asked in almost a whisper.

"But I did not! I decided not to tell him." He paused. "Look at me, Natalie. Do you realize what I am saying to you? I had no intention of telling this man that he had fathered a child! I would never have told him and it would have been a terrible deception."

"Who, then?" I said.

"You can guess the answer."

A chill ran through me. "Vidanne."

He nodded.

"Before he brought her body back to Paris, Vidanne called your father and announced that he had a six-year-old daughter."

"But why?" My voice caught in my throat. "What business was it of his?"

He let out a soft, bitter laugh. "You do not understand how Vidanne felt about your mother. She *was* his business. Perhaps he was jealous. Of me and of you. And then of death. But who was I as an adversary? I was young, and you were only a child. All he had to do to hurt us was to pick up the telephone." He looked down at his hands, as if the memory of it made him ashamed.

"Once your father knew of you, there was no chance for me to keep you. He could never unknow such a thing. He had a daughter. It was a simple matter. So I sent you to America to live with him. *Fin d'histoire.*"

We sat there for a long time, and the morning sun crept over the roof of the inn and filled the garden with shadows. I didn't know if it was the sun or the story Claudel had just told me, but I felt warm for the first time since I'd awakened.

"However, it was not the end of the story for me," he said. "And now I see it also was not the end for you."

"It was—" I began, but he closed his eyes and put up a finger to stop me, stifling a smile.

"Just one more minute, I am almost finished. I cannot imagine your loss, or how your life has been, growing up with your father. I hope you will share with me as much as you feel you can. But I have known for many years that if I were ever to see you again, it would be, necessarily, you who found me. From curiosity, if nothing else, but I did not know what your memories of me would be. And so, when you called on Friday night, I was ecstatic. I canceled all my plans and came to you."

He sat up straight and looked at me.

"But the sight of you, Natalie! My God, the sight of you. Not that your face was like hers, not that I saw her in you. I want you to understand this: It was you. You, grown into this fierce, vulnerable young woman." His hands were open in front of him, as if he were offering them to me. He clasped them together, and they fell clumsily in his lap. For a minute he was silent. "After our lunch yesterday, I was hopeful. I thought it was possible that we could be friends. Did you?"

I nodded. He looked at me for a long moment before he spoke.

"But when you told me about meeting Vidanne—all afternoon I was on the phone to business associates, trying to locate him myself. I cannot say if it was for my curiosity or because your encounter with him had fueled a forgotten anger. My concerns are intertwined with the business of films, but in all this time, our paths have never crossed. He is reclusive to the point of *excentricité*. But even an eccentric must account for bad manners."

He reached up briefly and squeezed the bridge of his nose.

"It is clear to me that we cannot ignore him. Perhaps we will even have to face him again. But before we do either one or the other, we have unfinished business, you and I. Balzac said that before we can embrace the living, the ghost must die. And that is why we are here. I want for us to be friends, but without the past to crush us."

I looked up at the mountain and back at him.

"Yes, the mountain. But more than that. You must try to trust me, and not argue every step of the way." There was a twinkle in his eyes, but I knew he was serious.

"Okay," I said. He took my hand and laid it in his open palm, holding it tightly.

"So. Your turn. *Vas-y!*"

Now that I was free to speak, I found I had nothing left to say. "You have stunned me to silence," I said.

A smile spread slowly across his face until it lit up the courtyard.

In May twenty-five years before, when I was six years old, the rugged mountains of France's High Alps of High Provence were the southern tip of a six-hundred-mile chain of massive mountain peaks that ran from Liechtenstein to France, through Slovenia, Germany, Austria, Italy, and all the way to the Mediterranean. The climate was the most dramatic and erratic in all of France, with long periods of drought, endless winter snows, and sudden summer storms that blew the roofs off houses. Twenty-five years later, none of it had changed. Only I had changed, and only on the outside.

It was after ten when we joined the path behind the inn, and

Claudel had bought two bottles of water and some bread and cheese and put them in a backpack. The sun warmed us while we sat in the courtyard, but on the mountain it was still chilly in the shade, and I was grateful that most of the path was open and free of trees. The air smelled faintly sweet—nothing like the dense pinewood fragrance of even the lower hills in the Rocky Mountains. Claudel took off in front of me, and he was a few steps ahead when I stopped suddenly.

"Wait, Claudel," I said. "I need to go back and check something."

He came to me and put his hands on my shoulders. "It is expected to be a clear and cloudless day. With no chance of rain or other storm activity."

He was standing uphill from me, and I had to tilt my head back to look him in the eye. I felt from him the breathtaking thrill of understanding, such an overpowering sensation I wanted to dissolve in it.

I forced a laugh instead. "Then what're we waiting for? We have a mountain to climb. *Tac-tac!*" And I laughed myself up the path.

The trees became denser as we continued to climb, and the forest seemed to move in around us. We'd been hiking hard for a little more than an hour, and we were both out of breath when we came to a sign beside the path.

—LAC HERIOT: 2
—PRÉ DE TRIOUX: 3 (interdit aux excursions
avril–septembre)
—SOMMET: 8 (élévation, 2183 M)

"The Pré de Trioux," I read out loud. "Is that . . . our meadow?"

"Yes," he said, "but why do you suppose it is closed from April to September?"

He pointed uphill, and we launched forward. When we reached the top, Lake Heriot lay before us, glistening in the sunlight. It was surrounded by mountains, as if a tiny canyon had filled with water and made a lake of itself. Claudel led me to the edge of the water, where he knelt and splashed water on his face. I watched as it trickled down his neck, and he closed his eyes and reveled in the sensation of it.

We sat on a rock. A thin green snake poked its head through the grass and slithered into the water.

"Why didn't we stay here to have our picnic? It feels so . . . picnicky."

"It wasn't quiet then," he said. "There was a group of noisy Germans who'd carried an inflatable canoe up the hill. We wanted someplace more isolated." He stared off into the distance. "I didn't know I remembered that."

He took a swig of water and washed it around in his mouth, then spat it out in the grass behind us. "Are there mountains near Crownpoint?"

I shook my head. "Only mesas—flat hills. They felt like mountains, until I found out what real mountains were." I unscrewed the top of my water bottle and screwed it back on. "And no lakes, for sure. It was so dry you had to put lotion on your feet all the time or your heels would crack. And the earth was red, so your socks and hair and under your fingernails, everything got tinted red. You could never wash it out. I couldn't wait to get out of Crownpoint, and when I left for college—"

"Where did you go to college?"

"In New Mexico. It was all we could afford. By then Pop—" I looked at Claudel and said, "My *father* was retired, so I got a scholarship, and he bought me a car."

There was a long silence before Claudel said, "What about your *droits de succession*?"

"My what?" I said.

"Your inheritance. What you received from your mother."

I laughed. "I didn't receive a thing from my mother."

Claudel frowned. "But she had a considerable trust, which they must have passed on to you."

"Who do you mean, 'they'?"

"The lawyers. Your father's lawyers. Your mother's lawyers. I think even Vidanne had lawyers, because their movie was still making money."

"Well, the lawyers must have gotten it all, then."

Claudel seemed to consider this. I picked up a pebble and tossed it into the lake. We watched the ripples lap against our rock.

"I have something for you," he said, taking a folded piece of yellowed newsprint from his shirt pocket. He unfolded it carefully. It was in good condition, but it was very old.

The headline read *Famille en Pique-nique Frappée par L'Éclair*. Picnicking Family Struck by Lightning. Under the headline were two pictures: a murky photo of a group of Boy Scouts—they looked to be in their early teens—and a picture of a small child, sitting up and smiling in a hospital bed. A handsome young man was standing beside her, holding her hand.

"That's you and me," I said under my breath.

"Read it aloud," he said.

I looked again at the picture of Claudel and me and felt the familiar sting of tears in my eyes as I read:

TRIOUX MEADOW—April 12. A family of three was struck by lightning as they laid out their picnic blanket in the grassy Trioux Meadow at 13:30. Michel Claudel, Kit Conway, and her 6-year-old daughter, Natalie, were vacationing from Paris when nature's worst nightmare interrupted their idyll. Thanks to eight intrepid scouts from the Toulon Scouts de France and their master Jean-Marie Breyard, the three unconscious victims were brought to the hospital of the Sisters of Sacred Heart in Briançon, where the mother remains unconscious after two days.

"We came to Briançon to flee from the chaos of Paris," Michel Claudel said from the hospital, where he was treated for minor burns. Asked if there was any warning that a storm was on its way, Claudel said, "There were a few clouds in the sky, but no, it was a beautiful, sunny day. We were taken completely by surprise."

Claudel, 26, is the owner of the Galérie Claudel in Paris. Conway, 26, is an American expatriate. Her daughter, Natalie, was born in Paris.

Doctors say the lightning apparently struck all three of the victims simultaneously, rendering them unconscious and leaving severe burns on mother and daughter. The mishap is the fourteenth in a series of similar accidents in the Trioux Meadow. (See story on page 7.)

"You brought this with you?" I said.

He nodded. "Keep it. I have a copy for myself."

I looked again at the picture of Claudel and me. Except for the gray hair at his temples, he looked exactly as he had then.

"That could be any little girl whose hand you're holding," I said. No matter how hard I stared at it, it wasn't familiar. "Tell me what you remember, after we came down from the meadow."

He shook his head slowly. "I awoke as they were moving me onto the sheets at the hospital, with no recollection of before. It took a full day for my life to return to my head, and even then it came in pieces. And the days were long, waiting to see what the lightning had done to you."

"When did Vidanne arrive?"

"Too soon—a matter of hours after he read the article. We had told no one where we were going, so he had no way of finding us. The nuns set up a room for us near her, and we did not leave the hospital. You were afraid to be outdoors, and we had to do it bit by bit—we called it 'making friends with the world.' Every day we spent a few more minutes in the garden." He opened his bottle of water and took a long, satisfying drink. "Balzac said that memory is history written in water. Perhaps he was right. What I remember clearly is that, in spite of the circumstances, waiting to see what would become of her, we were fine.

"Then Vidanne read the story in the Paris paper, and he was here in an instant, taking over our lives. I was still shaky, you know? I did not have the strength to fight him."

I could tell the memory of it made him sad, and without thinking, I reached out and put my hand on his cheek. The warmth of his skin against mine was stunning, and I took my hand away. He raised his eyebrows in surprise.

"I . . . are you hungry?" I said.

"Let's keep going," he said. "We can eat on the way back."

He helped me off the rock, and we found our way back to the path.

"By the way," I said. "What you were saying about memory and water?" He nodded. "Are you sure it was Balzac who said that? I think it was Victor Hugo or somebody."

His face broke out in a grin. "It might well have been Hugo. When I am unsure, I always guess Balzac. He wrote twice as many books as Shakespeare wrote plays, you know. So usually I am right."

"Nice system," I said, giving him a little jab.

We wound our way around the lake and the path began to climb again. At the top of the first incline, we lost sight of the lake. At the top of the next hill, we came upon another sign. It was as big as a standard movie poster and impossible to miss. The words were inscribed in a mosaic of ceramic tiles, which had been secured to a wooden frame. The message was written first in French and then in English:

ATTENTION HIKERS!
PRÉ DE TRIOUX CLOSURE

The Department of Forest Welfare of the High Alps of High
Provence extends a warning to all travelers! During the
months of April through September, the Trioux Meadow
is closed to all camping and hiking. The meadow and its
surrounding area emerges from an extensive deposit of
aluminum ore, which serves as a conductor of electrical
currents during storms. These storms can be sudden and
dramatic.

For your safety we ask your cooperation.

It was signed by Pierre Wiry, director of Forest Welfare of the
High Alps. On the left, a small wooden sign said "SOMMET: 6." We
stared at it for a time in silence.

Then I said, "Too late for us."

"I wonder how many 'accidents' occurred before they explored
the possibility that something other than the weather was at work?"

I glanced up the path that led to the meadow. "Well, that does it
for me," I said.

"We mustn't stop."

"You can go up there if you want, Claudel. I'm staying here."

"But look. There are no clouds. Not even a wisp."

"The same as the day of our picnic."

"I won't force you to do this, Natalie, but for me, it is necessary."

I watched Claudel grow smaller on the path and then I reread
the warning sign. Aluminum ore? The entire mountain where we'd
been picnicking was conducting the lightning to us? I leaned
against a tree, trying to imagine the three of us sitting on that blanket, unaware that the world was about to change for us forever. But
it was all in the past. What could Claudel possibly expect to accom-
plish by putting himself in harm's way now?

A breeze worked its way through the trees, and I held my arms in close, both for warmth and for comfort. Was Claudel's plan to look at the meadow and come right back? I felt the muscles in my stomach tighten and realized with a start that more than any-thing—more than logic, more than my own fear of the meadow—I wanted him safe. I slung the backpack onto my shoulder and started up the path.

He was already too far ahead to hear me call him. As I climbed faster I felt the sharp sting of panic. I could see the leaves of the trees moving around me, and—was I imagining it?—the tips of the taller trees seemed to be swaying. A wisp of cloud crept over the top of the hill like a long white finger.

As I approached the meadow, the hairs on my arms suddenly stood on end. The terrain began to flatten out, and through the shade of the tall trees I could see an uncanny green color, as if I were coming through the shadowy passageway in a sports stadium, and caught a glimpse of the field at the end of the tunnel. The meadow was thick with grass and tiny red wildflowers. I looked down at my watch and saw that it was dead on to noon. Claudel was nowhere in sight.

I waited at the edge of the meadow. I had a vague glimmer of familiarity with this place, but it looked like a hundred magazine photographs I'd seen of idyllic little meadows where people smoked menthol cigarettes or chewed mint gum, and I couldn't tell if it was memory or just commercial overload. I called Claudel's name again and waited. Nothing. I took off my watch and my ear-rings and put them in the front pouch of the backpack. I was grate-ful to be wearing pants without a metal zipper.

My eyes focused on the center of the green field as I came around the edge of the meadow. It was there, I was sure, where we had laid out the blanket for our picnic. Festive, unsuspecting. My throat felt constricted, thinking of it. I heard Claudel's voice.

"*Allo, chérie!*" he called. He was on the other side of the meadow, and when he saw me, he waved and started to walk slowly into the meadow.

"No, stop! Claudel!" I held my breath and waited, for what I wasn't sure. The sky was blue, the sun was shining; except for the wisp of cloud, there was no sign of any kind of peril.

Claudel continued on, and when he got to the middle of the meadow, he stopped and put out his hand for me to join him. I could see that he, too, had removed his watch. I didn't budge.

"This is silly, Natalie. Please."

If he was nervous about standing in the middle of that meadow, there was no trace of it in his face. He seemed unconcerned about where he was—all of his attention was on me. And finally I realized that if it happened again, if the worst thing I could imagine was going to happen, I wanted to be with him when it did. I took a step into the grass.

And nothing happened. The sun shone as it had the moment before. The trees fluttered indifferently above me. I took another step, and then another. And then, unaccountably, there I was in the middle of the meadow. Claudel was smiling when he put his arms around me.

"The problem with focusing on the past," he whispered, "is that it makes the future impossible."

After a moment he stepped back with his hands on my shoulders and said, "But you see? We have nothing to fear, even in this meadow."

We looked at each other, and at the sky, and grinned. We were safe. I thought I could hear the trees applaud.

Film is truth. 24 times a second.

Jean-Luc Godard, *Sunday Times,* 1966

10

Briançon, France

Sunday, May 11

*I*t was after one when we returned to the inn. I went to my room to gather my clothes and pillowcase while Claudel made some calls from the inn's front desk. When I came downstairs, he was hanging up the phone. He had a grin on his face that made me grin right back.

We were full of cheer as we set out for a walk along the main road toward Briançon, where heavy stone houses stood as resolutely as they had for centuries. We passed a gray stone church and stopped in front of the long stone building beside it, maison de santé: *l'Hôpital de l'Évangile.*

"Is this the hospital?" I said.

"A nursing home," he said, showing me the sidewalk that led to the building. "It was the closest facility when we were brought down from the mountain. *On y va?*"

The hospital was one more blank space in my memory. Thick

flowering bushes lined a sidewalk that led to a double-glassed front door. It was a one-story building, made of rough gray stone so that the exterior had the appearance of a long wall peppered with small windows at various intervals. It had a pitched roof to accommodate the snow that I imagined was the main feature of winters in the High Alps. None of it looked familiar.

"Is there anyone left who might remember us?" I asked as Claudel held the door for me.

"Only one doctor, named Von Cowenbergh," he said. "And he is now in retirement. But the sister in charge of medical records lives in her quarters behind the hospital. She agreed to meet with us."

We entered the foyer of the hospital, and Claudel let out a soft whistle. Instead of the small infirmary where we'd been treated, the hospital was now a substantial institution. A nurse, who had the plain and pinched demeanor of an unhappy nun, welcomed us at the office.

"Sister called to say she'll be here in no less than ten minutes. Would you like to wait in the lobby here? Can I get you a coffee? What is the nature of your visit with us? Have we seen you before?"

For a moment I thought Claudel was going to laugh. "We were patients here many years ago," he said. "We've come back to . . . to . . ."

"To reminisce," I finished.

"*Ah!* A short tour of the new addition, then," she said, leading us through heavy double doors behind the reception desk.

The crisp smell of healing hit us the second we stepped into the ward.

"Actually," I asked, "is the original hospital still in use?"

"Yes, mad'moiselle."

"Could we see it?" I asked.

She turned on her heel, her white rubber-soled shoes squeaking on the waxed-clean floor, and led us to another set of doors. As they parted, my whole body went stiff. A shaft of brilliant blue light stretched down a short hallway from a stained-glass window of Jesus Christ carrying a cross on his shoulder. It was the first thing that I remembered with absolute clarity.

A younger nurse stepped into the corridor and offered Claudel her hand. "Monsieur Claudel? I am Sister Monique."

We followed Sister Monique down the hall toward the stained-glass window. Sunlight shone through it and shot rays of cobalt blue over the hall's white linoleum floor. I stopped in front of the window and reached out to touch the stained glass: Jesus Christ. My old friend.

"Natalie," Sister Monique said, laying a soft hand on my shoulder. "Monsieur Claudel told me on the phone that you were brought down from the Trioux Meadow after an accident with lightning?"

"That's right," I said.

"Yes, it is well known here."

"Our particular accident is well known, or the incidence of lightning victims?" I said.

"Both, I'm sorry to say. And how can I be of service to you now?"

"We hoped we might look at our records," Claudel said. "For the three of us: Natalie Conway, Michel Claudel, and—"

"And my mother, Kit Conway," I finished.

"This way," Sister Monique said, opening a door marked medical records.

The room was about as big as my room at the inn, and it had the musty smell of a vault that hadn't been opened for a long time. It was lined on three walls with bookcases filled with medical charts.

"We have many of the newer charts on computer now, but this is where we keep the older ones, dating all the way back to the hospital's beginning."

Sister Monique walked directly to a row of stacks where each file was labeled with a tab of color: blue, red, yellow, or black. She moved her hand over the charts and removed a yellow-tabbed folder, followed by a blue one. Along the ceiling above us, the fluorescent lights flickered annoyingly.

"*Et feue Katherine Conway, n'est-ce pas?*" she asked me.

"Deceased," Claudel said, putting his palm against the small of my back.

"*Oui, feue,*" I said to Sister Monique.

She squeezed past us to get to the back wall, where all of the charts were tagged with black, in addition to red, yellow, or blue labels.

"*Non . . . non . . . non . . .*" she said, her fingers dancing over the charts. She went through them again. Then she pulled out a red-tagged folder. "*Le voici!*"

Claudel and I followed her to a small office adjacent to the medical records. She sat behind a simple wooden desk that had nothing on it but a rotary phone in one corner.

"Please sit down," she said. "These charts are the records of your stay with us." She used the word "*visite,*" as if we had stopped in for sandwiches one afternoon many years ago.

She opened Claudel's first and read through it quickly. "Yes, I see. You, Monsieur Claudel, were treated for a burn on your left wrist."

Claudel had taken his watch off earlier, at the Pré de Trioux, and now I noticed the thick scar that wrapped around his wrist. It was jagged and shiny, and he ran his finger over it absently. I looked up at him, and he answered with a faint smile.

"You had the usual symptoms: disorientation, severe headache, temporary blindness. But you were not admitted to the hospital." Claudel shook his head, and she closed his file and opened the yellow-tagged folder. "And you, mad'moiselle. You were unconscious for several hours and treated for a burn at the crown of your head." She read off a series of words that I guessed were names of ointments and medications. "And you also received treatment for another burn of eight centimeters on your abdomen. . . ."

From the corner of my eye, I could see Claudel looking at me, but I kept my eyes on Sister Monique.

"And you were discharged to the custody of"—she nodded in Claudel's direction—"Monsieur Michel Claudel." We both nodded.

"Now," she said, "this is the chart of Katherine Conway."

Sister Monique laid her hands flat on the open chart. It was an inch thicker than the other two folders. "Madame Conway was also unconscious at the time of admission. She was treated in Critical Care for a burn, also at the crown of her head. And another at her throat."

I looked at Claudel, remembering the necklace. His face was without expression.

"She was put on a respirator," Sister Monique continued, "as her breathing was erratic. Her vital signs were good, she remained unconscious from April tenth to . . . let's see . . . shock . . . May first . . . vital signs . . . ah . . . conscious . . . decision . . . seizure . . . diazepam . . ." Claudel and I sat forward in our chairs, listening carefully, trying to piece together something coherent from her garbled reading.

When she came to the last page, she said, "Yes, here it is. April thirtieth. She was removed from the respirator. Mmmm," she said, shaking her head. "That's curious."

Claudel's elbows were resting on his knees, and as Sister Monique came to the last page of the chart again, his hand covered his mouth, as if he had something to say and was trying to keep himself from saying it.

Sister Monique closed the chart and looked at me. "You said your mother, Madame Conway, was deceased?"

"Yes," I said.

"And it was your understanding that she died . . . in this hospital?"

"Yes, of course," Claudel said. "On May seventh."

"I'm sorry, Monsieur Claudel, yes, I understand. But according to her medical record, which was logged by two separate physicians, she regained consciousness on May second. The respirator was removed at . . . nine-oh-seven a.m. on May fourth. And three days later, on May seventh, her vital signs were exemplary."

Claudel shot out of his chair and took the chart from Sister Monique, who now sat uncomfortably with her hands folded on the desk in front of her. He flipped through the pages and, trying to calm himself, said, "Please, show me. . . ."

"Here," she said. "At the bottom. You see?"

Claudel stared at the paper. "*Mais non. Impossible.* It says a physician declared her in good health."

She tapped her finger on the spot. "It's signed by Dr. Von Cowenbergh. May seventh."

I listened to Claudel's and Sister Monique's loud protestations as if I were on the other side of a thick glass wall. I had the feeling that everything around me was changing shape, struggling to conform to this new reality, and if I didn't sit still while it happened, I'd be changed along with it, into something I didn't recognize.

Claudel's finger pounded on the chart as if he were hitting the "delete" key on a computer, but words had stopped coming out of his mouth. Sister Monique continued to defend her infallible hospital records, and as Claudel's eyes bore into hers, she matched his stare.

From some distant corner of my mind I heard myself say, "Come, Claudel, sit down." He looked at me with wide eyes. "*Viens,*" I said, and reached out to touch the arm of his empty chair.

Sister Monique looked up at him helplessly. "I'm sorry," she said. "I have no explanation for this. There should be further documentation."

Reluctantly, he sat, and Sister Monique said, "I see there is no record here of when or to whom she was discharged. Do you know who was responsible for her?" With or without documented evidence, both of us knew the answer to that question.

Claudel began to massage his eyes with his fingertips, as he had in the restaurant in Cannes the night before, and with an effort that felt like swimming through mud, I said to Sister Monique, "The physical was signed by a Dr. Von Cowenbergh?"

"Yes, Dr. Christian Von Cowenbergh. And the attending physician, Dr. Jean Grossman."

"Where are these physicians today?"

"Dr. Grossman died several years ago," Sister Monique said sadly.

"And the other one? Isn't he the doctor you told me was in retirement?" I asked Claudel.

Sister Monique answered, "Dr. Von Cowenbergh retired ten years ago. He lives alone now on the coast, in Saint-Tropez."

"That's just a few kilometers west of Cannes. Is he an old man, then?" I asked Sister Monique.

"Not so old," she said.

"I mean, is he lucid?"

Her face reddened. *"Oui, mad'moiselle, il est lucide."*

I looked at Claudel and then back at Sister Monique. "We will take my mother's chart to him."

She put her hands on top of the chart. "I cannot allow you to remove a patient's records from the hospital."

"Sister Monique," I said. "My father is a doctor. In the course of his professional life, he saw thousands of patients. If I asked him about one specific case, one that happened twenty-five years ago, I know he wouldn't remember details. Unless he had the patient's chart in front of him."

She shook her head slowly. "I am sorry, but it is against the rules."

I stood and leaned toward her, my hands on the desktop. "In America, a patient can obtain a copy of his medical records if he has the consent of a physician." Sister Monique's eyes went from me to the chart and back again. "Perhaps you could make a call to Dr. Von Cowenbergh," I suggested, glancing at the phone next to her, "and ask if he'd be willing to speak to us? I assume you have copying facilities in this hospital?"

Sister Monique nodded.

"Something tells me this is a case he'll want to remember." I raised my eyebrows and—slowly, slowly—took my seat. "We'll be happy to wait," I said.

For a minute, Sister Monique was still, staring at me angrily from the other side of the desk, and out of the corner of my eye I saw Claudel lift his head and look at me, too. Finally, she opened the drawer to her right and brought out a small book, lifted the receiver, and dialed.

Sister Monique had barely told Dr. Von Cowenbergh our names before he'd granted permission to release our charts. It was two-fifteen on Sunday afternoon, and the drive to Saint-Tropez would take at least four hours, so we checked out of the inn and in minutes we were winding down the steep hill into the valley of the Durance River. The river was headed in the same direction we were—to the sea—and as we passed over a bridge at the bottom of the hill, a rush of white water splashed onto the windshield. I watched the river in my side mirror for several minutes until it disappeared in the distance behind us.

Claudel's eyes seemed glazed as he watched the road ahead of him. From time to time I saw his grip tighten on the steering wheel and his arms go rigid. We drove for nearly an hour without exchanging so much as a sneeze. Every time I looked on my lap at the simple red tag on my mother's chart, it seemed that there wasn't enough air in the car.

I don't know how much time or how many mountain villages had passed before I heard Claudel say, *"Alors."* So.

I said nothing.

"God help us," he said. His face was flushed.

"*C'est rien,*" I said. It was a ridiculous statement, and I thought of Dustin Hoffman in *Wag the Dog,* telling the spin doctors, "This is *nothing,*" as everything around them fell to pieces.

"Talk to me."

But I didn't want to talk. I'd accused Claudel of this very act of avoidance the night before, but now the last thing I wanted to do was try to explain what I was feeling. Silence had suddenly become a narcotic, and I wanted more of it.

"Wouldn't you like to sleep?" I said. "You drove all night. You must be exhausted. Let me drive to Saint-Tropez."

For a moment he looked as if he was going to argue, but perhaps he heard the unspoken plea in my voice and pulled to the side of the road so we could change places.

When we were moving again, he said, "I am sorry I was unable to fight for you, or for your mother, to keep us together."

I said quietly, "Whatever we find in Saint-Tropez or in Cannes or wherever, none of it is your fault. We were victims of circumstance. Both of us."

Claudel leaned his head back on the headrest. In a moment his eyes closed.

The road was winding and steep and I had to fight myself to concentrate on driving. It felt as if my mind were full of snakes: Vidanne and Leland wound around my mother and Naomi; my father and even Draper slithered along the edge, mocking me for bad decisions and unfulfilled promises. Cannes seemed light-years away instead of merely hours, and I knew I'd have to return in the morning, like it or not.

But here beside me was Claudel, whose presence reminded me that, in spite of how it seemed, the world had not been overrun by snakes.

In only three hours we reached the eastern edge of the High Alps of High Provence and descended into the valley that led to Saint-Tropez. Claudel was sleeping with his arms crossed, and I put my hand on his shoulder to nudge him awake. He opened his eyes slowly.

"We're almost there."

"*Ho-la!* Already?" He stretched grandly and then he surveyed the landscape.

From the mountain pass, we had come into a street that was lined on both sides with expensive shops—clothing shops, jewelry shops, shoe shops, all with identically modest beige stone façades.

"The old man lives behind the Citadel, according to the directions. You see it, over there?" He pointed to a massive fortress on the hill overlooking the bay. "It was built in the sixteenth century, to defend the city from pirates and marauders from the south. Today the marauders come from the north. And from Southern California."

I tried not to smile.

He directed me onto a tiny cobblestone street that led up the hill, and I slowed in front of a bland three-story cement-faced apartment building that could have been found in any city in the world.

"Will you remember him?" I said.

"He may have changed more than I have. We'll see." He brushed a wisp of hair from my forehead with his fingertips, tucked it behind my ear, and in we went.

Dr. Von Cowenbergh opened the door so abruptly that he must have been peeking through the curtains as we came up the walk. He was a tiny man—his fluffy white head came just to my shoulder—but he would have been taller if his body had not been crippled by a dowager's hump and bent over at the waist. He seemed terribly frail as he rotated his head upward to look us in the eyes, but his voice was deep and commanding, as if it were coming from another body that was bigger and younger and full of health.

"May I offer you something to drink after your long journey?" he asked.

I started to refuse, but Claudel said, "With pleasure, monsieur," and I heard in his respectful tone the true meaning of the word: my sir.

The doctor led us to the living room, which was small and tidy, with furniture that looked as fragile as he did. I sat in a deep green armchair that almost swallowed me.

"Thank you for agreeing to see us," I said.

"But I'm delighted to have company," he said, passing me a glass of wine with one hand and brushing my thank-you into the lamp shade with the other. I took the glass and sipped: it was dry, but still sweet.

Claudel sat at one end of a plum-colored sofa and reached across a doily-covered coffee table to give the charts to the doctor. Seated, the man's bent body looked almost normal.

"And how is Sister Monique?" he asked. "I had the distinct impression she was troubled by your visit."

"*We* were troubled by our visit, Dr. Von Cowenbergh," I said.

"Yes, my dear, I'm quite sure you were. Delving into the past is like Hercules mucking out the Augean stables. It can be a very dirty business."

Without opening my chart he looked over his glasses at me and smiled.

I sat up as best I could in the billows of velvet.

"How is the scar on your abdomen, mademoiselle?"

"Natalie," I said. "It's big."

"Not bigger than it was then, I assure you. Scars do not grow, you know. Only in our unhappy imagination do they appear larger than they once were."

"I suppose," I said.

"May I see it, Natalie?" the doctor asked. "Your scar?"

After my disastrous high school experience, I had never voluntarily shown my scar to anyone. Even my father had only glimpsed it by accident, but it seemed perfectly natural in this odd little living room.

I stepped toward the sofa and lifted my shirt with one hand, pulling the elastic waistband of my sweatpants down below the scar with the other.

"It healed nicely, didn't it?" the old man said, moving his fingers over the surface of the scar. "It still looks like a little train track, crossing the abdomen. Nothing like any I've seen before or since. A lovely scar! On a lovely abdomen!" He looked up at me and smiled.

"Do you want to see it?" I asked Claudel. He nodded and I took a few steps toward him. Instead of touching it lightly, as the doctor had, he put one hand at the base of my back and pressed his other hand over the scar and left it there, as if he expected to feel it move beneath his palm. I felt my face flush. I glanced over at the doctor, who was studying the front of my chart.

I let go of my waistband and it snapped Claudel's hand away. When I was back in the armchair I couldn't look at him.

"You were with us for a long time, Natalie," the doctor said. "I remember you, too, Monsieur Claudel. Your wrist. Not an agonizing burn, as I recall." Claudel moved his watch up an inch or so and showed the old man his scar. "Nothing left but an echo," the doctor said with a sly smile. "Such wounds are more painful in the heart, I think."

"Can we ask about my mother?" I said.

"Your mother," he said to the pile of charts on his lap. "A stunning woman with a stubborn will." He opened my mother's chart and began reading it, running his hand over his white head as he read. "Yes, I remember. She fought for life for two, three—for almost four weeks. Three weeks before she was breathing on her own. A small miracle, I thought. She was a strong one." His finger followed a line on the page. "Removal from respirator, recovery, May seventh . . ." He flipped to the end of the folder, as Sister Monique had done, as if he were searching for something more. "Where is the last page?" he asked.

"This is all that Sister Monique found."

"The file is incomplete," the doctor said.

"Was she released from the hospital in good health?"

The doctor began to scratch the back of his head. "I am quite certain that she was," he said. And then his head popped up and he snapped his fingers in the air. "That was the day! There was a large party of tourists who were admitted, all at once. A crowd of tourists. Food poisoning. No, it wasn't food poisoning, something else. . . ." His eyes focused on a spot on the coffee table.

Claudel and I exchanged glances. "Dr. Von Cowenbergh, we buried my mother in Le Nôtre Cemetery in Paris on May eighth, twenty-five years ago."

He looked at me with a frown. "The next day?" He looked again in the chart. "I don't see how. She was breathing well, in good health," he said, pointing to the bottom of the last page of the chart. "I said so here." He looked at Claudel for help.

"That is why we have come to speak to you," Claudel said gently. "Because it makes no sense that she was released in good health on the same day her body was sent to us in Paris."

"Whose care was she released to, Doctor?" I asked.

He rubbed his forehead, as if a thought were stuck somewhere in the mêlée of his mind and he was struggling to pull it from his brain with his fingers. "I remember thinking . . . I felt she was not completely healed, I think. In cases such as hers, ventricular asystole—complete termination of the beating heart—if the rhythm picks up again, the respiratory arrest may cause a secondary cardiac arrest. Spinal artery syndromes, ischemia from vascular spasms are common. . . ."

The doctor must have seen my eyes glaze over at the unfamiliar medical terms in French because he said, "My apologies. My meaning is that much can happen after a blast of lightning which physicians cannot measure or correct. After such an accident even healthy survivors can develop nausea, ringing in the ears, an inability to sleep, headaches, personality changes—"

Almost in unison Claudel and I said, "We know all that." The doctor shook his head and raised his hands in the air, and I felt bad that we had come to disturb his peaceful Sunday.

"What I mean to say is that although my instinct was that she should be watched, I allowed Grossman to convince me that he would tend to her while I managed the admissions. He was confident that she would receive the necessary care."

"From whom?" Claudel asked. "There's nothing on the chart to indicate who it was."

Von Cowenbergh considered Claudel's question for a moment and then said, "But I believe it was your friend! He was with you for many days. Her husband."

I looked at Claudel, expecting to see the beginnings of another battle against his own head, but he was calm.

"Dr. Von Cowenbergh," he said, laying his hand on the doctor's shoulder. "I assure you with complete confidence that this man was not her husband. But please, do not bother yourself with this matter. What we want to know is, how did it happen that her release was not included in the medical file?"

The doctor hung his head over the folder, and Claudel lifted his eyebrows at me: it had been a long time, and perhaps we were asking too much of him.

The old man closed the folder. "Unless it was tampered with, I cannot imagine. If Grossman were alive, he could tell us. But he is dead these three years." He shook his head sadly. "I have offered you nothing."

"*Au contraire,* you have answered the questions you could answer," Claudel said. "You took good care of all of us. You see?" He gestured toward me, an offering of proof. "We are alive and well." He stood. "We will leave you now. We have a long drive tonight, and already it is late."

The doctor rose with a great deal of effort and carried his bent body to the door. "You should be proud of that scar, Miss Natalie. It is quite beautiful in its way."

As we were stepping onto the sidewalk, he called after us. "May I ask if you have consulted the national death records? It is now quite simple to do this kind of research if you have a computer."

Claudel sat in the driver's seat with the key in his hand, staring out the window into the darkness. I digested the image of Vidanne and my mother, twenty-five years younger, plotting her escape from her fettered life with me, negotiating it with the doctors, then pulling it off with an empty casket. The image of my motherless six-year-old self, mourning a phantom corpse, made me feel sick. I wished I had never started down this path.

"*On y va?*" I said. *Shall we go?*

On the road back to Cannes, we sped past a line of minivans making late-night deliveries along the Côte d'Azur, and I asked the question I'd been carrying around in my head for the last seven hours.

"Do you remember when the coffin arrived in Paris," I asked, "before the funeral? Did you open it? Did you look inside?"

"No, *chérie,*" he said. "Vidanne insisted that he take charge of the funeral, you see? A question of royalties from *Zeitgeist.* And I was in charge of you. But I did not want for you to see her. I thought it was the right thing." He looked at me with such remorse that I could hardly bear it.

"Please stop blaming yourself, Claudel. What good does that do either of us? We can only deal with what's happening today." It came out harsher than I'd meant it.

"*Bon*," he said, "I am now officially finished with regrets." He shifted the car into a lower gear as the engine propelled us loudly up a steep hill. "Frankly, it was a heavy burden, all that nonsense about wishing I could have made life better for you. Thank you for giving me your unqualified support to move on to less, shall we say, *piquant* matters."

"Okay, okay," I said. "I get it."

"Are you sure? Let me share something with you, Natalie, of which you may not be aware. I have, unequivocally, no feeling left for your mother." He glanced my way. "I am sorry if that is unkind, but I cannot pretend to feel anything at all for the woman I loved then, or the woman who may or may not be alive today. So why am I here? Why am I chasing this ghost with you, from one end of France to the other? I admit I do feel curiosity. And I feel a primitive rage at Jacques Vidanne that I thought was long dead. But those sentiments are nothing compared to my concern for you. I may not have been responsible for what happened, but I am the only man alive who truly understands what you lost, and how you lost it." He shifted to his lowest gear for the final push. There were no other cars in sight. We had left them all behind. "My regret is an annoyance that you will simply have to endure. For the present time, at least. Perhaps someday it will be replaced by something else."

The Citroën reached the top of the hill, and the sea appeared at our feet, black and magnificent with a silver streak of moonlight from the horizon to the shore. The car seemed to hover there at the pinnacle, as if it, too, were transfixed by the sight. The car began its descent down the hill, and I felt everything inside me turning upside down.

"I'll tell you something, Claudel. When I found her grave in Paris, I felt nothing, too. I didn't cry or anything. It was like she was nothing to me but stone."

He was quiet for a moment. Then he said slowly, "When you were a child, she was something for you then, I promise you. But she is little more than an idea for you now. You have lived a life in which she does not exist. It does not mean that you yourself have turned to stone."

I slumped down into the seat. Maybe that was exactly what I was afraid of.

It was midnight when we drove into Cannes. The moon and its reflection had followed us from Saint-Tropez along the Azure Coast, creating the illusion that we were connected at the hip to a romantic travel poster. We had both been silent for most of the drive, but I knew Claudel was thinking the same thing I was: if the public records confirmed no evidence of my mother's death, what then? Did I even want to find her?

We stopped at a traffic light at the edge of Cannes. "I keep a small apartment at the foot of the old city." He turned down the street on the left. I could see the castle at the top of the hill, keeping watch over the harbor. "And I have a computer."

The light turned green, but we hadn't moved. We were at some kind of crossroad. The street to the right led to the city, to the plaza and the Palais, which was no doubt teeming with people at this hour.

"Do you want me to take you to your hotel?" he asked evenly.

What I was thinking was that regardless of what had happened today, I had to get up at seven-thirty to make it to the morning screening of a movie called *Peppermill,* and I needed to shower and change clothes and pick up my bag before I went. However, what I said was, "Can you get me to the Palais by eight-thirty in the morning?"

He sighed. "I swear on my honor as a poster salesman."

And that was how I happened to find myself in Claudel's apartment. It was a small cottage in back of a larger house near the old city of Cannes—a pied-à-terre, surrounded by big trees, whose tired branches drooped over the gravel path that led to the door. The room was just large enough for a television and a brown leather couch against one wall and a kitchenette against another. There were two big windows, one behind the couch where a row of yellow silk flowers in clay pots lined the sill, and another above a small wooden desk.

The walls were bare except for a large oil painting—a busy jumble of red and blue angles, with an obscure black eye in the center. In the corner was a signature I recognized.

"Is this an original Paul Klee painting?" I couldn't believe he kept it here, in this little apartment.

"What do you think of it?"

I cocked my head to get a different perspective.

"It's horrible, isn't it?" he said before I could answer. "A good investment, but I can barely stand it. Never allow yourself to be impressed by a work of art that doesn't speak to you."

He gestured to a small refrigerator. "If you're hungry or thirsty, there are provisions."

"Let's do this now," I said, pointing to the laptop on the little desk. As it was booting up, he brought a wooden chair from beside the bed and set it next to the desk chair. I sat beside him, our thighs touching.

"*Bon*," he said. "Are you ready?"

I nodded, and he logged on to Google and typed in *Vital Records.* A long list of possibilities appeared, and he clicked on the first one, *Public Records Search: Worldwide Leader in Public Information.* At the prompt he typed *Katherine Kitredge Conway,* along with the date, department, and city in which the death occurred. A rectangle popped up. *No matches for this date. New search?*

"Try another date," I said.

He typed in *May 8.* The rectangle came up again.

"Maybe 'the event,' as they put it, happened in Paris."

Claudel typed in Paris, then did a broad search throughout France for that date. Nothing.

He returned to the original page and went through every site on the list. There was no record of the death of Katherine Kitredge Conway anywhere.

"Well, that's it," I said. After our visit to the hospital and to the doctor's house, this was what I suspected we'd find, but finding proof of it was still a shock. There was no place else to look, nothing more to say. Only Jacques Vidanne and my mother could answer the questions that remained.

Claudel was still typing, and a new page flickered on the screen: *Vital Records: MARRIAGE.* In small red letters inside a blue-outlined box were these words:

Mariage de Jacques Henri Vidanne et Katherine Kitredge Conway
PROVENCE: Briançon, France
Le sept mai

Le sept mai. Vidanne and my mother had been married on the very day I believed she had died. It meant she and Vidanne had staged her death and her burial. And it meant something so awful I didn't want to think it. It meant that my mother had made a choice.

"Are you still with me?"

I nodded. Claudel left his chair and in a moment I felt his hands on my shoulders.

For the second time that day, I had the eerie feeling that everything around me was morphing slowly, the way the scenery in *Time Machine* shifts to accommodate the reality of each new century. I turned in the chair, almost convinced I could watch it happen.

But everything was the same: Claudel's bag by the door, the yellow flowers on the sill, the couch, the television. Everything was just as I'd seen it moments ago. Claudel gave my shoulders a squeeze and then closed the laptop. Then he took a videotape from his bag.

"A present for you," he said.

"Is that what I think it is?" I said.

Claudel nodded. "I brought it with me from Paris. It is what I have of her. When you called me, I thought it might be a pleasant surprise. After today, I am afraid perhaps this is no longer the case."

"No . . . I do," I said. "I want to see it."

"It is not a legal copy. Many years in a French prison for the viewer," he said. He put the video in the VCR, then gestured to the couch. "Let me give you something to think about as you watch this: there is a scene at the beginning, a field of lavender. You and I were standing at the edge of the field."

"We were on the set?"

"All day, watching and waiting. We were, neither of us, happy. You were hot and hungry, and I was absurdly jealous."

"Jealous why?"

He scratched his neck with his index finger. "Because I was a young man who was about to have his heart broken for the first time."

"How could you possibly have known that?"

"I don't mean the mountain. I could see that creating this character with Vidanne was intoxicating for her. It was the first time I even considered that I might lose her. She had left your father without remorse. Why not me?" He gave an exaggerated shiver and reached for the remote. "And with that gloomy thought . . ."

He clicked on the remote, and the image of an endless field of lavender popped onto the television screen. The camera panned up slowly to establish the vastness of the field, and suddenly there was the sound of frenzied breathing. For almost a minute there was no other visual but the lavender field rushing toward us, and no sound but the breathing. I tried to see myself as a six-year-old, watching this with Claudel, but it was an impossible stretch of the imagination.

Abruptly the camera cut to a pair of bare feet breaking a path through the flowers. It moved slowly from the feet to a full side shot of a young woman who was running through the flowers, her long blonde hair flowing in the air behind her. It was my mother, younger than I was now, her strained breathing mixed with the rushing sound of her legs through the flowers. She wore a simple yellow print dress, and beads of sweat glistened on her forehead. She glanced over her shoulder with wide, frightened eyes.

"*Zeitgeist*" appeared in tall slanted script in front of her. And then, as if she were running into the letters and erasing them with her own body, they vanished—a flashy technique, even by today's standards. The camera swooped around to the front for a full-face close-up, and knowing that in a moment there would be a rack shot to pull her out of focus and reveal what she was running from, I leaned in closer so I could see her better. Claudel pushed "pause" and the image froze.

Her face was the movie star version of mine—not the way I looked now, or at any other time that I could remember—it was the way I looked when I imagined my most attractive self.

Claudel smiled. "You can almost sympathize with Vidanne, *n'est-ce pas*? Can you imagine his astonishment when you stepped onto his boat?"

I couldn't take my eyes from her face. "Remember you told me you had no feeling for her?" He nodded. "Can you honestly say that now? Even seeing her again like this?"

He looked at the screen for a moment.

"No. I cannot. I have many feelings for the woman she was. But only because it is tied to the memory of who I was then. I have as much affection for that hopeful young man as I ever had for her. But the woman I loved, she exists only in the past."

He rested his head on the back of the couch and looked at the ceiling.

"What?" I asked.

"I am thinking of something Balzac said." I could see his wry smile. "He said there is no escape from what lies within the heart. Once an emotion finds its way in—sorrow, love—it is always there."

"Like a scar."

"Perhaps. We must each decide if it is merely a scar or if it is evidence that a life has been lived."

For a minute we sat in silence, and the burden of the last twenty-four hours became too intense to bear. I didn't want to watch the rest of her movie. I didn't want to think of her, weighing the balance of her life with me and choosing Vidanne instead. All I wanted to do was sleep. I reached for the remote, clicked off the television.

"I think I have some wine," Claudel said.

"Honestly, you French," I said, trying to smile. "Always with the wine. I can't have anything more to drink, Claudel. I need to sleep."

He squeezed my hand gently and motioned to the bathroom.

I brushed my teeth, took a long, hot shower, and slipped into my nightgown. When I came out he'd turned down the bed for me and was shaking out a blanket over the couch. He was wearing cotton pajama bottoms and a white T-shirt. And no socks.

I crawled under the covers and watched him ready the room for sleep. I listened as his body settled onto the couch. The moon was so bright it shone through the window, bathing the cottage in blue light.

For a while I tried to make out a sign of his breathing, anything that would prove to me that he was still there.

"Claudel?" I said, trying to keep my voice steady. I didn't know what I was expecting. All I knew was that I wanted him close to me. I was lying on my side, and he came and sat on the edge of the bed. He put his hand on my hip and left it there. I couldn't catch my breath.

For several minutes we stayed that way, not daring to move or to speak. The warmth of his hand burned into my skin. I could only see the silhouette of his body against the blue light from the moon.

"I think . . ." he said slowly. "I think this is too important for us to be careless." He paused for a moment and then said, "Do you agree?"

Well, I did and I didn't. But I felt something almost like panic at the thought of him moving his hand.

"Please stay with me," I said.

"Can you sleep, do you think, if I stay?"

I nodded again.

He sat back so he was leaning against the wall and lifted his arm for me to settle my head on his shoulder. I tried to feel it as a platonic gesture, chaste and tender, but the scent of his body, mingled with the remembered fragrance of the meadow, with the hospital and the courtyard in Briançon, made me want to melt into him.

He took my hand and held it as if he were afraid to let it go, and I felt my breathing slow and finally return to normal. Sometime before dawn, I fell asleep listening to the steady sound of his heart.

'Tis said of love that it . . . wounds one,
another it kills. Like lightning it begins
and ends in the same moment.

Miguel de Cervantes Saavedra, 1547–1616

11

Cannes, France

Monday, May 12

*R*ain was falling softly on the cottage roof. The air in the room had the sweet smell of damp wood, and a thin ray of sunlight broke through a cloud and onto the bed. It seemed to work its way into the covers as if it were part of the fabric, unfolding slowly over Claudel's chest.

I slithered out from under his arm. I tiptoed across the cold stone floor to the computer and opened the lid of the laptop.

The monitor whirred softly to life, and the site we'd been looking at, *Vital Records: MARRIAGE,* popped onto the screen. It was 6:47 a.m., according to the digital clock in the corner of the monitor, when I felt Claudel behind me.

"*Te voilà,*" he said in a groggy, morning voice. I couldn't think what to do with my hands.

"Sleep well?"

"Well enough," he said, leaning down to give me a *bise* on my cheek. His skin smelled musky and his lips were so warm. He massaged my shoulders and whispered in my ear, "I see where you are."

I didn't answer, but he must have felt my body stiffen. "Come with me, Natalie," he said, taking my hand, lifting me from the chair, and guiding me to the sofa as if I were suddenly blind. "I will tell you my thoughts about this, and then you tell me yours."

"I have no thoughts, Claudel," I said without emotion. "And I'm not . . . I think we should leave it alone." I stood up suddenly and looked around the room for my pillowcase. I wanted to get out of the cottage, get out of Cannes, out of France, out of my own skin.

Claudel took my wrist and pulled me gently down to sit beside him. "Just listen," he said, moving closer and taking both my hands. "I have been trying to imagine how Vidanne could have brought this all to pass without my knowledge. I was young, yes, and I was not myself, but could I have been so naive?"

"Please—" I began.

"This is not about regret, Natalie. I am trying to be as logical as a man can be. Here is the question that came to me in the early hours of the morning: are you absolutely certain that you received nothing from your mother's estate?"

I'd never even heard about my mother's estate until Claudel had mentioned it yesterday on the mountain. "Absolutely positive. Unless my father kept it for me without my knowledge. He wanted to erase France from my mind, but he would never have turned down money that was rightfully mine."

"How do you know that? You were a child."

"You don't know my father."

Claudel winced.

"I mean, not the best part of him. There were so many times when I needed money—for my education or my house. Public Health Service doctors make almost nothing, and he borrowed from his own pension to help me. If he'd had access to a fund for me, believe me, he would have accessed it." I frowned at him. "Why?"

He paused for a moment and said, "They say there is a crime at the beginning of all great fortunes."

"So?"

"*Zeitgeist* was a big success—in a small way. Do you see what I mean?"

"Sure. Campy independent movies in America are the same. They have passionate fans, but they barely earn back the money it costs to make them."

"Precisely. And Vidanne chose not to release the movie on video, even though, with a big media push, it might have been even more successful as a video. It could have brought him a lot of money—at any rate, the money a movie like that can always count on. But he has not released it, even to this day."

"Why not?"

"*Qui sait?* I always thought it was a kind of reverence for the dead. But perhaps there is another reason."

My empty stomach tensed. "You're thinking he wanted to keep her face out of the public consciousness."

"It is a possibility, *n'est-ce pas*? And why did he not need the money that *Zeitgeist* would have brought him? Building an entire studio is an expensive operation. And Éclair appeared soon after your mother's death."

As I caught the irony in his use of the word, I felt the beginning of a nasty kind of anger welling up inside me. "He started the studio the same year!"

Claudel nodded. "I wonder where he got his money, don't you?"

"How much did she have? Enough to start a movie studio?"

"I don't know for sure. My memory is that it was old money, passed down to her from several generations. Lumber and furniture, something like that. And she was the only heir."

"How could they get away with it, though? Really. Someone must have investigated. . . ."

"There was no one to oppose him," he said. He let go of my hand and moved from the couch to the kitchenette, talking almost to himself as he opened cupboards and drawers. "I was no threat," he said, pulling an espresso machine and a bag of coffee beans out of the cupboard. "You were a child, and she was just another American. Her lawyers were all the way across the Atlantic. Your father, too, was half the world away, and in the short time they were together, I seriously doubt that she ever confided to him that she had inherited a fortune."

"But the lawyers. You said everyone had lawyers."

He scooped up some coffee beans with a small cup. "That is what I have been thinking about all night. And I cannot remember now if I ever actually saw them. Did I have a conversation with a lawyer? Or did I only hear that they were involved? I cannot remember."

He pushed a button and the grinder set to work, filling the room with the rich morning fragrance of coffee. The steamer sputtered, and a murky stream of brown sludge dribbled out of the espresso machine into a small cup.

"How is it that I have no memory of Vidanne?" I said suddenly. "I have a vague image of a man in the hospital in a white suit, but I've always thought it was a doctor. Maybe that was Vidanne."

"Probably. He was always in white. Still today, in photographs, he is always in white."

"But if he followed us everywhere, why have I no memories of him?"

He stopped himself in the middle of tightening the coffee press and said, "Because, *chérie,* he had no interest in you."

I let out a bitter little laugh. "Evidently."

"How much do you remember," he said gently, "from before the accident?"

"All I've ever had of her was a picture. But I remember her brushing my hair. I've never cut it short, because I remembered that she loved it long. And I remember sitting on her lap in the movie theater."

"These are your memories?" he said.

I nodded.

"I have to say, Natalie, that this is a surprise for me. I never once—and I am certain of this—saw your mother brushing your hair. That was for me to do. And as for sitting on her lap . . . I also doubt such a thing ever occurred."

"What do you mean?"

"How can I say this? She was not a woman of warmth, particularly with children. She was a sexual being, that was undeniable. But not affectionate. And she never treated you as a child—she wanted you to grow up. Immediately, if possible."

That was an unpleasant thought: an unaffectionate, impatient mother. In my mind Claudel had given me away. My father was distant. Could it be I'd made her up, conjured the memory of a loving parent?

"Did she . . . ," I began, not at all sure I wanted to finish. "Did *she* have any interest in me?"

"Of course she did. You were irresistible," he said with a smile. "I'm making you a *café crème*. With lots of *crème*."

"How can you be so calm about all this?"

The machine made a loud *whoosh,* and steam shot from the metal spigot. The milk began to bubble. "Because now it is I who am in control!" He brought me the foaming cup and offered the sugar bowl. "That is to say, it is *we* who are in control."

The coffee tasted delicious, exactly the way I liked it: hot, melted coffee ice cream. "How do you figure that we're in control of anything?"

Claudel joined me on the couch. "Because no matter how long

it takes to find them or what we have to do to stand before them face-to-face, we know."

I held the hot cup with the tips of my fingers. My enthusiasm for finding them was not as keen as Claudel's. "Maybe we should leave it to a lawyer."

"What could a lawyer do for us? What law have they broken? You cannot prosecute a man and woman for getting married, Natalie. She was legally divorced from your father, and she was not married to me. All they did was deceive us."

"But the cemetery—they buried an empty coffin."

"Perhaps you are right. But we still have to find them."

I felt the now-familiar sting in my eyes and heard my father's voice: "Swallow if you think you're going to cry, Buff. You can't cry if you're swallowing, it's a physical impossibility...."

I took a big gulp of coffee, and the stinging subsided. I said, "I don't know, Claudel. Maybe we should leave it."

"What?" he said, astonished. "How can we?"

"Because they don't *want* us to find them!"

"*Ah, bon,*" he said, sarcasm boiling in his voice. "So we leave them forever to enjoy their deception in peace? You have to face them."

"I don't!" My eyes filled with tears. Another gulp, and then another, until my cup was empty. "I don't *have* to do anything!"

For a moment he was silent. Then he put his hand on my knee and said, "If you do nothing, you will never be free of the past."

I brushed his hand from my knee and jumped off the couch, setting the cup on top of the tiny refrigerator. I should never have gotten into Claudel's car.

"I'm sick of the whole thing," I said.

"Natalie—"

"Please, Claudel! I don't want to find them. Let me go and do my work and forget this ever happened."

"But you cannot pretend you are still in ignorance."

"I can ignore them," I said, in a pretty turn of phrase that sounded false even to me. I looked at my watch. "Damn! You see? It's after eight already!"

"*T'en fais pas*," Claudel said, watching me dig through my pillowcase and come out with the lone dress I had brought. It was peach-colored and slightly wrinkled, but it was made of a good knit fabric that would relax as the day progressed. "There is plenty of time to get you to the Palais. But Natalie . . ." He took hold of my shoulders, forcing me to look him in the eye. "You must ask yourself seriously if you can return to the festival."

"Of course I can," I said dismissively. "It's why I'm here. I can do it blindfolded. Believe me, it'll be a relief, after everything that's happened in the last two days." I tried to move out of his grasp, but he held my shoulders.

"No one will think less of you if you withdraw."

"Right," I said. "No one but my editor and my mortgage company. I have to work, Claudel. Nothing has changed except a few facts."

"Are you absolutely sure? Natalie, look at me."

I looked at him, all right. "Am I sure of what, Claudel? Four days ago I was sure that my mother was dead. I was sure that you'd sent me out of your life and then forgotten me. I was sure my mother had loved me, that my father had taken me in only because he'd been forced to." I glared into his eyes, anger pinching my voice. "And I was absolutely sure I could never trust anyone enough to want . . ." I didn't dare finish that sentence. "Everything I was sure of is in . . . in . . ."

"*Tumulte?*" Claudel offered.

"No," I said. "In . . ."

"*Devastation?*"

"No! In . . . in . . ."

"*Chaos?*"

"*No!*" I said furiously. "It's in *ruins!*"

I shrugged out of his grasp and yanked my bra out of the tangle in my pillowcase. I pulled my arms out of my nightgown while I continued to rant.

"But am I sure I can sit in a theater filled with two thousand nameless journalists?" Under the tent of my nightgown I wrapped the bra around my waist and hooked it in front. "And watch five movies in one day?" I twisted the bra around and lifted it over my breasts. "And talk to a dozen actors and directors about their performances and the social climate that made their trivial little movies possible?" I shoved my arms furiously through the straps of the bra and grabbed my dress. "You bet I can!"

I stepped into the dress and jammed my arms into the short sleeves. In one swoop I tore off my nightgown, kicked it dramatically with my foot, and caught it in midair. "What else can I do?"

I was now fully clothed and breathing hard, and Claudel looked at me as if I'd just performed a complicated tap dance.

He took my nightgown, stuffed it into the pillowcase, and dropped it on the floor. And then he put his arms around me. After a minute he said in my ear, with a voice that would have calmed a rabid dog, "I will not force you, but I believe we must do this."

I stood stiffly for a minute, but then my body began to relax, and I nodded my head and laid it on his chest. He kissed my hair. He lifted my chin and kissed my forehead and my cheeks and my eyes. And I felt the weight of everything that had infuriated me a moment before lift and disappear.

"I'm sorry," I said when I'd recovered my voice. "It's not you I'm angry with."

"I know," he said. "And your anger does not worry me. In any case, don't let go of it entirely. It will help you to face the world— God help the world."

"Very funny."

He smiled, and brushed his lips across my forehead. When he started to loosen his embrace, I held on to him tightly.

"Don't let go."

"I am not going anywhere," he said.

"When you hold me, I feel like everything can be made right."

"But holding you will not make things right, Natalie. You cannot hide in my arms, any more than I can hide in yours."

Ten minutes later, I leapt out of Claudel's car with a promise to meet for the three-fifteen screening of *Le Vol*. Rain fell in a heavy stream as I ran up the majestic front stairway of the Palais. Every step made a loud squishing sound on the soaking red carpet.

The Grande Salle des Lumières was dimming its lights when I slipped into a seat in the last row of the mezzanine. *Peppermill* was a raucously funny animated American comedy about the life and times of the *Snow White* dwarf Sneezy. It was a movie you could enjoy without actually admiring it, which was exactly the opposite of how I'd felt about *Face of Peace*. Just the kind of mindless fizz I was looking for.

When it was over, I kept my eyes on the floor as I headed to my mailbox, afraid of running into Leland, whom I hadn't spoken to since I'd interrupted him in the middle of ringing Naomi's chimes.

The glitter and glow of Sunday's party had faded. While my life was being turned inside out, everything at the Palais seemed to have continued exactly as I'd left it on Saturday. Journalists still moved like ants from one screening room to another, and eager young directors wove through the crowd carrying heavy cans of film.

A mound of press notes and invitations spilled out of my mailbox. An envelope with *Éclair* printed in the upper left-hand corner landed on top, a single bolt of lightning passing through the word. I felt a rush of nerves at the thought of sitting across from Jacques Vidanne, but then I opened the envelope. It was a handwritten note that said they were sincerely sorry but they could not include me in the luncheon because I was not French. Only French journalists were invited. Many excuses, with profound regrets, etc. The note surprised me, but had I really believed he would speak to me?

The mound also included a note from Draper instructing me to phone him immediately, and I vowed to follow his orders to the letter. I shoved his note and the Éclair rejection into my bag and made my way to the phones.

"What?" Draper whined sleepily into the phone.

"I got a note that said I should phone you immediately."

"It's two in the morning."

" 'Immediately,' it said."

"Where the devil are you?"

"Cannes, France," I said.

"Where've you been?"

"Did you get my stories? I sent four of them."

"Of course I got them. Why haven't you checked your e-mail or answered your phone?"

For a moment I was afraid he was going to make me account for where I'd been. But I'd sent him more than I'd promised. "It was Sunday," I said. "The day the Lord set aside for—"

"There's no *resting* in journalism! There's no resting in journalism!"

I said, "What do you need, Draper? Is there something specific you need me to do that I haven't done?"

"No," he said heavily. "Just check your e-mail." And he hung up the phone.

I replaced the receiver, making a mental note to time all future calls to Draper so I woke him up. I climbed the stairs to Jack's. I was safe, I thought. Draper had been too tired to harass me, and Éclair had refused my request to attend the luncheon. I would not be forced to make myself vulnerable to Vidanne after all.

I sat for half an hour in Jack's, sipping coffee and listening to journalists talk about the parties from the night before—to which none of them had been invited, but about which all of them had an opinion. I recorded in my notebook all the facts I could strain to overhear:

- The jeweler Cartier spent twenty million euros at Cannes and hosted a dinner for six hundred VIPs.

    Note to self: Did the dinner cost twenty million euros, or did they contribute twenty million to the festival?
- Ingmar Bergman was awarded a one-time prize for his lifetime contribution to film because he's never won the Golden Palm. His daughter Linn, with her mother, Liv, accepted the award because Bergman was too old to come to Cannes.

    Note to self: Liv Ullmann was my age and Bergman was twenty-one years older when they began the affair that produced Linn. Was their age difference a scandal? A crime against nature? And why do I suddenly care?
- Julia Roberts is pregnant and has stopped smoking. Again.

    Note to self: wait for confirmation from her gynecologist before printing.
- Two Web sites are offering a twenty-four-hour fixed-camera view of the Palais:

    www.perceptualrobotics.com makes it possible for viewers to move the camera angle and zoom in on the festival action.

    www.plus.fr has a camera fixed six meters over the Palais.

    Note to self: Huh?

After three coffees, I packed up my mound of mail and went downstairs to install myself in the front row for the *Peppermill* press conference.

In five minutes most of the room was filled, but the seat beside me was still empty. When Leland appeared at the door, I moved all the papers from my lap to the empty seat. I watched him take in the room and then walk straight to me.

"You saved me a seat! How thoughtful. Those are yours, don't be coy," he said, pointing at the papers on the seat.

"Find another seat," I said.

"I thought we were friends."

"I don't think I want to be friends with you."

"Sure you do. I'm adorable. And you'll think I'm more adorable when I tell you what I've learned about Jacques Vidanne."

For a moment I hesitated, and then I picked up my pile of mail in one hand. It dropped all over the floor.

"Relax. I'll get them," he said, arranging the papers in a neat stack. "The mention of Vidanne's name threw you into a little tizzy. What's going on there?"

"None of your business," I said. I folded back the straps of the *Inu to Nekko* bag and slipped it under my chair.

"It is my business if I have information you want."

"How do you know I want the information you have?"

He sat down next to me and shoved his case under his seat. "Because you told Naomi you wanted it, that's how."

"What do you know?"

"Don't play games with me, Nattie. I really have something."

"Then tell me. You're the one playing games."

He laughed his nasal laugh. "You are the most impossible woman—"

"Forget it!" I said, pulling a yellow legal pad from the bag under my chair. I couldn't bear to explain everything to Leland.

He leaned in to me, an expression of concern on his face, and whispered, "It never occurred to me—are you in some kind of trouble?"

I made a sour face. "It's nothing like that. It's . . . personal."

"Good God. This Vidanne must be a real Svengali."

At that moment, the door opened and the moderator, Henri Behar, walked into the room, followed by Mike Myers, Antonio Banderas, the director Robert Zemeckis, and the rest of the cast. They sat themselves down behind the long table at the front of the room and adjusted their microphones. For a minute or two they spoke among themselves and laughed casually, as if a hundred journalists were not watching their every move.

As Behar leaned in to the mike, Leland whispered into my ear, "Did you have a thing with him?"

"I don't even know Jacques Vidanne!" I whispered, much too loudly. I thought I saw Mike Myers look my way. "Just tell me!"

"Fine!" Leland glanced toward Behar and gave him a little smile and a wave of acknowledgment. To me he said sotto voce, "First of all, Vidanne is married."

"I know that," I said. "But who cares whether he is or isn't?"

"You do! I mean, you did."

"I found out some things." That was an understatement.

"Well, he lives on Corsica, near a town called Bonifacio."

I stared at him. At the front of the room, Henri Behar tapped on his microphone and welcomed the journalists, in French and in English.

"It's an island, about a hundred miles off the coast." Leland strained for me to hear him without actually making his vocal cords vibrate.

"I *know* what Corsica is! Why does he live in Corsica?"

"*On* Corsica. Who knows? He moved there a couple of decades ago, and everyone I've talked to—"

"You've talked to people about Jacques Vidanne? Why would you do that?"

"Oh, come on. A French producer with his own yacht in the harbor at Cannes? He entertains a sexy little number like Naomi just for the pleasure of her company, without approaching her in any way for physical remuneration—doesn't that tweak your curiosity?"

"So what did 'everyone' say?"

He leaned closer to me, and I bent my head so his lips were only inches from my ear. Leland was in his element now—intimacies were his specialty. "For starters, he apparently isn't even French. He was born on Corsica, like Napoleon. And you probably know this, but his wife isn't—"

Leland and I both nearly jumped out of our seats when Henri Behar blasted into his microphone, "I think we'll begin the questions this morning with Leland Dunne from Toronto." Leland looked up at Behar and got a smile in return that said *Pay attention or die.*

Leland took the mike with one hand and pinched the other in his armpit—a nervous stance common to question-asking journalists at press conferences but totally uncharacteristic of the suave Leland Dunne.

"Good morning. I'd like to address my question to Mr. Myers." Sounding as if he'd been waiting for this opportunity for days, he asked Myers a long, probing question about rumors that he'd been paid five million dollars to do the voice work for Sneezy and whether he'd have settled for less. Leland was a skunk, but he was a good interviewer.

I listened to Myers's answer: he'd gladly have settled for one million, because he usually spent hours putting on costumes and makeup for a role. "But this time," he said, "I didn't even have to take a shower." I dutifully wrote it all down. Leland sat.

Some cutesy banter between the actors followed Leland's question, and I waited for him to finish the sentence Behar had interrupted. All the way in the back row, a man from the Netherlands stumbled through a question in French, which Behar translated perfectly, about what it was like to play the character of Grumpy.

"What was it like?" is a request for a simile I'd always avoided, because most actors are unable to handle such a broad question. Banderas, however, said something witty about the similarities between Grumpy and some of his other roles, like Zorro and Desperado. Everyone laughed except Leland and me.

"So, Jacques Vidanne's wife," he whispered to me. "She isn't French, either. She's Swedish, or Norwegian, or something blonde. And very reclusive. None of the French media have pictures of her on file, and that's the way Vidanne wants it. He's never talked about her publicly."

"How do you know that?" I whispered back to him.

The mike screeched as it was being handed to a woman in the row behind us—the piercing whistle that usually means someone is asleep at the controls. A hundred journalists grimaced and plugged their ears with their fingers.

"I talked to a French journalist who's been trying to get an interview with him for years. No dice. She said he's charming and well read—a self-made man from a peasant family. He speaks out a lot about racial biases, very bitter about the treatment of Corsicans by the French. But no personal interviews. Ever."

Henri Behar shot daggers at us from the stage, but Leland continued to whisper, "Plus, I looked him up on LexisNexis. And Google. *And* the Internet Movie Database: nothing but professional facts for you, toots." Then he shut up like a good boy.

The woman behind us was from a magazine I'd never heard of in London, and as she was speaking, I realized I'd seen her before, in the Éclair hospitality suite. Her question, to Myers, was whether he had another Austin Powers movie up his sleeve. Myers asked her if she was interested in a shag.

There were about twenty more questions, and then Behar wrapped up the conference in a neat little bow and sent the *Peppermill* actors out the door. We applauded and began to stream out through the opposite side of the room. I told Leland I'd meet him outside and hurried to the door, where the woman from London was caught in the exit squeeze. I reminded her that we'd almost met.

"Did you get an invitation to the luncheon tomorrow for *Le Vol*?" I asked. From behind, someone shoved me, and I bumped into the person in front of me and apologized.

"Of course," she said, as if she were addressing an insect.

"You didn't get a letter saying only French journalists were invited?"

"I told you, I received an invitation."

"But you're an English journalist," I said.

"Brilliant," she said, and joined the crowd pushing through the door.

I was scowling in the woman's direction when Leland tapped me on the shoulder. "You want some coffee?"

"I have to file by three," I said, "and there's a screening at three-fifteen," but my mind was stuck on the fact that Vidanne had singled me out.

"Plenty of time," Leland said.

"Why are you trying to be nice to me?" I asked.

He held the door open for me. "Actually, love, you're the one who should be trying to be nice to *me*."

"Don't start. You were an ass on the phone. From Naomi's bed, for God's sake." He followed me through the door.

"Two consenting adults. Or maybe just one adult. But we were both consenting."

I glared at him. We walked side by side up two flights of stairs without speaking. "You know I'm not talking about having sex with her. What do I care who you have sex with? But you only boinked her to get her permission for the pictures."

This made him furious. "How do you know why I boinked her?" Then his mouth curled in a grin. "And anyway, nobody says 'boinked' except horny teenagers."

I tried to sneer at him.

"I'm a little tired of you looking at me like you found me in a petri dish," he said.

He was right. If it wasn't my business who Leland slept with, it wasn't my business why he slept with them, either.

I sent two stories to Draper: one piercingly dull piece about the *Peppermill* press conference, and a second chatty little story filled with glitter and glam about the festival parties I'd attended only by rumor. Draper's e-mails were filled with instructions to see movies I already had on my schedule, so I sent him a note that said *Having a wonderful time, wish you were here.*

At five minutes after three, my anticipation of finding Claudel in the last row of the Salle Debussy was so overwhelming I nearly sprinted through the Palais.

When I finally stepped into the theater, I scanned the last row for Claudel, and there he was, sitting on the aisle against the back wall, exactly as he'd promised.

He was wearing black pants and a charcoal-gray V-neck sweater, the thin micro-knit that American men find too insubstantial to be fashionable. When he saw me, a smile crept over his face, so soft and slow that it was still growing when I arrived beside him. He looked at me as if he couldn't believe I'd found him, as if we hadn't spent the weekend sifting through the ashes of the last twenty-five years. As if we were a man and a woman, meeting at a movie theater, with the possibility of dinner and a future stretching out before us.

"I missed you," he said. He gave me a single *bise* that lingered on my cheek. I sat beside him, and he put his hand on mine, and we smiled idiotically at each other. It felt so good to see him, I forgot that I'd meant to share with him what Leland had told me. The only thing I could think about at the moment was that his hand was touching mine. On purpose.

Vidanne's movie was charming—like a valentine for adults, as Claudel described it—and when it was over, we applauded enthusiastically. I was amazed, as I always am, that artistic excellence—a fine performance or a truly beautiful painting—can transcend your personal feelings about the artists themselves. You couldn't hate *The Fugitive* just because Tommy Lee Jones, one of the all-time meanest interviews in the business, was in it. *Le Vol* was enchanting, no matter who had produced it.

The director, Edgar Loos, and the entire cast came onto the stage, and the audience continued to applaud for several minutes. Loos was a little man with a little head and little arms who stood just a few inches taller than the blond ethereal child-actor who had played the Little Prince.

People began filing out of the theater, and Claudel's hand slipped back into mine. The movie had been in French, with English subtitles so that American journalists could follow it, but the cast and director were about to speak in French, so there seemed to be no reason for Americans to stay. I recognized Rex Reed and Steve from VH1 in the exodus. And then I saw Leland coming up the aisle toward us. He took one look at me and his eyes dropped to my lap, where Claudel's hand lay clasped in mine. He stopped and greeted me with his nasal snigger.

"I take it you filed in time," he said with a grin, which he punctuated with a Groucho Marx spasm of his eyebrows.

My first thought was to pretend I didn't know him, but instead I behaved like a grown-up. I said to Claudel, "This is an old colleague of mine from Canada, Leland Dunne. This is my friend Michel Claudel."

"My pleasure," Claudel said in English. He let go of my hand to shake Leland's. "Natalie has spoken about you."

I don't know whether it was my surprise at hearing Claudel speak English or the fact that he'd remembered Leland's name, but I stared at Claudel in wonder. Without hesitation, he took my hand again.

"She has?" Leland said.

Claudel's next comment threw him completely off guard. "I understand you are a photographer." He pronounced it "photo grapher," but Leland understood.

He looked blankly at Claudel and then slowly realized he'd been had. He laughed through his nose.

On the stage, Edgar Loos began thanking the audience for its warm reception.

"*Enchanté*," Claudel said to Leland, who was still laughing as he left the theater.

Loos said a few words about the harsh realities of filming in the Sahara Desert and made a grand gesture of thanks to the estate of Antoine de Saint-Exupéry for permitting the movie to be made.

Jean-Paul Tournat, who had played the aviator, made a quick mention of the magic of *The Little Prince,* which he said was until recently the third most read book in the world.

"The first is the Bible. The second is the Koran. And our *Little Prince* is third!" No mention of the little wizard.

The audience cheered loudly and applauded, and the unearthly young boy, Philippe Couronne, smiled in shy approval. Loos thanked his crew and his wife. And then he began a long *merci* to his good friend and benefactor, Jacques Vidanne.

"*Fichons le camp!*" Claudel said. And we got the hell out of there.

The rain had stopped, and the street smelled crisp and new. We walked down the Palais stairs and onto the Croisette, where two little boys dressed in identical black shorts and suspenders were stomping around in the center of a big puddle, splashing water everywhere. Claudel held my hand as if it belonged to him.

His car was parked in front of the gallery, but we decided to walk up the hill to a restaurant near my hotel instead of staying on the Croisette. I took my pillowcase out of the car, and Claudel pulled me into the gallery.

"I have a surprise for you," he said.

On a large table, he opened a standard-sized poster of the movie *Zeitgeist*. It had been folded four times and frayed to nothing where the folds intersected. In the center of the poster was a sexy brunette—Lynette Hamilton, I assumed—caught in a pose like the woman on mud flaps over the back wheels of American trucks. The crystal-blue Mediterranean formed the background, and to her left was a young man who looked forlorn. To her right, a ghostly presence, was an old man, holding the hand of another beautiful girl in a short skirt, her long blonde hair caught in a breeze that had no doubt been manufactured expressly for the photo shoot. She was facing the camera, and there was no question about who she was. Even with the frayed line of the fold cutting off her right side, she was recognizable as my mother.

"Where did you find it?" I asked Claudel. He had opened it carefully and laid it out on the big table in the gallery.

"A colleague in Paris. There is always someone somewhere who is saving something on the remote chance that someone else will want to buy it."

I ran my hand over the photograph, barely ten inches high, of my mother.

"If you'd like, I can have it restored. You can do it in America, but it will be very expensive. Perhaps I will bring it to you myself."

It must have been the reminder that this week would have an end that stopped me. I was touched by his thoughtfulness for having searched for the poster, and truly I wanted him to come to America. But I wanted so much more that his suggestion of less made me want nothing at all.

"That's very kind, but I don't think I want to restore it. I'll take it back with me the way it is. But thank you." I stood there, staring at the poster, wondering what I would do with it once I got it home. I wanted not to be reminded of her, or of her movie, or of the things I now knew that I wished I'd never learned.

I knew my response was not at all what Claudel was expecting, but I was unable to muster the generosity of spirit to be anything more than polite. We walked up the hill to the restaurant in silence.

We took a table at the little restaurant in the courtyard of the Chalet d'Isere, and he agreed to order for us both while I went to my attic room to unpack my pillowcase. I found two notes tacked to my door. One was a fax from Draper that said *800. Not 826.*

The second note was a message that had just arrived from Leland:

I need to ask you a favor for Friday 2 p.m.
Don't say yes to anything else.

My little room looked sad and lonely, and the only evidence of life was the mound of papers and press notes scattered on the floor. I took a quick shower, towel-dried my hair, and looked at myself in the mirror. My eyebrows suddenly looked freakish to me. I tried to soften them, combing them down at the top with my fingers and up at the sides, but they remained stubbornly pointed.

As I was leaving, I took the photo of my mother from my big travel bag and locked the door behind me.

Claudel stood up when I arrived—a quintessentially un-American gesture, and one so gentlemanly, I blushed.

"I have something I want you to see," I said, handing him the picture I'd hidden in the zippered compartment.

He looked at it for a minute and smiled weakly.

"This is your father, I suppose?"

"Yes."

"And the mother—always onstage." It was not an unkind remark, but he'd dropped the pretense of respect he'd shown when we first spoke of her. He looked at it again and handed it back to me.

"It's the only picture I'd ever seen of her," I said, glancing at the picture before I slipped it back in my purse. "I wish I'd never heard of Jacques Vidanne." What I didn't acknowledge was that if not for Jacques Vidanne, I'd never have rediscovered Claudel, and that would have been a calamity of its own. But I was too absorbed in myself to notice his discomfort.

"I got a letter about the press luncheon for *Le Vol* today," I said.

"So, you'll sit with Vidanne tomorrow, face-to—"

"No, I won't."

Claudel sat up at attention. "He's canceled his participation in the festival?"

"No, as it happens. The letter apologized sincerely that they were unable to include me, but there was so much interest in the film, etc., etc., and they could only make the interviews available to print journalists from France."

"That seems reasonable."

I shook my head. "Apparently they've only canceled their availability to me. I spoke to an English journalist who was still invited."

"Are you going to make a protest?" he asked. He picked up a book of matches from the ashtray and began turning it over, end to end, on the table.

"No," I said.

"*Mais pourquoi pas?*" he asked. "It doesn't make you angry? That he feels he can dismiss you?"

"But he *has* dismissed me."

"Natalie—"

"Claudel. Please. I just want to drop it."

"*Bon,*" he said, tossing the book of matches on the table and putting his hands up in a gesture of surrender. "No more argument."

He finished a full glass of wine before our dinner arrived—a delicious *coq au vin* with fresh asparagus, which the waiter served with a fork and spoon in one hand, scooping up the juice and dribbling it over the chicken. We talked about silly things as we ate, movies and spotted goldfish and a French actor who'd bought a poster of his latest movie and burned it to ashes—he was miffed at the director—on the sidewalk. It felt as if we were on a first date, learning about the daily details of each other's lives. But when his little cup of espresso arrived, Claudel became quiet. He seemed to be turning something over in his mind.

"I am returning to Paris," he said finally.

"What?" I said. "Are you serious?"

"Very serious indeed."

"When?"

"Tomorrow morning, I think."

"But why?" I asked, knowing that any answer was bound to make me unhappy.

He took a sip of his espresso and leaned toward me. "I could tell you that I must return to work, and that would be partially true. One can always find work to do, in order to escape a painful circumstance. But the entire truth is that I have done enough damage here already."

"What does that mean?" I said, feeling myself begin to panic.

"We cannot extricate ourselves from all that has come before, and it is obvious I was naive to think so. I cannot compel you to pursue your mother and Vidanne."

"Why would you ask that of me?" I said, unable to mask the anger in my voice. "What does my not wanting to chase after my mother—who incidentally does not want me in her life, if you remember—what does that have to do with your leaving? What we are has nothing to do with her, or with Vidanne, does it?" I looked across the table, and he returned my glance with an expression of terrible sadness. "Please, Claudel, I don't understand what you're saying."

He put his cup in the small saucer and took my hand. "It was clear to me last night when you were sleeping that my feelings for you cannot remain as they are. You are not a child. And I am a man who has loved you longer than your memory can reach. It is perhaps natural that I should want to continue loving you, but is it natural for two who began as we did to care for each other as a man and a woman?"

"But it feels—"

"In any case," he interrupted. "What I mean to say is that I have no interest in any kind of relationship with you that hovers over the surface."

"I don't want that, either!"

"And yet you have just told me—and I think this is truly what you want—that you have no intention of facing Vidanne and your mother." He waited for me to disagree. When I didn't, he said, "You see, the surface is precisely where you wish to remain. I understand that your life has taught you it is easier to ignore unpleasantness than to face it. But you must understand, our misfortune on the mountain taught me precisely the opposite. I cannot live without facing what is before me. I must absorb what is real and live with it. You are free to live the way you must. But your way is not possible for me."

"But that's not fair! I was the one who called you."

"Ah, that is true. But it was curiosity, *n'est-ce pas*? The stakes were not as high as they are today. Now you must take a risk."

"Are you making me choose between you and my own sanity?"

"A little simplified, but if you believe you are protecting yourself by ignoring what is before you, then yes."

Claudel fell silent. He was so calm, I felt myself recoil from him.

"*Eh bien. C'est ça*," I said. That's it. I folded my napkin and placed it carefully on the table. Slowly, slowly, I said to myself. "The screening of *A Gathering of Men* starts in thirty minutes. I'd better hurry." I took the last gulp of my wine, picked up my purse, and stood up. Claudel stood, too.

"Let me pay for dinner, and we'll go to the screening together."

"No, thank you. I'm going alone."

"Don't be melodramatic, Natalie. We are not terminating this relationship."

"I think we are. You won't even try to understand that I can't make myself vulnerable to them again."

"But I do understand. And I think you have as much courage as you need."

I shook my head and turned away, but he grabbed my arm and pulled me to him.

"I am not abandoning you," he said forcefully. "But I also must do what I must do."

I pulled myself away, my arms limp at my sides. "There's something I have to say to you," I said, although I had no idea what it was I had to say. His eyes widened, and I dug my nails into my palms while I tried to think of something brave and sophisticated to say in farewell. But nothing came. Even lines from my favorite movies deserted me. There was a pain in my chest that made it impossible to think, so I said the first thing that came into my head.

"For your information," I said, squaring my shoulders, "it was Balzac who said the thing about great fortunes beginning with a crime. Mario Puzo used that quote in *The Godfather*."

"*Et bien?*" he said, trying to smile. "You see? Always Balzac."

I tried to smile, too, as I adjusted my purse strap on my shoulder. And then I turned toward the harbor.

"I am here for you if you need me," he said to my back. "For anything. You have my phone numbers. . . ."

I walked as fast as I could down the hill. I had to be careful on the cobblestones, but when I reached the flat easy surface of the sidewalk, I didn't look back.

Bolts of lightning follow the path of least resistance
to electrical neutrality—they strike either the closest
or the strongest center of opposite charge. The secret
to avoiding lightning is not to be either.

Beach Safety: Protect Yourself from Lightning
by James M. Falk

12

Cannes, France

Friday, May 16

Without the wire service archives as evidence, I could easily be convinced that I spent the next three days in a coma. I returned to my empty room on Monday night and lay in bed for a long time contemplating connections. I'd felt hollow when I left Claudel at the restaurant, but there's always a movie to amplify your most miserable view of the world. *A Gathering of Men* had been a portrait of crafty misogyny, of men bewitching and then abandoning women, and by the end of it, I felt hollower still.

And I thought that loving another human being was such a leap of faith—of faith in one's own judgment, faith in the vagaries of the heart, faith in the frailty of life itself—that it seemed impossible to me that people went around loving each other every day, as if there were nothing to it.

I had not been sent away to America and then forgotten—Claudel had shown me that. And he had made me feel for the first time in my life that I was connected to another human being. But what he was asking of me was impossible. He also had been deceived by my mother and Vidanne, but he had loved again, and had made a successful life. I was alone. And I could barely support myself.

I resolved to finish the job I was hired to do. I'd already survived half of the festival, and there were only five more days before I could return to the safety of my own home, with enough money to see me through another summer. And if I could stand to be in the same office with Vince Draper, I would even have a job. I'd lived without Claudel and my mother and France for the last twenty-five years; I could live without them for the rest of my life.

With that decision under my belt, I closed shop, as they say in the emotional retail biz. I floated through Tuesday and Wednesday on automatic pilot.

By Thursday evening I'd done thirty-six interviews with movie stars and seen thirteen movies, including *Off the Record,* a film about ruthless reporters that made me squirm. The other twelve were even darker, directed by men who'd obviously been frightened by a happy ending at an early age: their movies evolved from sad to sadder until the final credits rolled over lonely characters caught in the icy jaws of reality.

According to Draper's e-mails, the stories I sent him were cleverly probing ("When I asked if the rumor was true, Branagh seemed so itchy I felt I should scratch him myself") and devilishly insightful ("A movie that's not worth making is not worth making well"), but they were written by the cold-blooded robot who'd moved into my brain.

By Thursday night, when Steve from VH1 plopped down next

to me for the midnight screening of *Faust*, I'd have sold my own soul for a screening of *Legally Blonde*.

"When do you get to go home?" Steve asked me wearily.

"I can't remember where I live," I said.

Friday morning's screening was Sean Penn's movie *Ain't She Sweet*, an excruciating drama about love that won't die, no matter how sick it is. As I stepped out to get a glimpse of sun with the rest of the survivors, I was wondering why all the movies in competition for the Golden Palm had to be so depressing when I heard my name from the other side of the stairway. I squinted and saw Leland standing on the cement handrail, waving at me.

"What in the world?" I said as he swam through the crowd toward me. It took a moment to register that Naomi Paul was swimming with him. She was wearing a huge grin and a skirt so short it barely qualified as clothing. We said "Hi" to each other in unison.

"How does a person find you?" Leland whined. "I've been leaving messages all over Europe."

"I didn't . . ." I began, and then remembered the notes he'd left me. I had never called him back. "I'm a rat," I said as we were all swept down the stairs by the crowd. "What did you want?"

"I made a stupid mistake," he said. "I promised to cover a movie that wasn't on my schedule, but it's going to be the festival sleeper. I usually leave the interviews with French speakers to someone else. But this movie . . ." he said, glancing at Naomi, who had held her grin all the way down the stairs.

"And you want me to do the interviews."

"I heard you spewing French at the airport. And nobody in this movie speaks English. It's this afternoon."

"But there are a thousand translators in Cannes. Doesn't your producer speak French?"

"It was my idea!" Naomi said, so excited she looked like she might implode.

"Trust me, Nattie. This is win-win for both of us." Leland put his arm around Naomi's waist. "We'll probably use fifteen seconds of the interviews, but we have to do all of them. It'll take three hours, start to finish. What do you say?"

"Maybe I can use it for my own story. What's the movie?" From the other side of a palm tree, Shawn the cameraperson called Leland's name. He put up a finger to indicate he'd be right with her.

"*Le Vol,*" he said, and then grinned ridiculously at me.

I gulped. "You're kidding me."

He handed me the press kit as he and Naomi moved toward Shawn. "The interviews are at the Hôtel du Cap—paradise! There'll be a car for you in front of the Carlton at two!"

Naomi was all smiles. "You're a goddess!" she said, as they backed into the crowd.

I stared at the *Le Vol* press kit. Fate was messing with me. In spite of everything I'd said to Claudel, I was going to have to meet Vidanne face-to-face.

"A goddess!" Leland shouted as they disappeared.

I sat through a vicious meditation on the ethics of killing called *Assassination* before I caught Leland's car. Apart from planting ideas in my head for possible ways to approach Vidanne, the movie was easily forgotten.

The ride to the Hôtel du Cap was thirty minutes along the rocky coastline of the Mediterranean, through an unending forest of upscale clothing shops and into a tunnel of dense trees. Leland and his crew had left for the hotel before me, but the driver was sure I'd be thrilled to be spending a couple of hours at hotel swank.

"It's where F. Scott Fitzgerald set *Tender Is the Night,* you know," he said.

"I didn't know that," I said, feeling sort of warm and fuzzy that Leland and Naomi had conspired together to bring me to Vidanne without even asking why it meant so much to me.

"It's right in the middle of a twenty-acre park of pine trees," the driver was saying. "From the swimming pool you can dive right into the sea."

"Hmm," I said, barely listening. But as we turned the corner onto the cape, the hotel came into view for the first time, and I got the picture. It was a fortress of luxury across turquoise water, seemingly carved into the rock of the promontory of the Cap d'Antibes.

"Isn't this the best?" Naomi said when I got out of the car. She led me through the garden and stopped in front of two tall, ornate glass doors.

Leland held a door open for me. "If you trade in one of your original Rembrandts, you, too, can afford to stay here for a night."

Leland had hired the infamous cameraperson Shawn. His producer Rock—a big man with curly black hair—banged through the glass doors carrying most of her equipment. We were met in the foyer by a solemn bellman who checked Leland's name with a list that had been prepared by the concierge. His voice echoed in the airy, high-ceilinged alcove, which had apparently been built as a holding tank for visitors whose status as guests was still pending.

Naomi took my hand and led me to a corner of the foyer. "I'm going to my room," she said quietly. "I can't run into Mashure V'don, you know?" She gave me a hug that was surprising in its intensity.

"I don't . . . know what to say, Naomi," I stammered.

"Don't have to. Whatever it is you want from him, I hope you get it."

I nodded my thanks, and Leland came up behind her and gave her a wet kiss on her cheek. She giggled and headed up a gilded stairway.

Leland watched her until she disappeared, and I watched him watching her. When he turned to me, he was blushing.

"Be nice," I said.

"I'm always nice," he said with a grin.

The concierge joined us and escorted us to the lobby, where we parked our equipment and waited on satiny tapestry-covered chairs for a studio representative to find us. I was beginning to feel very nervous.

I whispered to Leland, "If you have to introduce me, don't say my name."

"Why not?"

"Trust me on this. Just say I'm your interpreter."

"If you say so," he said. He handed me a small piece of paper. "I have a couple of questions for you to ask the actors. They're my story. Loos and Vidanne are all yours." My stomach flipped at the mention of Vidanne's name.

A purposeful blonde woman entered the lobby, followed by a small entourage of men in dark suits and women in tailored pants. Stealthily hidden in the center of the entourage like a traveling dignitary was Eddie Murphy, handsome and slim in black slacks and shirt, and gesticulating to someone about something. We watched them pass without comment, even though Murphy would certainly have recognized Leland. But we both knew the unwritten law of dealing with celebrities and unfamiliar children: never speak unless spoken to.

Murphy's entourage exited through a door to a glass-walled room next to the lobby. They were followed by a smaller delegation with Tim Robbins in the center, and straggling in behind them was a cheery French person, perhaps the only frumpy woman in France, who welcomed us all and led us through a door at the back of the hotel. The clean scent of pine filled my nostrils as we shuffled through a small forest, but when we started down the gravel path to the beach, a pungent seaweed smell replaced it.

A string of small, simple wood cabins had been built at the edge of the water, in the hotel's effort to trump its own exclusivity. We followed the Éclair rep to the first of the cabins, onto a terrace that stretched out over the water.

"To arrange your equipment here, and to employ all furniture," she said in halting English, indicating a set of six sturdy cast-iron chairs and a round table, where several bottles of water had been arranged on a silver tray. "I will lead our actors here two times. You have Jean-Paul Tournat and Philippe Couronne, together. And Edgar Loos with Jacques Vidanne."

Leland thanked her, and she headed up the hill again, back to the hotel. I faced the Mediterranean and the high rocky promontory on which the hotel had been built. There was no wind and no boating activity to clutter the horizon. A trio of pelicans flew over the cabin, and one by one they dived into the water, disappeared, and then popped up to the surface to float there. The sky was as blue as the water, not a cloud in any direction, and I was marveling at the power of a cloudless sky to soothe my nerves when a loud explosion sent me into the cabin for cover.

Leland whistled. "Whoa, there, Nellie!" he said, guiding me back out to the veranda. He pointed in the direction of the cliff wall. "It was just a wave crashing against the rocks."

I looked toward the cliff and saw the water receding, but I couldn't get control of my nerves. I breathed in the raw sea air. I breathed it out. I felt like one of the Earp boys at the O.K. Corral, with no weapons to protect myself. It was a beautiful spot for a showdown, but I wished I'd told Leland no.

"How . . . the hell . . . am I . . . supposed to mask . . . that . . . sound?" Shawn said as another wave hit the rocks.

"Don't worry about it. We'll have Nattie facing this way," Leland said, sitting me in a chair with a view of the water. "And the talent can face away from the sea. You'll get the sun, Nattie. Can you handle it?"

The sun was glaring directly into my eyes, and I shaded them with my hand.

"Why don't I wear my sunglasses?"

"It's bad TV etiquette, for one thing," Rock the producer said, speaking for the first time.

"She's not on camera," Leland said. "What do they care?"

Rock shrugged and went to work with Shawn setting up the TV paraphernalia. I felt so jittery I went into the cabin to look over the questions Leland had given me. They were standard questions—what was the hardest thing about working in the desert, what did *The Little Prince* mean to you as you were growing up, what does it mean as an adult—but I wanted to have them on the tip of my tongue, in case my mind went blank. I couldn't mention his wife or the interview would be over. Could I make a reference to our meeting on his boat? How could I do that? My fear of asking "hard" questions was why I'd lost my job in the first place. Of course, all of this could be a waste of time. When Vidanne saw me, he could easily decide to end the interview before it had even begun.

I heard footsteps coming down the path, and Rock came into the cabin to find me. "Showtime!" he said.

I set my big purse on the floor beside my chair and was about to sit down when the frumpy Frenchwoman brought Couronne and Tournat onto the veranda. Leland shook hands with them and introduced himself, and the two actors looked confused and said helplessly, "No English."

Leland motioned in my direction and said, "My interpreter . . ." and gave me a huge smile.

"*Enchantée*," I said, greeting each of them with an abrupt single shake of the hand. "This is Leland Dunne, the star of the program, but I'll be asking the questions."

"*Heureusement pour nous*," Couronne said. Happily for us.

We settled into our seats, and Rock said, "Speed!" which was television talk for "go." Philippe Couronne was eight years old, with the kind of perfectly beautiful face from which light seems to radiate. If it was possible, he was more nervous than I, and most of my questions were answered by Tournat.

We talked for twenty minutes, and I was beginning to hit a comfortable momentum when I heard footsteps coming down the path again. My mind went blank. I thanked Tournat and Couronne politely, and they left the terrace.

"Was that good?" Leland asked me. "What did they say?"

I could hear the actors talking with other voices on the other side of the cabin. Vidanne was just around the corner. "They were great. We'll go over the tape later, okay? I'll tell you what they said."

I grabbed my purse and found a brush to run through my hair. I turned to Leland. "Am I okay?"

Leland looked at me. "Great. You look sort of cute and bouncy with your hair all curly like that."

"Are the frigging glasses necessary?" Rock said to Leland as if I weren't there. "They're jumbo, man. They cover half her face. Lose the glasses."

"If she wants to wear them . . ." But Leland was interrupted when the Éclair rep stepped onto the veranda with two men: the diminutive Edgar Loos in Levi's and a stylish gray shirt, and on his right, dressed in a white suit, single button straining over his large abdomen, was Jacques Vidanne. I tried to stand to greet them, but my legs wouldn't hold me. I dropped back into my chair.

Leland took Loos's hand and then Vidanne's, and when he welcomed them in English, Loos said to Vidanne, in French, "I thought this would be conducted in French." To Leland he said, in English, "Sorry, I have not English."

Leland turned and was startled to find me still sitting in my chair. I stood up immediately.

"My interpreter," he said.

"*Oui, bonjour, messieurs,*" I said, pushing my sunglasses up the bridge of my nose until they were almost embedded between my eyes. French words began to spill out of me indiscriminately. "Please sit down and excuse my glasses the sun is very bright and in any case the camera will not see me can I offer you something to drink a bottle of water perhaps make yourselves as comfortable as possible in these painful iron chairs and then we'll get started I know you're very busy I enjoyed your movie so much."

During this barrage of words, Loos and Vidanne sat in their chairs, and Rock hooked the tiny mikes onto their lapels. I was afraid to look at Vidanne, and I kept my eyes on Leland, who was standing behind the filmmakers, frowning at me as if I'd lost my marbles. Loos and Vidanne twisted around in their chairs until they found a position that didn't hurt. Slowly, slowly, I said to myself.

A wave crashed against the stone wall of the promontory, and Vidanne and Loos jumped slightly and glanced over their shoulders. From behind the camera I heard Shawn utter a mild expletive about the white balance, now that a person dressed entirely in white had entered the picture, and Rock stepped between me and Vidanne with a piece of white paper for Shawn to balance her color.

We sat in awkward silence: Loos watched the camera, Vidanne watched the water, and I watched Vidanne. The sun shone off his bald head so it seemed to glow, and in profile it looked like the head of a caesar, a head that belonged on a coin instead of this round, undistinguished body. It seemed impossible that this odd little man had wielded his blade so deftly that with a single stroke he had sliced my life into pieces. And now here he sat, gazing at the water as if the view were his, as if he deserved to bask in the pleasure of it.

Suddenly Vidanne leaned in to Loos and whispered, "Cue the sea!" In the next second, another wave exploded on the rocks. Loos let out a guffaw of pleasure and applauded.

Rock removed the paper and said, "Speed!" and both Loos and Vidanne sat up at attention.

My heart was in my throat. For a minute I was frozen, thinking I'd have to look down and read the questions on my lap, but I heard myself pulling out the clichéd interview opener: "First let me thank you for *Le Vol*." Vidanne and Loos smiled politely and thanked me for my kindness. I stared at Vidanne. It was clear that he had no idea who I was. He looked at me through a mask of feigned interest, a façade designed to conceal the fact that his only intention was to answer my questions about the movie and then flee. Loos wore the same mask. It was part of the territory. But it made me furious that Jacques Vidanne had the audacity to wear it now.

Somewhere in my head, I heard Claudel's voice. "It's like a valentine for grown-ups," he'd said, and I repeated it out loud. "A reminder that there are truths that never go out of fashion."

It wasn't exactly profound, but both Loos and Vidanne took the bait. They began to rhapsodize about *The Little Prince* and every child who ever had the good fortune to cross paths with Saint-Exupéry.

"Well said!" Loos gushed. "No one on earth has been untouched by *The Little Prince*! When I was a child in Périgueux . . ."

"Our precise motivation!" Vidanne said. "As a young boy on Corsica . . ."

They were animated and exuberant about their movie, just as a hundred other actors and moviemakers had been in interviews about a hundred other movies.

"We wanted to give this to the millions of moviegoers around the world . . . ," Loos said, and he seemed to mean it. And I wondered suddenly if there was something I'd missed in other interviews I'd had with moviemakers, most of them raving about their movies as if they had transformed the cinema. I'd always assumed that their enthusiasm was all part of a publicity game that both of us hated. But I wondered now if some of them had genuinely wanted to share their creation for reasons other than box-office returns. Maybe the fact that the next movie would be a transformation of cinema all over again didn't mean that they were lying to us. Maybe it only meant that human beings could love something today, and believe in the necessity of its existence for their survival—and then tomorrow, by some oddity of nature, move on to something else.

It might have been at that moment when the balance began to

shift for me, when everything around me slowed down to a speed I could handle and I stopped being afraid of Jacques Vidanne. Another wave hit the cliff wall, but the sound of it seemed muted to me. Only Vidanne was on my radar. Startled from his poetic rendering by the crashing surf, he said to the camera, "Should I say that again? Could you hear me?" And the words came out of his mouth sluggishly, as if I could watch them hang in the air between us and then evaporate.

One thing I've learned from interviewing movie stars is that the quickest way to get the upper hand in an interview is to make the other person feel like an idiot. I'd had it done to me so many times I could do it in my sleep, and I decided to do it now. I leaned forward, enjoying this, and said, *"Ne vous en faites pas, Monsieur Vidanne."* Don't let it bother you. "If you concentrate on what we're saying here, you won't notice the sound of the surf or the camera or anything else around you." I reached out and patted his knee. Loos was silent. Vidanne cocked his head, a slow movement as if he were putting two and two together and still getting five. I continued to lean on my elbows, which brought my body even closer to his.

"Tell me, Monsieur Vidanne, you began your career as a director—of a movie that would make even a seasoned director proud."

"I thank you," he said. "But you are so young. You have not seen the movie yourself."

"No, I've never had the pleasure. Because you have never released the movie on video. Why is that?"

He stiffened. This was not the first time he'd been asked this question. "The original print was lost," he said. "And only a handful of copies remain. I exercise my right as the movie's director to choose not to dilute the power of the film for the sake of—"

"Why was it that you never returned to directing?" I interrupted.

"Because my dream was to produce films, not to direct them."

I nodded. "You realize, I assume, how unusual that is?"

"Of course I do. Most producers dream of directing, not the other way around. But I wanted to have control of the movies I made."

"But can a producer claim total control?" I squinted my eyes slightly, as if I were unclear about his meaning.

"Not exactly. Only the producer who owns the studio can do that."

I responded with a pleasant smile. "Ah yes, the studio. And you own the studio, do you not?"

He lifted his head to give me a nod, but before he had time to bring it forward, I said, "Your studio, which was born shortly after *Zeitgeist* was released?"

"Yes," he said. "Shortly after."

Another wave crashed magnificently against the rocks, and I turned my head to watch the aftermath. Vidanne followed my gaze as a fine spray of water fell on the rocks. In the calm, I paused for a moment as his eyes returned to mine.

In a soft even voice I said, "And why did you choose the name 'Éclair' for your studio, Monsieur Vidanne?"

That was when it happened, I could see it in his face, when two and two suddenly made four. When, in spite of his efforts to prevent it from happening, he had found himself sitting inches from me, in a professional setting before a television camera, where he was forced to remain civil. Another wave crashed against the rocks, but he didn't seem to notice. He looked up at Leland and then at his watch and apparently registered that there was no graceful escape.

"I should think that is obvious," he said coldly, sitting up and readjusting the button of his white coat. "I chose the name 'Éclair' because light is the fundamental ingredient of film, the capturing and controlled diffusion of light. Without light, we have no images. Without images, we have no cinema."

"That's very poetic."

"It has nothing to do with poetry, it is merely—"

"Capturing light? This is not poetic?"

"Yes, perhaps there is a certain—"

"But I think it was more than the poetry of diffused light, *n'est-ce pas?*"

"Not in the least. It was a matter of simple science."

"And you're certain there was no other reason?"

"*Aucune quelconque!*" he shouted. None whatsoever. He sat back and folded his arms across his large stomach.

Edgar Loos, realizing that his friend was in trouble, said, "Perhaps we could return—"

I interrupted Loos and said to Vidanne, "But you can't capture lightning, can you, Monsieur Vidanne?"

"You cannot, Mademoiselle Conway. It strikes where it chooses." His gaze was fixed on me, and for a long moment neither of us spoke. Loos stared at Vidanne and then at me. Leland looked baffled at Vidanne's use of my name. Out of the corner of my eye, I could see Rock throw up his hands in frustration.

"Excuse me," Edgar Loos said. "Let us perhaps return to the movie."

I shook my gaze from Vidanne and said to Loos, "Why not? I have a question for you. This story is basically a collection of Saint-Exupéry's philosophies, disguised as a book for children, do you agree?"

Loos considered my question and said, "Yes, perhaps."

"And the most famous of all your Little Prince's philosophies is the idea that what is essential is invisible to the eye."

"Yes, definitely," Loos agreed.

"How do you reconcile this idea, that the essential is invisible, with the very fact of cinema, which is, as Monsieur Vidanne has just said, nothing but visual images?"

Poor Edgar Loos. He understood that something had gone terribly wrong, but he had no idea when it had happened. He said, "A very good question. If we have done our job, there should be—"

But I interrupted him again. "I have a better question. At the end of the film, when the snake bites the Little Prince and he falls—without a sound—does he die, do you think?"

Loos began, "That is a question—" but Vidanne put up his hand to stop him.

"Mad'moiselle Conway is asking *me.*" He looked me straight in the eye. "What do you think, Natalie? Is the Little Prince dead?"

I held my eyes on Vidanne, but my head was filled with the image of myself at six years old, watching helplessly as the casket disappeared into the ground, and I wanted to avert my eyes, from the memory and from Vidanne.

What I said was this: "I will tell you, *Monsieur* Vidanne, that until recently, I have believed that the Little Prince died in the end. But now I see clearly that he did not."

He fumbled to unclip his clip-on mike and said, "Don't be so certain, mad'moiselle." I held my gaze on him for just a moment. Then my eyes escaped to his pudgy fingers as they pulled the mike from his white lapel. It was long enough to flood my head with memories of Vidanne in his white suit, waiting in the hospital with Claudel, waiting outside a restaurant, Vidanne always waiting in the background.

He was pulling himself up from his chair, and I realized this was my last chance. I wasn't ready for him to walk away from me.

"Wait, Monsieur Vidanne," I said, "I have a gift for you." And I reached into my purse for the plastic bag that held the blades of grass from my mother's grave.

He was standing when he took the bag. "What is this?"

"A souvenir from Le Nôtre Cemetery in Paris."

He was heading for the steps before Edgar Loos had figured out how to remove his mike.

"What the hell was that about?" Rock said when the veranda was finally free of Frenchmen.

"You got what you need," I said.

"But what made him so angry?"

"I guess you were right about the sunglasses."

I had left the Hôtel du Cap feeling more alive than I'd ever felt. It was like winning a barroom brawl: I was bruised, but I'd landed the final punch.

Leland had stayed behind to join Naomi in her room, and after we transcribed the actors' interview, he'd given me a high five. As I was climbing into the car, he said, "Are you okay now? You don't want to tell me what this was all about?"

"I'm good," I said.

" 'Good,' huh? That's your story?"

"It's a long one. Call me when you get to the other side."

With a flash of his perfect teeth, he said, "It's what I live for," and threw me a kiss. I stared out the car window all the way back to Cannes.

I wrote an insanely personal review of the splendor of the Cap d'Antibes as a watering hole for the glitterati and sent it to Draper. I was feeling proud of myself, and though I didn't know it then, I was gearing up for another fight.

I dragged myself to a crazy Spanish comedy by Pedro Almodóvar about forbidden sex in a pizza parlor, and when the movie was over, I made my way back toward the pressroom. I wanted desperately to talk to Claudel. I wanted to describe to him the look in Vidanne's eyes when he realized who I was. If I couldn't tell Claudel, who could I tell?

For the first time in days, I thought about my father. I'd been feeling so detached from him after what Claudel had told me, I couldn't even bear to relate to him in even the most superficial way—which, according to both Claudel and Leland, seemed to be my specialty.

At the foot of the pressroom stairs, the phones were all in use.

I sat on the black vinyl seats that stretched along the wall of windows overlooking the harbor and looked out at the night. It had begun to rain. The pier glistened under the lights, and when the wind shifted, a barrage of drops splattered against the window. I could see a few hundred sopping spectators huddled together in front of the Palais.

I floated to a French movie called *La Femme Défendue,* which turned out to be my favorite film of the festival. It was a ridiculously simple story about a twenty-two-year-old woman named Muriel who has an affair with a thirty-nine-year-old man named François—a perfectly reasonable age difference, I thought. What made the movie interesting was that the whole story was seen through the eyes of François, whom we never saw. François was the camera, and therefore so were we, all voyeurs in Muriel's life.

By the end of the movie, the rain had stopped and stars had popped out between wisps of luminescent clouds. A warm breeze had followed the rain, but I felt chilled to the bone from loneliness, and I had an overwhelming need to talk to someone.

Under the massive eaves at the press entrance to the Palais, a phone was free. Surrounded by the after-rain hangover of water dripping all around me, I used my phone card and punched in the first number that came into my head. After three rings, I heard a husky old voice.

"Hiya, Pop," I said.

"Well, well. She lives."

"What time is it there?"

"I don't know, but I'm hungry for lunch."

"It's bedtime here."

There was a long pause.

"How you doing?" I asked.

"Good. How's the Cannes festival?" He pronounced it "can."

"Fine," I said. "The movies are depressing. Most of them, anyway. I just saw a silly one, but it's like the Oscars, you know, nobody takes a funny movie seriously." There was another pause.

"And it's raining," I added.

"How bad?"

"Just rain. There was a thing on the plane, but nothing here. Don't worry. It's all okay." Another pause. "I only called to say hi."

"Well, it's a pleasant surprise."

We hung on the line without speaking for almost a minute, and I wondered how much the silence was costing, halfway around the world. I couldn't remember why I'd called him—maybe to be reminded that there was someone permanent in my life—but I was thinking of asking him again how he was, just to fill the silence, when he asked a question that stunned me.

"Have you found that Frenchman over there?" he asked.

"You mean Michel Claudel?"

He didn't answer, and I knew he was waiting for me to tell him the truth.

"Yes, Pop, I have."

"Well, then," he said. And the conversation screeched to a halt. Just like old times.

"Actually, Pop? I was kind of wondering if you could tell me something, about when—when I came to you."

He paused. I waited. "Don't expect details. My pencil-sharp memory is duller than it was, you know."

"Not as dull as you think. But do you remember, did you have to talk to lawyers back then?"

"Why would I talk to lawyers? You were my child," he said fiercely. "You *are* my child."

"But custody lawyers, maybe. Or money lawyers, about arrangements with . . . her estate, maybe."

"Nossir. There was no estate and no lawyers. You landed here with your birth certificate and some clothes."

"So you never spoke to a lawyer?"

"Is this a bad connection or something? I talked to the Frenchman."

Vidanne, I thought. And later, Claudel.

"Okay," I said. "Sorry I brought it up."

"It's up for good now. No sense pretending it's not."

There was no anger in his voice, and it was such an obvious fact that I thought I must have been blind not to see it myself.

I felt a spurt of bitterness toward him now, for refusing to let me communicate with Claudel and for keeping even my mother's memory from me. But I was wrong to think of him as any kind of villain in my life. He had accepted responsibility for me and given me a stable home in an unstable world. He'd done the best he could. But he'd been waging a battle of his own against my mother's memory, and I had simply been caught in the crossfire.

"Pop?" I said. "I wanted you to know . . ." I could hear a sigh of impatience on the other end of the line. I cleared my throat and said, "I wanted you to know that you did a real good job with me."

I heard him take in a breath. "That's a nice thing to say."

"And I'm going to be just fine."

"I know you are, Nattie-girl," he said, and his voice was soft.

"Thanks, Pop. I mean for everything."

"Sure enough," he said, and the connection went dead.

"Good-bye, Pop," I said to an empty line.

For several minutes I sat and listened to the sound of people walking on the wet pavement, talking into cell phones, living their lives.

There had been no lawyers. No estate. No doubt about what my mother had chosen to do with her money. I could feel something stirring in me that had begun this afternoon while I was talking to Vidanne. Pop was right, and Claudel had been right, too. "It" was up for good, and I was a fool to think I could pretend otherwise.

I took out the notebook where I'd written Claudel's information and punched his personal number into the phone. It rang five times before his voice mail picked up. I left a short message: "It's me, Natalie. I had an interview with Vidanne today. I'm going to Corsica."

Hamish: Where are you going?
William Wallace: I'm going to pick a fight.
Hamish: Well, we didn't get dressed up for nothing.

Braveheart

13

Corsica

Saturday, May 17

hen I tried to convert 162 kilometers to miles so I could calculate how long it would take to get to Corsica, the ticket
agent said, *"Ce n'est pas de science de fusée, mad'moiselle.* It will take
one minute and thirty seconds per kilometer, whether you convert
it to miles or not."

I'd climbed out of bed that morning at the usual hour, but the
night had been one long anxiety attack, interrupted occasionally by
a moment of sleep. I'd packed my big travel bag with toiletries and
spent the morning in the Palais, gathering all the news and gossip I
could glean from early trade publications and my fellow reporters
at the American Pavilion. Then I'd sent it all to Draper.

By ten o'clock I was boarding a private boat to Corsica. In line at
the ticket booth, I'd met a honeymooning couple from Austria
making an overnight visit to Bonifacio, on the southern tip of the
island where Leland had said Vidanne lived. It was risky for me to

leave Cannes—I still had one more story to write after the closing ceremonies the next evening or Draper would go ballistic—but the Austrians assured me we'd be back in time, and it was a risk I was willing to take. The round-trip fare had left me $95 to feed myself for the next three days.

The water between Cannes and Corsica was choppy, and five minutes from shore I was already seasick. My head began to spin and the smell of the water . . . well, I lost interest in Vidanne and my mother and even in Claudel, and concentrated on holding on to my breakfast. I lay on my back on a bench at the back of the boat, reading a brochure about Corsica, just to keep my mind off my body.

Poor Corsica had a long embattled history of invasions, from the Greek occupation in 560 B.C. to its infiltration by Algerians in the 1960s. It was a history that had created a ferociously independent population with its own language, whose sole contribution to the English language was the word "vendetta."

The brochure described the island as a "mountain growing out of the sea," and the polar opposite of the Côte d'Azur, where beautiful people flock to see and be seen. *Corsica,* it said, *is a place where people go to get away from it all.*

I may have slept during the four-and-a-half-hour voyage, but I was still queasy when we pulled into the Bonifacio harbor. The town of Bonifacio was built at the top of an immense and rugged white-chalk cliff, and as we drew closer we could see that part of the cliff had broken away from the mainland, the cliff city still standing on top of it. The port of Bonifacio was shielded from view by the island, and as we rounded the wall and floated into the tiny harbor, we passed jetties with chunks of cement missing, where battered fishing boats and a few sailboats were moored. As we drew closer to shore I could see sprigs of green growing everywhere—between stones in the path that led to the dock, even poking through cracks in the high limestone wall: life, finding a way.

Legs wobbly, I stepped off the boat and was greeted by two scrawny brown dogs with no collars. The wind was so fierce I had to stay close to walls and benches just to stay upright, and I was leaning against a stone piling when I was approached—accosted was more like it—by a short man who must have been part of the jobless castrati. His voice was tinny and thin, and his shiny black hair was slicked back with some kind of petroleum product. He planted himself in front of me and wouldn't let me pass.

"You want a car?" he asked.

"You mean a taxi?" I said. I was still a little daffy after the boat ride.

"Sure, sure, a taxi," he said. "I will take you through the forest to Ajaccio to see Napoleon's birthplace. Beautiful forests." He spoke in a high-pitched French hybrid.

"I don't want to see Napoleon's birthplace, or forests," I said. "I'm looking for some people, and I don't know where they live." I tried to walk past him, but he stepped in front of me.

"Easy, easy, madame," he said. "If they live on Corsica, I will find them. I will take you to them. What is the name of your people?"

He was so eager, he made me smile. "His name is Vidanne. He makes movies."

"Vidanne! Yes, madame. He resides on Corsica, for certain. I will find exactly where. Stay. I will return for you." And he scurried off on a gravel road before I could tell him that I had no intention of going anywhere with him.

Fighting the wind and my own balance, I continued gingerly along the cobblestone quai through the old port town, past broken plastic Pepsi signs and tourist shops advertising boat excursions to Ajaccio and bus tours through the *haute ville* at the top of the cliff.

I looked up the long stairway that had been carved into the cliff wall and felt queasy all over again, so I sat on the first horizontal surface I came upon, which happened to be a chair at a small round table on the patio of a lazy café. The moment I sat, the mongrel dogs descended upon me, sniffing at my feet for food. I could hardly believe this place was connected by a little stretch of water to the splendor of Cannes.

The wind was like a mild, persistent headache. Cement walls built on either side of the café's patio provided ineffective protection. White tablecloths were secured to the tables with clamps, and the ashtrays—the only item on the tabletops—were heavy little beanbags supporting ash-stained plastic bowls. I had to hold my hair at the back of my neck to keep strands of it from whipping into my eyes.

"And you would like?" asked a small wizened waiter, swatting a leaf off my table with his towel.

"A Coke with ice and a ham sandwich, *s'il vous plaît*. And is there a phone book for the island?"

"Of course," he said. When he returned with my order, I was tying my hair back with a rubber band I'd found at the bottom of my purse.

"Is it always this windy?" I asked.

"Normalement," he said. "In Corsica we say that the wind gives speech to trees." He held his finger in the air, an invitation to listen: the trees that towered over the café seemed to hum. He handed me the thin Corsican phone book.

Neither Vidanne nor anyone with the surname Conway was listed. Surely, I thought, with only 250,000 people on the entire island, I should be able to find someone who could point me in Vidanne's direction.

"Excuse me," I asked the waiter. "How would you go about finding a house in Corsica if you knew only the name of the owner and not the location?"

"And who would I be looking for?" he asked, pouring Coke from a bottle over tiny squares of ice.

"Monsieur and Madame Jacques Vidanne," I said.

The waiter stopped in midpour and raised his eyebrows. "And

why would I wish to find them, may I ask?" It was a question to which, I now realized, I should have prepared an answer.

"I am a relative of Madame Vidanne's," I said, honesty being the least complicated policy.

He stared at me and passed his hand vaguely over his face. "I can see that you might be."

"You know her?" I asked.

"Yes, naturally," he said. "I live here."

"How can I find them?"

He crossed his arms and patted one hand against his upper arm, considering. He scrutinized me, top to bottom. I knew my hair was a tangled mess, but I hoped the rest of me was presentable.

"I am not at liberty to share such information with a stranger," he said.

"Why not?" I asked.

"Because Monsieur Vidanne is an important man, and there is a reason he inhabits Corsica."

I took a deep breath. "I would be willing to pay for these directions," I said, trying not to make it sound like a proposition to assassinate the pope.

The old man stared at me with an open mouth, and after a moment he said, "Will you excuse me, please? I must make a brief phone call."

For a second I thought he might be calling the police to have me thrown in jail for attempting to bribe a waiter, but then I decided we were too close to Sicily for such a thing to be a serious offense. I took a bite of my sandwich. The dogs sat up at attention, hoping for scraps, but my stomach was settled enough that I finished the long baguette without their help.

I was slipping a ten-euro note under my plate when I happened to glance into the street beyond the café and saw something that stopped me cold. Bobbing up and down past a travel agency window was a scrawny ponytail that stuck out from the back of a woman's head like a tuft of pine needles. In the second it took me to place its owner, she darted out of sight. The waiter came out of the café as I grabbed my bag and hurried across the street.

The waiter tried to stop me. *"Arrête, mad'moiselle!"* he shouted, but I threw my bag over my shoulder and ran as fast as I could in the pine-needle ponytail's direction. When I caught up with her, I put my hand on her arm.

The woman, who was several inches taller than I was, whirled her head around and gave a little gasp when she saw my face.

"Pardon me," I said. "I saw you on Monsieur Vidanne's yacht last week, in the harbor at Cannes." Her mouth made a tiny O shape and she stepped around me to escape down the street, but I caught up with her and stood in her way.

"Please. My name is Natalie Conway, and I believe Madame Vidanne is—"

"I cannot," she said under her breath, and tried again to pass me, but from out of nowhere the intense small body of the squeaky-voiced man from the harbor planted itself between me and the woman.

"There you are, madame!" said the little castrato. "I have searched for you everywhere."

The ponytail seized the opportunity to flee. She swerved around me and rushed down the street, and the little man stood firmly in my path.

"Madame, you will be very pleased!"

"I beg you, let me go!" I said to him, as if he were twice my size and holding me in shackles.

"I happily have found—" he began, but I pushed him aside and ran after the ponytail, which had now disappeared completely.

"Damn!" I said in English. The little castrato had followed me to the corner, and he tapped me gently on the arm.

"Madame, I can take you to the house of your friend." He gave me a grimy piece of paper and a toothy grin.

The note was almost unreadable, except for the letters *V-A-D-I-N*.

"The name is *Vidanne*."

"Just so, madame. Jacques. And the yellow-haired woman. The house is high in the hills near Propriano, at the edge of the Forêt National."

"But how? How can you take me there?"

He motioned across the street to a tiny white Fiat. It had no front bumper, and the side window had been patched with cardboard.

"How much?" I asked.

"Forty euros, to go and to return."

Counting the sandwich I'd just paid for, that left me exactly fifty-five euros for the rest of my stay.

"Thirty-five," I said.

"Acceptable, madame."

"And you'll pick me up there in the morning?"

"Same place."

"How far is it?"

"Sixty kilometers. But for you, forty." He gave me a toothy grin.

The road from Bonifacio was bumpy and the Fiat had long ago donated its shock absorbers to posterity, but the scenery was spectacular: deep wooded gorges at the foot of jagged mountain precipices dropped straight into the gulf sea, which sparkled like the cover of a book on a coffee table. I'd never seen scenery so dramatic, unless you counted the miles of flat desert sand and rocky buttes that jutted out of the landscape of the American Southwest.

My little driver, who sat on four thick pillows so he could see over the steering wheel, kept a well-rehearsed tourist monologue going during the forty-five minutes it took to bounce from Bonifacio to Propriano.

As we came around a craggy corner, he turned to me and said, "Now we are passing through the maquis!"

"I beg your pardon?" I said.

"Madame has not heard of the maquis?" He looked in his rearview mirror and saw me shake my head. He pointed to the thick forest on our right.

"The forest?" I asked.

"Ooo," he said ominously. "It is more than a forest, madame. It is the maquis! An impenetrable jungle in which a man can become lost forever." He strained his neck to glance at me in the mirror. "But not a Corsican. During the war, the soldiers' cry was *'Prendre le maquis!'* They hid themselves in the maquis to outsmart the Germans. The Germans went in, but they never came out. Now there are bandits who inhabit the maquis."

My stomach twisted: Bandits—Germans—the maquis. I peered through the broken window at a wooded landscape so dense the entire mountainside seemed to be painted green. What kind of place is this? I thought. Did Vidanne and my mother live in the maquis, where no one was meant to find them?

When he finally pulled into Propriano, my little driver stopped in front of a small stuccoed house with a red roof—all of the houses seemed to be small and stuccoed with red roofs—and a wooden sign that said "Bureau de Poste." He turned off the ignition.

"Why have you stopped?" I said uneasily.

"Tomorrow I wait for you here. What time?"

"But you're not leaving me here."

"Yes, madame, the post office," he said, pleased to have brought me to such a fine location. "The youth hostel is there, next to the Bains de Baracci—world's most praiseworthy hot springs. The post office is altogether *convenable*."

"But you said you'd take me to Vidanne's house!" I could feel the bitter taste of panic on my tongue.

He shook his head and said, "No, madame, sadly I cannot. The road is steep and full of bumps, and my car is delicate." That was an understatement. "You must find the house alone."

"But I don't know where it is!" I said, completely furious. "You promised me—"

"No, no. The house is near. You can walk, only some minutes, not hours. You see?" He pointed to a narrow dirt road that took off into the woods from a point behind the post office. "This is the roadway of your friends. You will follow it until you reach a gate. A spectacular gate, I am told, but no cars allowed, very private. And you must stay on the road, in any case. Do not go into the maquis."

Into the maquis? Did he think I was nuts?

I was still fuming as I paid him half of his thirty-five euros, and he promised to meet me at the Bureau de Poste at eleven a.m. the next day. A cool wind was blowing over the streets of Propriano. I stuck an arm through each of the straps of my travel bag like a backpack and started toward the road.

An ornately carved wooden sign had been nailed to a tree at the bottom of the road: DÉFENSE DE PASSER SOUS PEINE D'AMENDE—a medieval version of "No Trespassing."

I had to walk along the edge of the deeply rutted road in order to keep my footing. In minutes I was climbing upward into a forest of thick green trees and bushes so close together I couldn't see ten feet from the road. The wind made the tops of the trees purr, and several times I tripped and staggered a few steps before I caught my balance.

I'd been walking for half an hour when suddenly the air was filled with a soft thwacking noise. I stopped and looked up, searching the sky for the source of the sound, and caught sight of the round black belly of a helicopter floating over the trees and then disappearing from view. The helicopter hummed loudly for a moment, and as it moved into the distance ahead of me, the sound began to fade and then died completely.

Twenty minutes later, sweating and breathing hard, I reached the gate. It was a tightly spaced wrought-iron barricade with sharp *fleur-de-lis* tips on the ends of each post so that bandits and other unwanted visitors would be impaled by iron lilies while attempting to climb over it. My traitorous castrato had warned me about the gate, but he'd neglected to mention the wall that went with it.

It was impossibly high—I could barely have reached the top of it if I'd stood on the seat of a bicycle—and made of heavy white stone the color of the cliff face that dominated the harbor in Bonifacio. There was no visible lock on the gate—only a small rectangle of numbered buttons, which had been embedded in the wall to the left of the gate.

Without the combination, I could see at once that there was no hope of opening the gate. I walked a few yards into the maquis on either side of the road and realized there was no way to climb over the wall. I could see the wind bending the tops of the trees, and I felt a chill, even though the air was warm. I knew it was my body's way of telling me that a sensible person would, at this point, admit defeat.

For the first time since I'd arrived on the island, I considered the possibility that I'd made a mistake. Even if I could get past the gate, what did I plan to do? Present myself at my mother's door like a Christmas ham?

It was five o'clock. The sun was still breaking through the dense branches of the maquis in dusty streams, but it wouldn't for long. I guessed I had two more hours of daylight before the forest went completely black. Whatever I was going to do, I had to do it soon. I decided to focus on getting inside and to worry later about what I would do once I was in.

I was entertaining the possibility of climbing a tree when I heard a car engine in the distance straining up the hill. My first instinct was to step into the road and wait for the driver to let me through the gate, but I knew that if it was Vidanne at the wheel, he would send me away without an argument. He might even have me arrested. I crept to the edge of the road and crouched behind a bush that was close enough to the wall for me to see the electronic panel.

The brown Range Rover finally rounded the corner and sent a blinding beam of reflected light straight into my eyes.

The car pulled up to the gate, and I held my breath. I listened to the click of the latch, the sound of the car door being opened. The slowing of time was palpable, and the foot coming out of the car took forever to reveal itself. My mind was moving slowly along with it, pausing to see if maybe, perhaps, it could possibly be that this was my mother and I would step out onto the road and announce to her that I had found her at last.

But the moment the other foot touched the road, time stumbled forward in its usual pace. The black pants and white blouse belonged to the pine-needle ponytail, obviously returning from her visit in Bonifacio. She left the car door open and approached the wall.

She was a hunt-and-peck typist, so I could see the buttons she was punching. I watched her press 0, 7, another 0. The fourth number was pressed too fast to see. A motor hummed to life and the gate rolled slowly to the right. She returned to the car and waited for the portal to open all the way.

I considered leaping through behind the car, but some corner of logic opened in my head, and I knew she would see me in her rearview mirror.

The gate inched its way at a snail's pace and finally clanked closed. When the car was out of sight I approached the wall and its numbered panel. I hadn't seen the last number, but there were only ten to choose from. I punched in 0-7-0-1 and then 0-7-0-2. Nothing happened. Then 0-7-0-3. Still nothing. And then I remembered: the European way of writing dates was the opposite of the American system. Month first, day second.

Claudel hadn't been exaggerating when he said Vidanne was

obsessed with my mother. The numbers 7-5 had to be *le sept mai*. I punched in the final 5. The motor whirred into motion, and the gate began to roll.

When the whirring stopped and the gate was open all the way, I stepped across the threshold, into my mother's world.

The forest on the other side of the wall was more densely overgrown and gnarled than the one I'd left behind. I saw the taillights of the Range Rover disappearing around a curve, and I ran up the narrow road to follow it. But as I neared the curve, the road split into three even narrower paths, all of which seemed to lead straight into the inscrutable maquis.

Without any good reason, I chose the path that forked to the right. I followed what looked like a break in the bushes, but within seconds I was surrounded by a tangle of trees and branches. In my head I heard the little taxi driver's warning to stay out of the maquis. I turned to take a step, but I couldn't find where I'd come from. The trees were so dense, there wasn't enough light to illuminate the path.

Every direction I turned seemed to drag me deeper into the maquis. Sounds seemed to be coming at me from all directions.

I felt the prickly sting of fear along my arms, and I was working myself into a full-blown panic when I heard the sound of a car door slamming shut through the trees behind me.

A woman shouted, *"J'arrive!"* and I crept gingerly into the bushes in her direction. Through the leaves I could see a gray tiled roof, and I ducked under branches toward it, snagging a hole in the sleeve of my blouse as I pushed through the dense underbrush.

I was squinting into the bushes, thinking I saw a patch of light, when the ground flew out from under me. I fell with a thud onto my back and slipped down a sharp embankment, bumping over vines and small stones, until the trunk of a tall tree stopped me.

I lay for a moment with my feet against the tree and listened. There was no sound.

Nothing seemed to hurt, but on the other side of the tree that had broken my fall, the slope ended abruptly and disappeared over a rocky cliff. I grabbed a low branch and leaned out to look over the edge.

I was standing on the upper ridge of a deep, narrow, incomprehensibly green valley. A thin cascade of water trickled over the edge of the rock face into a clear pond ten or twenty feet below. The water spilled out of the pond, past an enormous ivy-covered stone house, over rocks and ground cover, and into a larger stream that flowed through the middle of the valley.

Growing up as I had where the ground was red dirt and sagebrush was the only form of vegetation, I could hardly fathom so much green. I stood for a moment, awed by the simple, unexpected beauty of it.

I climbed down the steep slope, stepping clumsily from one level to the next and stopping after each step to listen for voices. At the bottom, I washed my hands in the warm water of the pond. The Range Rover was parked at the end of a gravel drive that led to a courtyard at the front of the house. I made my way through the courtyard, and then I took a deep breath and pounded the heavy brass knocker at the center of the front door.

No answer. I knocked again. Still nothing. I heard a loud gust of wind and stepped out of the courtyard to look up at the sky.

For a moment the suggestion of bad weather drowned out all thoughts of Vidanne, but as I was looking at the sky, I noticed something peculiar. At the upper edge of the surrounding forest, not far from where I'd slipped down the hill, I saw the silhouette of a tall metal tower. I thought at first it was a power transformer to bring electricity to the house, but there were more of them around the perimeter—three visible from where I stood, bending ominously toward the center of the house.

I hurried toward the back of the house, past a curtained window framed by strips of aluminum that looked like part of a security system. I peeked in the window, and through a small gap in heavy lace curtains I could make out the shapes of things: a couple of chairs, a table, possibly a bed.

Peering through the thick double-paned window, I shaded my eyes against the reflection of the patio over my shoulder. At the far end of the room, I could barely recognize a round, white-suited body—Jacques Vidanne, I assumed—pacing around a high-backed armchair.

My first impulse was to hide. What if my mother was sitting in the chair? I imagined her turning toward the sound at the window and, with the slow recognition that the daughter she had jettisoned twenty-five years earlier was trying to move back into her life, turning away to resume her conversation.

Tears stung my eyes. What was I doing here? I cursed Leland Dunne for dragging me to the gala, where Naomi had led me to my mother and Vidanne and finally to this unfriendly place. My heart suddenly ached for Claudel. Where was he now, when I needed him most? I'd done what he wanted me to do, hadn't I? And what had it gotten me?

The answer was simple. It had gotten me exactly what I'd brought with me to France: no Claudel, no mother, no answers, and no peace of mind. All I had for sure was an aging father and the possibility of a job I didn't even want. Nothing had changed.

I looked through the window, at Vidanne in his white suit, inside his comfortable house, where he lived with the mother he had stolen from me, and inside me something snapped. I had nothing to lose. I made a fist and rapped my knuckles against the window. Vidanne looked up from his conversation and glanced in the direction of the window. For a moment I thought he was going to signal me to come in through the door, but instead he turned back to his conversation with the flowered armchair. I knocked again, urgently, the way a person knocks on a door when a fire is creeping into a burning building. Vidanne's head spun around in alarm, and I hit the window one more time, as hard as I could, so hard my fist shattered the outer pane.

The second my hand broke the glass the world exploded in a flash of light so brilliant I thought it had come from inside my memory. My body went rigid. I felt shards of glass in my knuckles and heard a piercing crackle of electric energy that made the hairs on my arm stand on end. I sensed glass in my hair, between my fingers, flying over my shoulder. I turned my head to protect my eyes, and was almost blinded by a second explosion of light.

For a moment I was paralyzed, my arm extended into the cracked window with my bloodied fist at the end of it. And then several things happened at once: through the dizzying spots before my eyes I saw the outline of Vidanne's body run from the room, and the figure in the armchair turned to look in my direction. I heard a door slam as the ponytailed woman emerged from the back of the house.

I took all of this in as if it were on a movie screen split into three separate sections, and then a third explosion of light took the wind out of my chest. My knees buckled under me, and I staggered away from the window and fell backward onto the stone patio. My throat closed.

The woman with the ponytail was the first to reach me. I felt her fingers on my throat. The last thing I remember was looking up at the underside of Jacques Vidanne's linen-covered belly.

"*Éteingnez l'éclair*," he said. "And bring her inside."

> The reason lightning doesn't strike twice
> in the same place is that the same place
> doesn't exist the second time.
>
> Willie Tyler, comedian

14

Corsica

Saturday, May 17

When I opened my eyes, I was in darkness so complete it took several minutes to realize I hadn't slipped into the afterlife. I was lying on complicated whorls of lace. A soft pillow. All I could see was a thin slice of light peeking in through the bottom of a door. I pulled myself to a sitting position. The darkness was unsettling.

I felt around me and my hand found a rounded corner, a smooth surface—a bedside table?—and an electrical wire—a lamp? I followed the wire with my fingers, but I was too eager: the lamp fell to the floor with a loud crash. Footsteps on the other side of the door. Light! I had to cover my eyes at the sudden glare. When I took my hand away, all I could make out was the rounded silhouette of Jacques Vidanne standing at the open door.

"We did not expect you to arrive so quickly," he said in a voice that was not quite welcoming.

I sat with my back flat against the wall.

"You made quite an impression in Bonifacio," he said. "We received several phone calls."

My eyes stayed fixed on Vidanne's silhouette. "Where am I?" I said.

"In your mother's house."

He flicked on the light switch, and my eyes pinched half closed. The wall facing me was an enormous mirror, floor to ceiling. I felt myself recoil from it in a kind of horror. It was an expansive reflection that gave the impression of endless space and absolute seclusion, all at once. The sight of myself on the bed in the middle of this otherwise small, uncluttered space made me feel strangely isolated.

"When . . . I mean, what time is it?"

"Just after seven. You left us for only a short time."

"What happened to me? Was I— Did the lightning—"

"You were never in danger. It was your fear alone that frightened you."

Vidanne took a step into the room, and I put up my hand.

"As you wish," he said, raising his own hands in surrender.

I remembered the maquis, the nausea of the boat ride, the little castrato. And here I was. Where was my mother? I swung my feet over the edge of the bed and stood on the hardwood floor. "I want to see her."

"Of course. And you will, in a moment. Please." He moved to the side and gestured for me to leave the bedroom, and I stepped past him into an enormous living area.

As Vidanne closed the door behind him, I tried to take in the room, but it was impossible in one glance. It was a space that didn't end. The ceiling was two full stories high, and it seemed to include everything that most houses require several rooms to encompass: a kitchen, a sitting area with a couch and chairs around a glass coffee table, a dining space, a library, an exercise area with weights and pulleys, and a large window through which I could clearly see, in the fading evening light, the terrace and the rosebushes in back of the house. To the left of the door was a smaller window, and I felt myself flush with embarrassment when I saw the broken pane.

It seemed that a person could live an entire life in this room. It was a space that might have been created by a set designer, where all the dramatic action of a three-act play could take place without changing a single piece of furniture. The only thing that was missing was a place to sleep.

I could feel Vidanne watching me as I took it all in. A long spiral stairway in a far corner wound its way to a balcony along the back wall. Beside the staircase, a dark-skinned man, wearing a black shirt with sleeves rolled up to his biceps, stood over a pot of boiling water with a handful of spaghetti. He was whistling "La Marseillaise"—the French national anthem. Vidanne gave the man a withering look, and he grinned shyly in return and then stopped whistling.

"Natalie, I present to you Gérard, my right arm. Gérard is French, you see. Hence, his affection for the 'La Marseillaise.' Sometimes he forgets he now lives on *Corsica*."

Gérard broke the pasta in half and waved it at me. I thought, Vidanne, my mother, the ponytailed woman, Gérard . . . who else lived in this peculiar place?

Vidanne motioned for me to sit in a white leather chair.

"So. Here we are again," he said grandly, pulling a straight-backed chair from the dining table. "Your arrival was nearly simultaneous with mine. If you had found your way onto the property a few minutes earlier, we might have run into each other, and none of this would have happened."

Automatically I touched the top of my head, and then my stomach.

"You are unharmed," Vidanne said wearily. "Sédrine, whom you met again in Bonifacio, has put salve on your beleaguered hand."

I touched the raw skin on my knuckles. Only when I made a fist was it tender.

"It was not lightning at all," he said.

I looked at him blankly.

"It is an antiquated system of security." He leaned as far forward as his extensive abdomen permitted. "My studio technicians installed it years ago: movie magic, lights so bright they can blind you temporarily if you stare into them. At one time it was necessary, but it has not been activated in years. As you can see, it is still quite functional. I apologize for your unpleasant experience."

"I want to see my mother," I said.

Vidanne nodded. *"Absolument.* But there are some things you should know first. I ask your indulgence for a mere five minutes. And then I will take you to her."

I sat down and held my hands so tightly I could feel the sting on my knuckles. It reminded me that anger would get me nowhere.

"Alors," he said. "Our unexpected meeting at the Hôtel du Cap was awkward in the extreme, but I must say you behaved professionally, under the circumstances. Most impressive."

I squeezed my hands together. Was he actually trying to compliment me?

"When it was over," he continued, "I realized the time had come for me to respond to the deluge of phone calls Michel had made to my office."

"You talked to Claudel?"

"This morning. He informed me that you were on your way to us." Vidanne took a deep breath, then began to brush at a piece of lint on his pant leg. "You cannot imagine my surprise, finding you on the deck of the *Éclair.* Your mother and I go out so rarely together, but the chance to see the lights of Cannes—" He stopped suddenly and reached for a glass of red wine that was sitting on the coffee table. "May I offer you some wine?" he asked.

"No, you may not," I said, jaws clenched.

He shrugged and took an infuriatingly slow sip. "Frankly, I am badly prepared for an encounter such as this. I took every precaution to protect you."

"You are deranged if you believe you have protected me in any way."

He shook his head. "Such certainty. I wish only to emphasize that at the time of our decision, there was no intention of causing you pain. I was urgently in love with your mother." He paused. "And she loved me, in her way."

I said evenly, "I'm sure you can understand that what you felt for my mother is of no comfort to me."

"Of course. But let me apologize for any distress you might have suffered."

"Apologize?" I couldn't believe my ears.

"You must not blame your mother. It was I who felt that a new arrangement would be easier—"

"This is insane," I interrupted. "I have not come all this way to grant you forgiveness, Vidanne! Or to listen to your apologies!" Summoning every ounce of control I could muster, I stood up. "My mother is alive. Can you possibly imagine what that means to me?"

Vidanne started to speak but stopped himself. He pursed his lips, and I had the feeling that this scene was not playing out as he had written it in his mind.

I relaxed my hands at my sides and felt the sting on my knuckles fade away. "I'm her daughter. You can't keep me from her."

"Natalie—"

"Please!"

"*Bon*," he said finally. He stood, placed his glass on the table, and nodded toward the back door. I followed him to the patio.

The light was gone completely, but I could see a glow on the other side of the wall as we crossed the terrace. Beyond the roses I heard water splashing. Vidanne opened the iron latch on the gate and motioned for me to pass through it.

A wave of fear stopped me as I approached the gate. All at once it dawned on me what was happening—that after twenty-five years of yearning, I was actually going to see my mother—and I realized I was totally unprepared. For all my planning, I hadn't really expected to get this far. A jumble of questions I hadn't thought to ask flooded my head. What did she know about my life? Would I be what she expected? Would she see any of herself in me? Be proud of how I'd turned out? Angry that I'd found her? She'd rejected me once. I wasn't sure I wanted to go through that again.

But more urgently, I wanted her to see me and to know that she had made a terrible mistake. I tried to catch a glimpse of myself in the window, but it was too far to see myself clearly. I ran my fingers through my hair and pulled it back as neatly as I could.

"Natalie?" Vidanne said, still holding the gate for me.

I thought of what Claudel had said, about the unwelcome responsibility of taking care of a child and how my mother had wanted me to grow up, immediately if possible. Well, here I was, a grown woman. I had finally become what she'd wanted.

The gate was open. In defiance of Vidanne and my mother and all the years I'd spent missing her, I stepped through it. Three stairs led from the patio to the pond, and they were the hardest steps I'd ever taken. Vidanne waited until I reached the bottom before he closed the gate behind him.

I saw the ponytailed Sédrine first, standing waist-deep in the pool of water. As I approached, she looked up at me and nodded.

And then I stopped moving. Vidanne stood so close to me our shoulders were touching.

On the surface of the water, a woman lay, her face toward the sky, supported by Sédrine's hands in the center of her back. The woman's blonde hair floated around her head. Her eyes were closed, and the corners of her mouth were lifted in the trace of a smile. She was wearing a white one-piece bathing suit, and the toenails of one foot, which poked out of the water slightly, were painted a brilliant red. She was still as lovely as she'd been in Vidanne's film and in the picture I'd stolen from my father.

The only light was an uncanny blue glow from around the pool. White skin, white fabric. Her eyebrows arched perfectly over her closed eyes.

I choked back tears.

She kicked her foot in a slow luxurious circle and moved her arms as if she were making an angel in the snow.

In a soft, even voice, Vidanne said, *"Katherine?"*

My mother's head lifted, and she opened her eyes to see me standing above her.

Her smile vanished.

For a moment she stared at me vacantly, and I thought she was going to speak. I didn't want to take my eyes from her, afraid of missing a clue to what she was thinking. The tension between us was palpable, and for a horrifying moment I wondered if Vidanne had even told her I was here. I waited, thinking that even if she didn't want me in her life, she would at least have to respond to my presence.

I said to myself, You're a grown-up now. Act like a grown-up. But I didn't feel like one. I felt like a frightened six-year-old.

I took a deep breath. In English, I said, "I am Natalie, your daughter."

She began to move back in the pool but lost her footing in the water. Sédrine helped to steady her. Her eyes never left my face.

I came closer, and it was a moment before I realized that she was not looking at me at all, but past me, just over my shoulder. I glanced behind me, but no one was there.

And then, to my astonishment, she turned her head to Sédrine and leaned back in the water.

I turned helplessly to Vidanne. He met my gaze and then briskly clapped his hands to get Sédrine's attention, exactly as he'd done on the *Éclair*. He twirled his finger in the air: Wrap it up.

Sédrine brought my mother to a standing position, but my mother refused to stay there. She let herself fall backward, and her mouth twisted into a determined grimace as she slapped her hands on the surface of the water. Sédrine lifted her by the shoulders, and my mother tried to wrench out of her grasp, but Sédrine was taller and much stronger: she turned her until they were face-to-face. When my mother continued to fight, Sédrine leaned in close and shook her head. *"Arrêtez."* Stop.

My mother stopped struggling. Sédrine led her to the rock steps at the end of the pool and she sat on the top stair.

Her face wasn't perfect. I could see twenty-five years of fine lines on her forehead and around her eyes. But her features were delicate and perfectly symmetrical, and her lips, so different from my own, were full and sensuous. Her blonde hair hung in wet strings around her face, which began to take on a strange scowl when she saw me watching her. It was not the expression of a woman whose unwanted daughter had surprised her in the swimming pool. It was the look of an animal in a trap.

A moment ago I'd been frightened by her indifference. Now I had no idea what to feel. I turned again to Vidanne, but he put up his hand.

"Please," he said almost in a whisper. "Wait until she is gone." He handed me a towel and motioned for me to take it to her. I wrapped the towel over my mother's shoulders. Without looking up at me, she pulled it tightly around her.

"Katherine," Vidanne said, and the sound of his voice was so tender, I had to look to be sure it had come from him.

My mother lifted her head to him.

"Je te présente Natalie," he said.

A tiny movement of her head in my direction.

Vidanne motioned to Sédrine, who stepped around the corner of the pool and took my mother's hand. She stepped out of the pool—her legs long and slender beneath the towel—and with Sédrine's hand barely touching the middle of her back, she set off toward the stairs to the patio. She stopped at the foot of the steps, and I wondered if she was waiting for help. But Sédrine said, "*Allez-y,*" and my mother continued up the stairs. She and Sédrine disappeared through the gate.

For a minute neither of us spoke. Vidanne broke the silence.

"I had hoped to prepare you. But perhaps it was better for you to see her for yourself."

"What's wrong with her?"

"*Évidemment,* she sustained extensive damage from the accident. It is a condition known as Broca's aphasia. A difficulty in producing and comprehending speech."

"She can't talk?"

"She is able to use words of content—verbs, nouns, adjectives. But her vocabulary is not extensive." Vidanne cleared his throat. "The lightning damaged this hemisphere of her frontal lobe," he said, touching the left side of his head, "the region of speech function."

"But we talked to one of her doctors. He said her recovery was a miracle."

"And so it was. Miraculous that she regained consciousness at all. But she was not as lucky as you were, Natalie."

On the patio above us, the door to the house slammed. I turned in the direction of the stairs, as if she might materialize again, but there was only darkness.

"She doesn't even remember me," I said.

He shook his head almost imperceptibly and said, "Please sit down. I understand that it is awkward to speak of these things. But there is a great deal to explain." He gestured to a chair beside the pool, and I sat without protest. Vidanne flicked a switch on the wall and an eerie light shone from the rock face and flooded the area around us.

As I watched him position the furniture and adjust the lighting for this encounter, I tried to piece together the scene in the hospital when my mother had awakened. How had he managed everything that followed?

"In Briançon," I said. "Was she like this when she woke up?"

"*Ah, non,* much, much worse. In the beginning, she was unable to speak at all. It has taken many years of hard work for her to regain even the most rudimentary of skills. We have concentrated only on French. She has no memory of English, I am afraid." He paused for a moment and lowered his head, remembering. "She was also terrified."

"Of what?" I asked, although I had a memory of the moment I'd awakened in the hospital. I'd been frightened, too.

He sighed audibly. "What do you know about lightning?" he asked.

I stared at him incredulously.

"Please. I am not referring to personal knowledge. Of course you are uniquely informed by your own experience. My question is general in nature. Do you know the range of destruction that lightning can cause to the human body? It can affect the brain, the central nervous system. The immediate effects can be minimal, or they can be more dramatic, as they are with Katherine. They can be temporary, or they can subside with time." He crossed his arms over his large abdomen. "But you must be aware that there are other complications that may arise from these accidents, which are, if you will permit me to borrow a line from Saint-Exupéry, 'invisible to the eye.' "

I shifted uneasily in my chair, and Vidanne looked down at his hands as if choosing his words carefully. "You were perhaps too young to remember, but she was very fond of attention. The adulation of others was almost, *comment dirais-je,* an aphrodisiac."

It was hardly the kind of thing I wanted to hear about my mother, but I thought of what Claudel had said about her loving the fuss that was made when *Zeitgeist* was released.

Vidanne continued. "After the accident, her pleasure in crowds became distorted. Where once she had taken delight, she felt only dread. She was agitated in public places and with unfamiliar people. We wanted to believe that she would recover. Therapies, medications. But it was an unrealistic fiction. She remained in a state of almost constant panic. And so I removed her from the world, because her fear of it had become unbearable."

I looked at Vidanne through narrowed eyes. "But she does go into public places. You took her to Cannes; the people in Bonifacio know her—"

"And over time she came to know them. Which is precisely why I am able to take her there, on rare occasions. You may have noticed that Bonifacio is not a bustling metropolis. To a certain extent, I am able to control the surroundings there." With an indulgent smile he said, "And she trusts me, Natalie. It is as complex and as simple as that.

"As you see, she is good-natured. And calm, unless she is asked to do something she does not wish to do. Most of the time I would even describe her as contented. Her only residual fear is of lightning. Hence the system of security."

I felt a chill across my shoulders. It made perfect sense.

"The lightning," I said, "is to keep her in, not to keep people out."

He nodded. "Initially, when I brought her here, we worried that once she grew comfortable she might begin to wander. The system turned out to be necessary only once, partly because we do not leave her alone. We stay with her until she is asleep and keep careful watch should she awaken and become frightened. Her needs are taken care of. She is fond of Sédrine and Gérard. But she has no initiative."

"What does that mean?"

"She cannot make the connection between something she wants and how to get it." He leaned forward with his hands on his knees. "For example, she loves the feel of the water. But she would never make the necessary connections required to move from the house to the swimming pool. If she is instructed at each interval, she will change from her clothing to her swimming suit, walk to the pool, step into the water . . . you see what I am saying? She will do whatever she is told to do. But without external prompting, she will remain indefinitely. She will stay in the sun until she is badly burned or forget to drink water unless we give it to her."

"I don't understand how they let you leave the hospital with her."

He folded his arms over his abdomen and sat back in his chair. "You might say it was dumb luck: a convergence of fortune and necessity. There was an emergency of some sort, many injuries. The hospital was small, and they needed her bed. And she was in perfect physical health. In such a remote area, there was nothing more they could do for her. The doctors in Briançon recommended better facilities, extensive therapies, all of which I promised, and provided. In endless quantities."

"You told them you were her husband."

"It was merely a matter of timing: hours later, on the same day. A small stretch of the truth."

I felt as if his words had slapped me. "A small stretch? You lied to everyone! My father, Claudel."

"You think I should be ashamed? I am not. Michel had taken you to Paris. The opportunity presented itself, so I took it. Arranging the funeral was nothing. I am a producer of films. It is my business to create illusions. And there was no one to care for her as I could. I loved her, even as she was. I knew her best chance for recovery was with me."

"I don't believe you. It was because she had money."

An impatient smile crept across his face and he leaned closer. "Silly girl. Every centime that was hers has been returned to her estate. And caring for her has dominated my life. This valley was designed for her. If I wanted nothing but her money, would I have bothered to create this environment for her, lived the way I have lived? I have never enjoyed the affection from her that a man can expect from a normal woman. We have never lived as husband and wife. But, as you can see, I remain with her."

"I would have remained with her," I said pathetically, "but you never gave me the chance." It was senseless to argue with him, but I couldn't stop myself. "You ruined my life."

"I? I ruined your life?" He laughed. "I did no such thing! The lightning struck you, I did not."

"You turned everything I cared about into a lie!" I was nearly shaking I was so angry. "And then you turned it into a movie!"

"*Aimée* ended happily, did it not?"

"It was a *movie*! You stopped her story when she was five years old—I have lived my whole life. And no one told me the truth."

"The truth," he said, as if it were irrelevant. "The only truth that matters is that your mother is comfortable." He held his shoulders back in a position of pride. "I defy you to tell me otherwise, and I will take your punishment. But ask yourself"—and here he softened—"what kind of life would you have wanted for her? For *her*, I ask you. Who would have cared for her like this? You were only a child. Your friend Michel, perhaps? He was in no condition to care for anyone."

"He would have cared for *me*. You made that impossible."

"*Ah, oui, ça,*" he scoffed. "Do you mean to say it would have been acceptable to deceive the innocent father, but unacceptable to tell the handsome young lover a lie?"

It was an infuriating argument, but even Claudel had come to that realization. I stood up and stepped away from Vidanne. I wrapped my arms around myself.

"I assumed the responsibility for her," he said to my back, "and gave you the freedom to live your lives."

I wheeled around and glared at Vidanne. He believed what he

was saying! In his view, he had saved me from a fate worse than being torn from Claudel and my mother: he had protected me from the burden of her care.

He put his hands flat on his knees and said, "I will leave you now. Perhaps it will be easier to digest these facts without my interference." He paused for a moment and added, "Believe me when I say that I understand how alarming this must be for you."

I felt as if he'd thrown a heavy stone at my chest. I squeezed my hands into fists, and, feeling the now-familiar sting that reminded me to control my temper, wondered how in the broadest stretch of his self-centered, misguided imagination Jacques Vidanne could possibly comprehend how alarming this was for me.

Vidanne had wielded power over me for my entire life, and I hadn't even known it. I felt sore, inside and out. And as he raised himself to his full, round height until he was standing only inches from the edge of the pool, I did the only thing within *my* power: I put the palm of my hand on his shoulder and pushed him as hard as I could in the direction of the water.

It wasn't a violent shove, but he was so top-heavy, his body careened to the side and all his weight shifted to the leg closest to the pool. His other leg flew up to counterbalance him, and his arms flailed unsuccessfully in an effort to right his equilibrium. And in a slow, graceful arc, his arms still flapping in the air as if flight would save him, he fell into the water with a fantastic splash that caused a minor deluge around my feet.

There was a deep *whomp* as his bulk created a vacuum that enveloped him. He was barely submerged when the spatter began to fall, landing like little aquatic pellets on the surface of the water. Then the pool was silent.

For a moment nothing happened. The handkerchief that had protruded proudly from his breast pocket seconds before was floating near the edge, and I bent over to rescue it. Still there was no movement from under the water. And then, so slowly I might have thought he'd planned it just for the effect of dignity it created, his head emerged from the water and he walked straight to the stairs and out of the pool.

He took the last step onto the deck and stood, sopping wet from the tip of his nose to the cuffs of his pants. We faced each other for a long moment, and then I did something that surprised even me. I took the soggy handkerchief and twisted it until all the water had been squeezed from it. Then I spread it on the palm of my hand and wiped the droplets of water from his face.

Vidanne's eyes were huge as I moved the handkerchief across his chin, his lips, and under his nose, until not even a sheen of dampness remained on his face. Then I pinched the handkerchief at the center of the fabric with the tips of my fingers, shook it once to loosen the corners, and eased it carefully into his pocket.

He watched every gesture without saying a word, as if it were all part of a necessary ritual, and when it was over, he looked me straight in the eye.

"*Eh bien,*" he said, bowing his head slightly. He brushed the excess moisture from the lapels of his coat with the fingers of one hand. "We will expect you for dinner." He set off toward the patio. He'd only taken a few steps before he turned to me again. "Perhaps your childhood was not ideal. But you will find that it was a small part of your life."

He turned and made his way through the darkness to his house. I watched him climb the stairs and then disappear. When the door slammed I leaned against the wall. I slid down until I was sitting on cold stones. My childhood. A lifetime of questions. And now, what difference did knowing the answers make?

Vidanne, my mother, and Sédrine were sitting at the table when I came into the house. The curtains were drawn over the broken window. Vidanne had changed into a clean, dry white suit, and

Sédrine had done her job well: my mother was elegant in a soft blue dress, with a diamond choker around her neck. She was perfectly made up—a little mascara, some light coral lipstick— and her blonde hair fell in natural waves just to her shoulders. She looked like any attractive middle-aged woman dressed up for dinner.

Vidanne pulled out a chair for me, directly across the table from my mother.

The meal was shrimp and pasta salad prepared by Gérard, who stayed in the kitchen corner. As he tapped his wooden spoon on the edge of a pan, he began to whistle the "La Marseillaise" again, in a slow, dirgelike rhythm. When I turned to look at him, he waved with his spoon. Vidanne saw the wave, tore off a piece of his baguette, and pitched it across the room at the cook.

The man put up his spoon just in time to deflect the morsel and gave a little laugh. Vidanne chuckled to himself and returned to his meal without comment. It was hard to imagine Vidanne with a sense of humor, but there it was.

The table was set with splendid crystal and elaborate silver settings that sparkled in the candlelight. Vidanne poured a clear white wine into our glasses like an amiable host, as if he'd invited me to dinner on purpose. My mother's glass was filled with water.

Since it was apparently necessary to avoid speaking about my mother in her presence, our dinner conversation was as innocuous as one overheard in a post office.

"How is the festival, from the perspective of an American journalist?" Vidanne asked.

"Exhausting. Frantic," I said carefully. My mother turned her eyes on me, but when I glanced directly at her, they darted away. "And frustrating, as I imagine it is even for French journalists. But the films are good."

Vidanne said, "And what a fine occasion for me to ask an insider: what was the critical response to *Le Vol?*"

"The audience seemed to love it," I said. Across the table my mother was pointing her spoon at me.

Sédrine saw her and patted her hand down. With a smile she said to me, "She wants so much to be a part of things."

"And you, Natalie? How did you find *Le Vol*?" Vidanne said.

"As I told you yesterday, it's a beautiful film. I hope it does well."

"Thank you," he said politely.

I followed Vidanne's lead of gracious decorum, out of respect, or awe perhaps, for this new creature who was at once my mother and not my mother. It was a pleasant meal, in spite of the fact that Vidanne was the director of this scene. I answered his questions courteously, watching my mother's eyes on every word.

The only time she spoke was when dessert was served. She picked up her spoon again and pointed it across the table, straight at me. With a serious purse to her lips, she said, "Crème brûlée."

It was very funny, but I felt it would be wrong to laugh at her. Vidanne, on the other hand, burst out in a throaty guffaw and then dabbed his mouth with his napkin.

"Do you like crème brûlée?" I said, but she was already spooning the dessert into her mouth.

When the serving dish of crème brûlée had been scraped clean, Gérard brought us coffee and Vidanne began to tell a story about filming *Le Vol*. My mother was not listening to Vidanne. She'd begun again to point at me—this time with her finger at the table's edge, subtly aimed in my direction—while she stared at my blouse. When Sédrine saw her, she laughed and rose from her seat, nodding politely to the rest of us, and together they left the table. I watched my mother glide across the room—it was hard not to watch her, she was so lovely. They disappeared into the bedroom where I had awakened a lifetime ago, and I turned to Vidanne.

"May I ask . . ." I said, and Vidanne looked up, as if he'd forgotten I was there, "what that was all about? Why did she keep pointing at me?"

He laughed softly. "I do not pretend to understand what goes through her mind—there is no examination to dissect a human thought, is there? But Sédrine takes such pains with her appearance, I can easily imagine that she was alarmed at the condition of your clothing." I looked down. My blouse was now badly wrinkled and smudged with dirt. One of the sleeves was torn in two places, and there were spots of blood on the front of it from my encounter with the window. I put my hand over the blood.

"I apologize," Vidanne said. "I should have offered you a change of clothes the moment you awakened." There was a long pause, and he looked at me through narrowed eyes, as if he were trying to see me through a lens. "She acknowledged you," he said. "That was something."

He held his glass at the stem and moved it in a slow circle. I was surprised at the sadness in his face. I was thinking about his lonely life, into which the occasional appearance of someone like Naomi must have seemed like the Hallelujah Chorus, when Sédrine appeared at the bedroom door and beckoned to me with a wave.

"She wants Natalie to join us."

Vidanne raised an eyebrow.

"What should I do?" I asked him.

"*Allez-y,*" he said to me with enthusiasm. Go ahead.

In the bedroom, Sédrine closed the door behind us. My mother was moving past the enormous mirror I'd noticed earlier, to a bank of drawers set into the wall.

"The top," Sédrine said, and my mother picked something out of the top drawer. "You can give it to her, Katherine," she said, but my mother remained by the drawers without moving. "Come and give it to her."

She crossed the room without looking at me, handed me a soft green velveteen sweat suit, and pointed at my blouse.

"Thank you," I said. Apart from this unexpected generosity, I

was delighted to have something clean to wear. Sédrine motioned
to me to feel free to change.

My mother clasped her hands behind her and watched me
remove my blouse and step out of my slacks. When I stood straight,
with nothing left but my underwear, she gasped and pointed at my
abdomen. My scar was in full view.

"*C'est une cicatrice,*" I said. She stepped toward me, and I held
my breath. With her index finger she reached out hesitantly to
touch my scar. I said, "It doesn't hurt anymore. I had an accident,
with lightning."

My mother's mouth opened in surprise. She touched the diamond necklace she was wearing and struggled to pull it off. Sédrine
reached quickly to unhook it, and my mother ran her fingers over
a thin scar that wrapped around her neck like a choker. I hadn't
noticed it in the pool. It was narrower, but like mine it was slightly
shiny, and paler than the surrounding skin.

"*La même,*" she said. *The same.*

I swallowed hard. "*Oui. La même.*"

Her smile was filled with shared pleasure, and I could barely
keep myself from putting my arms around her. I reached over and
touched the scar around her neck.

She flinched a little and then pointed again at my filthy blouse.
I put the sweat suit on without hesitation. As I pulled the shirt over
my head, Sédrine pulled down the zipper of my mother's dress. The
dress and the silk slip underneath fell to her feet in a rumpled heap
of fabric. My mother turned her back to me modestly and Sédrine
removed her bra and stockings.

And as she stood there, waiting for Sédrine to bring her nightgown, her naked body slender and lovely despite the years and the
trauma it had endured, she turned and stole a glance over her
shoulder at her image in the mirror.

It was a tiny gesture, so brief I might have missed it had I not
been watching every movement she made, but the look in her eye

as she caught herself in the mirror froze my heart. Suddenly I was six again, and back in the sunny Paris apartment. I was pulling at the hem of her skirt, trying to get her attention, pleading with her to notice me. But she was transfixed by her mirror, as if I weren't there at all.

The image lasted only a second, but it was so vivid, I had to hold the door for support.

In her nightgown, my mother looked almost regal. The gown was made of soft blue satiny material, and it was long and sleeveless with a high neck. She moved her hands over the curves of her hips and thighs—a gesture of sensation, I thought, to feel the fabric more than to feel her body—and smiled at her reflection. Sédrine gave her a little nudge, and, still smiling and smoothing the gown over her body, my mother disappeared into the adjoining bathroom.

Quietly, Sédrine said to me, "I will tell Monsieur that she is ready."

Vidanne came into the room and my mother stepped out of the bathroom. I watched as he gave her a tender *bise* on each cheek.

"*Bisous*," she said. Little kisses. He laughed and waited as Sédrine helped her into bed. It was as if I were observing them through a one-way mirror: a nightly ritual that belonged to the three of them. I was completely forgotten. There was something haunting about the whole scene, but I knew my perception of it was mingled with newly remembered gloom. When she'd been carefully tucked under her covers, Vidanne led me back into the living area, where we'd sat awkwardly earlier in the evening.

"You may make yourself comfortable here." He motioned to the leather sofa and a pile of blankets and pillows Sédrine had prepared for me. "There is a small *toilette*, which you are welcome to use. As we never have guests, we have only enough beds for the four of us. But these chairs are designed for maximum comfort. You should have no problem finding a restful sleep."

I hardly thought that was likely, but I thanked him politely, and he bowed ridiculously from his pudgy middle. "Until tomorrow," he said.

I found my way to the *toilette*, and when I was returning to the couch, I saw that the door to my mother's room was open a tiny crack. When I pushed, it swung open silently.

My mother lay peacefully under her covers, and I tiptoed to the bed, careful not to wake her. I knew that if she were to wake up and find me standing over her, she would not be so calm: I was a stranger to her, an aberration in her well-ordered world. Vidanne had directed the story of her life so that she had nothing to fear. Was anyone else's life as simple as that? And yet it seemed that we were all looking for that absolute sense that we were safe. I'd lived my whole life hoping for that assurance, waiting for even nature to swear allegiance to me. Was I so different from my mother? In her isolated, artificial world such promises were possible. She was utterly protected, totally confident that nothing would harm her. But it was hardly a life. I wanted something better for myself.

I leaned over and put my lips to her forehead, as softly as a human being could touch another. I could hardly find enough air to fill my lungs. The tears I'd been holding back since I'd first set eyes on Claudel seven days before began to stream from my eyes. I didn't try to stop them.

We accept the reality of the world
with which we're presented.

Ed Harris, in *The Truman Show*

15

Corsica

Sunday, May 18

$\mathcal{A}$nd now what? All I knew for sure was that the future was not what it used to be. Who had said that? Probably Balzac.

It was my first thought on waking in my mother's house, and it made me think of Claudel. I wondered where he was.

I left the couch and tiptoed to the *toilette*. When I saw myself in the mirror, I gasped. My eyes were pink and puffy, my hair was a disaster, and I was wearing a sweat suit of an awful green color. It was the dusty shade of a used tennis ball, the worst color I'd ever seen, but I remembered my mother choosing it for me, and I felt a strange sense of tenderness for her that made even chartreuse bearable.

I pulled my wayward hair back in a rubber band, splashed water on my face, and when I emerged the room was still empty, so I slipped out the front door to see the house in the morning light, while everything was quiet.

The valley Vidanne had built for my mother had the crisp green perfection of an expensive postcard. The water fell over the edge of the slope and into the swimming pool. From there the river snaked along the valley floor as if designed by a power higher than Vidanne. It practically glistened.

I was looking down on the moss- and ivy-covered slates of the roof when I realized that this was what movie directors were trying to convey when they pulled the camera up for an overhead shot: the God Shot, someone had called it, to give the audience a chance to step out of the action so they could see the whole picture, observe it from a loftier perspective.

And here was the whole picture of this house: a damaged woman living a solitary life, pampered and protected because a man had loved her. That was what it amounted to. It didn't matter that I hadn't known about it. It didn't matter what I thought about it now.

My father's words echoed in my ears: "In the natural world, everything is exactly where it belongs. The rocks, the animals, the predators, even the lightning falls where it must. . . . The trick for human beings is to figure out where they belong."

I looked out over the valley that Vidanne had claimed for my mother, at its insane, movie-poster perfection and the bizarre security system he'd created to keep her safe. I considered the isolated, obsessive genius of it, and realized that this was where she belonged. No one else was necessary in this life. Certainly not me.

For a moment I imagined myself disappearing through the maquis and out the gate to the other side of the wall, where my life was waiting, but I still had to say good-bye. Being a grown-up was going to take some getting used to.

When I walked through the front door, Gérard waved to me from the kitchen.

"Good morning, Natalie," Vidanne said, sipping gingerly from his café au lait. "Please join me. Did you have a pleasant walk?"

"*Oui*," I said.

Gérard arrived with a bowl of foam for me. I spooned in sugar. Except for the ticking of the clock, Vidanne and I sat in silence as my sugar dissolved.

"Monsieur Vidanne?" I said, and my voice pierced the stillness. "Where is my mother?"

"Sédrine has just taken her for their morning *plongement*. We will see her again soon," he said, offering me a baguette.

We ate with our eyes on our plates, and when my bowl was empty, Vidanne patted his chest with his pudgy hand. "*Voilà*. My heart is beginning to beat again." He stood and adjusted his coat with a couple of sharp tugs.

"Natalie," he said. "Will you please accompany me upstairs? It is a small business matter, and we will both feel more comfortable in my office."

I followed him up the staircase to a carpeted loft that over-looked the massive living room. It must surely have been con-structed so Vidanne had a clear view of my mother at all times. Through an open door I could see his bedroom, where a stack of screenplays was balanced on a table beside a bed.

"*Asseyez-vous*," he said, indicating the chair facing him. He took his seat behind a desk of thick glass.

I wasn't surprised to see the framed poster of *Zeitgeist*—the same one Claudel had given me—hanging on the wall behind his desk. And beside it two small video monitors, each the size of an average TV, set into the paneled wall. One was focused on my mother's bedroom; the other showed a full view of the swimming pool, where I could clearly see my mother and Sédrine. As Vidanne busied himself with something from his desk, I watched my mother move gracefully through the water as she'd done the night before. She was so lovely it was eerie to watch her.

"She looks younger than I expected," I said, almost to myself.

Vidanne turned to the monitor, where she lay peacefully on the water, like a portrait of Ophelia.

"A small advantage of her condition," he said with a bittersweet smile. "The autonomic nervous system is no longer controlled by the brain, so stress has no impact on the body. She is in flawless health."

He allowed me to watch the monitor for another moment, and then he said, "Which brings me to our business. I wish to propose an arrangement that will benefit both you and your mother."

That was enough to get my attention. He picked up a collapsible folder and snapped off the elastic band. It stretched open like an accordion, and he pulled out a document encased in blue paper and placed it on the desk between us. It was a calculated process; he was arranging the props, as he had the night before beside the pool, preparing the scene for what was to follow.

"*Bon*," he said, folding his hands on the desk. "Your arrival was so unexpected, I hardly had time to appreciate the implications of these new circumstances."

"What implications?" I said. "What circumstances?" As far as I could tell, nothing had changed for any of us except that I had learned the truth.

"You have found your mother," he said.

He paused, and I hoped he wasn't waiting for me to respond to the obvious—I had no idea what he was talking about.

"I am not an old man, Natalie, but Katherine is younger and, as I said, her body is also much healthier than mine." He sat back in his chair. "For several years, I have harbored a growing anxiety regarding the future. Sédrine and Gérard are devoted to Katherine's well-being, but I cannot expect them to live in this isolation forever."

He paused again, as if his proposition were so delicate he had to feed it to me in installments.

"You are your mother's only family."

It was true. There were no other relatives, as far as I knew. I started to nod in agreement, but all of a sudden I realized where this was going.

"Let me be clear," he said. "Should I precede her in death, I would like to offer you the opportunity to become her guardian." He placed his hand on the blue document, and I felt my face flush.

"Monsieur Vidanne . . . ," I began, and shook my head in amazement.

"I offer you the prospect of a connection with your mother. Who else will care for her as I have done? Even Sédrine and Gérard are here only because I pay them handsomely. But I have seen for myself your concern and affection. . . ." He watched my face carefully.

I didn't know what to say. What he was offering me was a second chance. I had been too small either to understand or to accept responsibility for her at the age of six. Now I was fully capable of both.

Still, it was an outrageous proposition. I couldn't even begin to imagine what was involved in her care. "Monsieur Vidanne," I said. "You're asking the wrong person here. You cannot possibly know how ill-equipped I am for a commitment like this."

"*Quelle bêtise,*" he scoffed. "Look what you have accomplished! A mystery unfolded. And never once did you run from your goal. You have come a very long way to where you are today, Natalie."

"You're wrong, Monsieur Vidanne. I—"

"Even in the face of my careful security, you found her. You have behaved in a civilized manner. I can think of no one more qualified."

Civilized? I'd pushed him into his own pool!

"This is ridiculous," I said. "I only accepted the job in Cannes because I'm on the verge of losing my house in America. I've been unemployed for almost a year. I can barely afford to take care of myself, let alone another human being."

He leaned forward with his arms on the desk. "Your naïveté is enchanting. Of course I know these things! Do you think I have been idle in the days since you appeared on my boat? Do you imagine I would make such an offer to someone whose life I had not investigated to the full extent of my capabilities? There is nothing about your finances, or the choices you have made in your life so far, that I do not know about . . ."

The thought of him probing into my life made my stomach tighten.

". . . and admire." For a perverse moment I almost wanted to thank him. "*En tout cas,* there will be money from both your mother's estate and my own. Many years ago I made the legal provision for those funds to be made available to her caregiver in perpetuity. Finances are of no concern."

My mother's inheritance, I thought. Vidanne's fortune. I tried to imagine a life in which finances were of no concern.

Vidanne's fingers drummed on the blue paper.

And in a moment of clarity that was like stepping out of a cave, I realized that Vidanne needed me, for reasons that had nothing to do with the ones he was giving. The balance of power that existed between us the evening before had undergone an overhaul: now I was in control. I could change the course of his life as quickly as he had changed the course of my life with that phone call to my father. With a single call to Vince Draper or even Leland Dunne, his reputation would be ruined. He might even end up in jail. He needed me to be on his side.

In my head I saw Vidanne in one of those maddening movie montages designed to illuminate the passage of time. I saw him at the hospital in Briançon, seizing the opportunity to spirit my mother away like Dustin Hoffman escaping with Katherine Ross in *The Graduate,* sure that his love was strong enough to make her well. I wondered if there had been a time when he believed his life with my mother might resemble a normal marriage. As the years wore on and there was little change, what must he have thought about the decision he'd made, which had bound him inexorably to her? My mother was his forever, even though she had not chosen him. He had gotten what he wanted. But look what it had cost him.

We looked at each other across the desk for a long moment before I said, "She may be my mother, but I don't know her at all."

The sides of his mouth raised microscopically. *"Bien sûr.* My demise is not imminent. I encourage you to return to Corsica whenever you can."

I nodded, but my mind had already left Vidanne's office. In the living area below I heard the clock chime and I looked at my watch: nine o'clock. I said, "There's a car coming for me at the post office in two hours, to take me back to Bonifacio."

"I will send Sédrine to compensate your driver."

"I need to go back to the festival," I said. "I have to finish what I started. Tonight the festival is over, and I need to file a story after the closing ceremonies."

Vidanne shrugged. "My helicopter will have you in Cannes in half an hour."

"That's very kind, Monsieur Vidanne, but I want to return the way I came. I have a lot to think about."

"Very well. Gérard will drive you to Bonifacio."

"Thank you." We sat without speaking for several minutes. I looked at the monitor over his shoulder. My mother was holding on to the edge of the pool and kicking her legs. Water splashed all around her, and Sédrine put her hands in the air in mock distress.

Vidanne watched me. "Would you like to sit with her before you go?"

"Yes, I would." I stood up and headed for the stairs.

"You must not frighten her," he said behind me.

I made my way to the terrace and stopped at the gate, with a full view of the pool below, where my mother was playing in the water with Sédrine. She lowered herself until she was completely submerged, and Sédrine tapped her on the head and she burst out of the water.

A heavy melancholy fell over me as I watched them. If something happened to Vidanne, someone would have to care for her here. She was bound to this place, but I was free to do whatever I chose with my life. My only obligation was to myself, and that was more valuable than a life with financial security.

Sédrine took hold of my mother's feet and she moved her arms as if she were swimming. After a few minutes, she made her way to the pool stairs, and Sédrine led her to a wrought-iron chaise longue. When I motioned to Sédrine to leave us alone, my mother's face showed signs of panic, but Sédrine assured her that she would not go far.

I sat on a rock next to her. Her hair was wet, and water still glistened on her cheeks. "Katherine?" I said, and the edges of her mouth turned up slightly. It looked like a genuine smile, but a moment later she turned away from me and stared at her fingernails, as if she were waiting for them to grow.

The memory I'd had the night before began to fade like a ghost beside me. I understood then that regardless of whether she knew who I was, whether her memory had been wiped clean by the lightning or she was simply choosing not to acknowledge me, I could tug on her skirt for the rest of my life and she would never give me what I needed.

I looked beyond her, beyond the gate, and saw Vidanne peering down at us from the roses. And then I took a deep breath and said to my mother, "I want to tell you something."

There was no reaction, not even a flicker of her eyelids to suggest she was listening. "I don't expect you to respond," I said, "and it doesn't matter if you don't understand me. But I want to tell you who I am. What has happened to me since we sat on top of that mountain, on your birthday."

So I told her about my life. I told her about growing up in the desert, about the work that had brought me back to France, and the bizarre circumstances that had led me to that boat. I told her that in spite of everything that had happened, in spite of the lightning and the fact that I'd done it without a mother, I had grown into a good person. I told her that I'd found Claudel again. And I thought one day soon I would find my way out of the desert.

As I spoke, she sat placidly in her chair. The only time she seemed to be listening was when I told her about my father. I said I knew he wasn't the most exciting man on the planet—and I thought I saw a bit of a smile when I said it.

"But I need to tell you that he's a decent man," I said. "And he was a good father to me. I thought you'd like to know that."

My mother turned to me, and for the tiniest second she looked me straight in the eye. Her glance was unreadable, but it chilled me to the bone.

I stayed beside her, not speaking, for a long time, as if I were keeping vigil at a deathbed.

After a while, I heard a car start in the driveway and realized it was time to go. Sédrine rose from her chair by the waterfall, and I gave her a little wave. I put my hand on my mother's shoulder, but she shrugged out of my grasp and then closed her eyes.

"Perhaps I'll come again," I said.

The "Marseillaise"-whistling Gérard was in the driver's seat of the Range Rover when I came out of the house, and Vidanne stood in the driveway.

"Natalie," he said. "Despite the difficulties, I have enjoyed our encounter. I hope you will return. You are welcome in this house."

"Thank you," I said.

He checked the status of the button on his jacket. "If you have need of anything—a job, perhaps, with Éclair—do not hesitate to call me. You would be a great asset."

"That's very generous," I said, wondering if I might consider working for his company if it were the last job on earth. "We'll see."

Gérard revved the engine. But Vidanne, as usual, was directing this scene. He grasped the handle of the car door and cleared his throat. "I'm afraid I was not much of a host," he said.

"Well," I said, "considering that I broke into your house, I suppose I was not much of a guest."

Neither of us spoke after that, and I felt the edgy loosening of tension that battling nations strive for: détente. I think perhaps Vidanne felt it, too, because his eyes had softened when he helped me into the back seat of the car.

Gérard put the car in gear, and we edged up the steep driveway. But as we were pulling to the top, I realized there was something else I needed to know.

"*Gérard, attendez!*" I said. Gérard took his foot off the gas, and we drifted back down the driveway. Leaning out the window, I said, "Monsieur Vidanne? What did you put in the casket? What was it we buried in Le Nôtre Cemetery?"

His face grew serious, and he rested both of his hands on the window edge. "*Eh bien,*" he said. "The original reels of *Zeitgeist*, of course." He bowed his head and patted the top of the car.

In a matter of seconds, the maquis folded in behind us until there was no hint that a house lay veiled within it.

Gérard looked at me in the rearview mirror and said, "You made your way through the maquis without knowing where you were going?"

I nodded, but I could hardly believe it myself. When I looked back, he was grinning.

"*Vous êtes bien courageuse, mademoiselle,*" he said. "Only a Corsican would have dared to journey into the maquis."

"Courageous? You think I'm courageous?" I rested my head on the back of the seat. "Well, that's a first," I said to myself.

After what seemed like only a heartbeat we came to the bottom of the bumpy road I'd struggled up the day before, and in another heartbeat we were through Propriano and out to the Bonifacio road, with the maquis on our left and a craggy outcropping of stone on the right that fell dramatically to the sea.

Soon after that I saw the old boats anchored to the pier and realized we had arrived in Bonifacio. I sat on the bench in the back of the boat where I'd tried to calm my stomach the day before, but I moved when the boat left the harbor. I preferred the sight of where I was going to the view of where I'd been.

I felt a fine mist on my face as the prow parted the water before us. The sky was the clear, endless, promising color of the sea, and there wasn't a cloud in sight. I was exactly where I belonged.

It was only three-thirty when the boat pulled into the harbor at Cannes and the captain helped us onto the solid surface of the pier. I set off down an adjacent jetty and headed to the Palais at the end of the main quai. I was thinking about returning to the bedlam of the festival, amazed that after all that had happened, I was still curious to find out who would win the Palme d'Or.

But I was also thinking about telephones. I had called Claudel two nights before from the foot of the stairs to the Salle Debussy. As soon as I reached the end of the quai, I'd call him again from the very same phone.

As I walked up the pier, I thought about what I would tell him. He had spoken to Vidanne; he would know the facts of my mother's condition and the circumstances that had led Vidanne to make the choices he'd made. But there was so much more.

A small crowd of people had gathered at the entrance to the

quai, all of them staring and pointing at a low balcony of the Palais, where Charlize Theron was waving, a battalion of photographers behind her. Cameras were clicking, lights were flashing, and the fans below waved back at her. She was wearing something black with no sleeves, and as beautiful as she was, she had that plastic look that people on balconies have when they're acknowledging the masses. Her arm swayed back and forth as if it were mechanized. She sparkled in the sunlight.

For a minute I stopped and watched her interacting with her fans. They whistled and yelled out her name, and her arm continued to move grandly from side to side. Then the photographers started calling for her to pose. She turned her back on the crowd below, arching her long body against the balcony wall as the fans watched in reverent silence.

I was standing in the middle of the quai, maybe twenty feet from the assembled Theron gazers, when I heard someone say from the middle of the crowd, "*Pardon. Excusez-moi. Pardon.*"

People in the crowd began to move aside, and others were bumped out of their Charlize stupor. One by one the throng parted to make way for a man in a simple white shirt who was rolling up his sleeves. He was taller than the others, and slightly graying at the temples, and he moved through the crowd with studied determination. He stopped when he caught my eye.

A few of Theron's fans turned in Claudel's direction and followed his gaze to me. A short woman in a knitted shawl was standing in front of him, and someone grabbed her arm and pulled her out of the way. His face broke out in a smile, and we stood apart, drinking in the sight of one another.

I wanted to run to him. I wanted to drop my heavy purse and let him fold me in his arms the way I'd dreamed of for twenty-five years. But this time I wasn't a little girl. My childhood was over.

More heads turned in my direction and stared from me to Claudel and back again. A few of them nudged their friends and pointed at me. For a moment I thought it was because I was wearing the most heinous color ever conceived, but it was clear that this moment was everybody's business. We were in France, after all, where love was a team sport! Passion was a virtue!

Someone whistled, and the short woman in the shawl shouted, *"Allez-y!"* at Claudel. I heard him laugh as a friendly hand from behind gave him a shove. He stepped onto the quai and started walking toward me, with a smile so big I could have drowned in it.

I started toward him, but his arms were around me before I'd taken a step. There was a small burst of applause from the surrounding crowd, and Claudel waved to them over his shoulder. Their sounds began to fade.

He took my hand and kissed the raw skin on my knuckles. I didn't say a word—I was grinning too hard, and there was plenty of time to tell him how I'd broken and entered into Vidanne's house.

He kissed my forehead and then moved his lips slowly toward mine and stopped, centimeters from the mark. It was the kiss that would change everything, and we both knew it.

I could feel his breath on my cheek, and he felt so good to me it was almost unbearable. But I pressed my forehead into his chest instead and closed my eyes.

"Thank you," I said into the folds of his shirt.

"For what?"

"For finding me."

I looked up at him with a smile, and he took my face in his hands and brushed his lips over mine.

A jolt shot through me that nearly straightened my eyebrows. I pulled away from him and looked up, expecting clouds.

"I thought that was . . ."

Claudel was also looking at the sky. It was a seamless blue.

"They're kissing . . .
do we have to read the kissing parts?"

Fred Savage, in *The Princess Bride*

EPILOGUE

From: nattieconway@yahoo.com

Subject: The End

Date: May 18 3:43:00PM PST

To: vincedraper@lanews.com

Vince—

Here is my closing-night story, exactly 800 words.

This will be my final contribution to journalism. I think it was Balzac who said "I have delighted you long enough."

All the best,

Natalie

CANNES—Sunday, May 18. I have nudged and elbowed my way through a thousand other journalists to find the last seat in the highest row of the nosebleed section in the elegant Salle Debussy. It is the second grandest theater in the Great Palace of Festivals at Cannes, and we have come to watch the awards ceremony for this year's Cannes Film Festival.

The ceremony itself is taking place next door in the opulent Salle des Lumières, which is named for the famous Lumière brothers, Louis and Auguste, who invented a camera called the cinématographe and in 1895 presented the first public screening of a motion picture.

Among their short films was a 50-second shot of a train pulling into a station. It had no story: it was all about the magic of light and the relishing of movement. But the audience had never seen anything like it, and many people ran from the room in fear as the train came barreling toward them. Even though their audience must have been mesmerized, Auguste and Louis believed that the cinématographe was an invention without a future.

But tonight in Cannes, glittering moviemakers from every corner of the planet have come to celebrate the cinema. Streaming out of limousines, they will pass through a mob of impassioned fans along the red carpet that leads to the Cinderella stairway of the Palais des Festivals. The Salle des Lumières will be aglow with stars.

We in the Salle Debussy are attending the ceremony via closed-circuit TV, and as the camera pans through the crowd of luminaries who are floating into the theater, I spot Tommy Lee Jones in a shiny black tuxedo that appears to itch; Andie MacDowell is moving like an ad for expensive hair-care products. Cleavage is rampant.

Gérard Depardieu steps onto the carpet, magnificent in white, and the entire crowd erupts in cheers. Then all eyes are on Uma Thurman in a metallic silver dress so sparse that when she is out of the picture we are unsure if she was wearing anything at all.

When the jewels of the global film industry are seated in their plush red seats, French actress Jeanne Moreau appears at the podium, and the crowd grows silent.

"Tell us the winner!" Moreau breathes into the microphone, in a mysterious velvet voice that makes the president of the Cannes festival jury forget temporarily how to read.

There is an audible gasp when the Palme d'Or winner is announced, a tie between the Iranian film *A Thirst for Rain,* which the director's own government had banned from competition until five days ago, and the Japanese cat and dog movie *Inu to Nekko.* Only a few times in the long history of the festival has there been a tie for the Palme d'Or. But after the original surprise, the gasp is forgotten and no protests are heard, either from the artists in the Salle des Lumières or from their shadow artists in the Salle Debussy.

The applause is more perfunctory than it is thunderous, which can only mean that the winners are not as obvious as in previous years, and the fact that the festival's highest honor should boil down to a draw is a reminder that we are soon to leave this world of absolutes, of good and evil, black and white, triumph and defeat.

Still, when the ceremony is over and we cram our wrinkled clothes into suitcases for the long journey back to reality, we know we've had a taste of something Auguste and Louis Lumière could never have imagined when they tamed the light and transformed it into film: we have become captives in a love affair with cinema. For eleven days we've been taken on adventures all around the world, and some of them have been bumpy rides. We are not afraid of bumps.

And do you wonder why? Look at the landscape the next time you leave the theater after a movie. Do you recognize it? It is the same landscape you left two hours before, but now it is changed. Once, it was inhabited only by you and your petty problems: your failed love affair, your backache, the sour waiter who served you prawns. Now it is a landscape in which Gypsies have lives you understand, in which wars are fought and won and suffering overcome. It is a landscape in which decent people can be hurt and be forgiven and any wound can heal.

And perhaps there is love for me after all, you think, if you've found the right movie. Perhaps I can embrace the world, knowing it will not be what I expect, knowing it is fleeting as a sunset. Or a childhood.

"Tell us the winner!" Jeanne Moreau says. But tonight there are no clear winners. There are only those who have dared to play.

ACKNOWLEDGMENTS

First, thanks to my brilliant agent and favorite Tootsie, Bess Reed, whose instincts, humor, and perseverance are infinite.

And to my editor, Marysue Rucci, whose editorial eye is flawless and whose taste is impeccable, thank you. I am so lucky you are mine.

Thanks to my mother, who gave me all that Nattie missed.

To my husband, Dayton, who fed and clothed me while this was being written and never lost faith.

To my children, who turned maternal when Best Read got tough.

And thank you to all of my patient, brainy friends who read this book, shared invaluable ideas, and jumped up and down with their pom-poms:

Jim O'Leary, who first took me seriously, and Marilyn, who picked up the gauntlet; Jefferson Davis, the handsomest of men, who made me write, and LeDoux Kesling; Jake and Susanne Page, generous souls indeed, who led me to Joe Regal; and Joe Regal himself—thank you for not becoming a rock star. To Molly Maycock, my inspiration, favorite screenwriter, and fellow Francophile.

To book groups in general and my bookies in particular: Amy, Ann, Denise, Laura, Marg, Peg, Shireen, and Susan, and to our honorary member, Fred Harris. To Lesley and Chuck McKee and all their various book groups, especially to Lesley, who is indiscriminant in my favor; my sister Jody and my brother Butch; to my dearest roomie Kathi "Grunie" George—she of the eagle eye and miraculous memory; to Jim Belshaw, who thinks you can't laugh and talk at the same time; to Mari Davis, who believed from the beginning; to my spiritual center, Robin King; to Pace and Nancy Van Devender, who make us believe in ball lightning; and to my friend of longest duration, Anne Peterson.

To Uli Merwart, who always gets things right; to my most revered film critic, Jay Carr; to Vladimir Nabokov (picnic, light-ning); and to all artists and shadow artists who labor for the love of film.

And finally, *à mes amis français—Christian, Jean, Michel, Monique, et Pierre—qui m'ont montré les merveilles de la France. Et surtout à ma courageuse amie Sédrine Wiry, qui est montée sans crainte dans la Rolls-Royce d'Elton John.*

Thanks also to the #8 bus in Denver, which took me to more movies than my parents ever knew about.

ABOUT THE AUTHOR

Sara Voorhees has been a film critic on television for twenty-five years and currently serves on the board of directors of the Broadcast Film Critics Association. She and her husband live in Corrales, New Mexico, where they have raised a son, a daughter, a dog, a cat, and eleven peacocks.

This is her first novel.